D1135488

The Witches of the Wild West

From the Chicken House

I couldn't wait to open the new Michael Molloy when it arrived on my desk - I knew it would be choc-a-bloc with fantastic adventures, excitement, wildly inventive characters and heart stopping tales of courage and skill! I couldn't guess what was around the next corner - and I wasn't disappointed.
Pure enjoyment is guaranteed.

Barry Cunningham
Publisher

The Witches of the Wild West

Michael Molloy

The Chicken House
An Egmont Joint Venture

For Sandy

First published in Great Britain in 2003 by
The Chicken House
2 Palmer Street, Frome, Somerset, BA11 1DS, United Kingdom
E-mail: chickenhouse@doublecluck.com
www.doublecluck.com

ISBN 1-903434-89-0
British Library Cataloguing in Publication data available.

Cover illustration by David Wyatt
Cover design by Ian Butterworth
Text design by Dorchester Typesetting Group Ltd
Printed and bound in Great Britain

Contents

The Coin in the Water

It was the week before Christmas and a fine winter's morning in Speller, the little seaside town where Abby Clover lived. Overnight, the Sea Witches had arranged for a thick fall of snow. The cobbled lanes and houses, which spread down the cliff-side to the harbour, were sparkling in the sunshine. The sky was a clear intense blue, except for a small bank of fluffy clouds over the cliff-tops.

Because the town's cottages were painted white, only their green bottle-glass windows and faint blue wisps of smoke curling up from log fires showed against the deep drifts of snow. The only other splashes of colour in the landscape were the rose-red hues of the town hall overlooking the square, and the honey-coloured stone walls of the church, which stood next to the harbour.

Traditionally, the Sea Witches always kept secret the day they would arrange for the first fall of snow. So when the children had opened their eyes that morning, even their bedrooms seemed to be filled with a magical light.

Abby Clover and her best friend Spike, who was staying with her, leaned out of the window of the old lighthouse

where Abby lived with her parents, and breathed in the cold air. The lighthouse overlooked the bay next to Speller and from the window they could just see the face of the town hall clock which began to chime eight. Already they could hear the excited voices of children drifting up from the town.

Despite their protests, Abby's mother insisted they each eat at least a piece of toast for breakfast before they rushed down to the town square where all the children of Speller were gathering for a great snowball fight.

After sides had been carefully chosen, the battle raged nearly all the morning with lots of happy shrieks of laughter until finally Mr Mainbrace the mayor appeared carrying a shovel and called for a truce.

'Time to put up the Christmas tree,' he cried. 'If you children want to continue your fight I suggest you all go up to the cliff-tops so I can get on with my work in peace.'

His announcement was greeted with a barrage of snowballs and more laughter. The mayor held up his hand. 'But if you want to stay and give me a hand, I don't mind.'

Declining his offer with a final flurry of snowballs, most of the children began to trudge up the lane.

'Are you and Spike going to help me, Abby?' Mr Mainbrace asked, surprised that the two had not gone with the others.

'I will if you want me to, Mr Mayor,' Abby replied. 'But we'll have to be quick. Spike and I are going to wait at the jetty for Captain Starlight. He's due in from

America this morning.'

'I know,' answered the mayor. 'Sir Chadwick and the Great Mandini are setting up my telescope to watch for his arrival.'

Abby looked up at the town hall balcony where two figures were making adjustments to the long brass instrument. They gave her a wave.

'So, where do you want the Christmas tree, Mr Mainbrace?' Abby asked.

The mayor looked thoughtful, stroking his chin in an uncertain manner, until a firm voice announced, 'Make a clear space in the snow twelve paces square, ten paces from the steps, please, Abby.'

'Very well, Mrs Mainbrace,' Abby replied to the mayor's wife, who was standing at the door of the town hall.

'Excellent,' said Mr Mainbrace, smiling at his wife. 'You always know exactly what to do, dearest.'

Abby paced out the distance and reached into her pocket for a single speck of Ice Dust. Like Spike, she was dressed from head to foot in an Atlantis cape, an extraordinary item of clothing that gave perfect protection in any sort of weather. Whatever the temperature, the cape was always comfortable. It could adapt itself to any style the wearer desired, and also change colour if camouflage were needed.

Abby and Spike were the same height but all similarity ended there. Abby wore her shiny chestnut-coloured hair in pigtails and her green eyes were the colour of fresh laurel leaves. Her longish face was always sun-tanned and today her cheeks glowed red in the cold air.

Spike looked quite different. His hair and complexion were as pale as the snow around them. No matter how long he stayed out in the heat of the sun or winter's cold his complexion never changed, and his eyes were the colour of blue ice.

Abby placed the mote of sparkling white dust on the shovel Mr Mainbrace held, and recited:

'Shovel do the work of ten,
Clear this snow, and when
The task is done,
Clear Speller's paths for everyone.'

Immediately, the shovel leaped from the mayor's hand and into the air as if it had a life of its own. In moments, it had cleared the space Abby had indicated. It gave a waggle, as if satisfied with the task it had performed, and set about furiously shovelling the snow off all the pavements of the little town.

'All that from one speck of Ice Dust,' Spike said, impressed.

'*And* my spell,' Abby said quickly. 'One won't work without the other.'

Spike nodded. He appreciated that most spells could only be performed with the aid of Ice Dust, and the more powerful the spell the greater the quantity of Ice Dust required.

'Excellent work,' said Mr Mainbrace, looking on with admiration. Like the rest of the townsfolk, Mr Mainbrace was a Sea Witch. Long ago they had given up being Light Witches because they preferred a life at sea. And although the Sea Witches had gradually lost most of their other powers, they could still control the weather.

Mr Mainbrace turned towards the town hall. 'Now, if you could just give me a hand to bring the tree up from the basement, children.'

Abby and Spike followed him into the foyer and down a wide flight of steps to the cellar. They entered a vast room filled with dusty crates, old ship tackle, stacks of chairs, and the huge marquee used by the citizens of Speller for festive occasions.

Along one wall, lying on its side, was a mighty Christmas tree planted in a massive pot.

'How did it get down here?' asked Spike.

'The Elves of Darkwood Forest bring us a tree every year,' replied the mayor. 'We never see them deliver it; you know what a shy lot they are. We just find it here in the basement. I'm told they call it the Elvin tree, after your famous ancestor, Jack Elvin, Abby.'

Abby nodded. She knew all about the friendship between her great-great-grandfather and the elves Mr Mainbrace spoke of. Although he hadn't been a Sea Witch, Jack Elvin had done a great deal for Speller. He had built the town hall and made the maze that protected the town from the outside world. Jack Elvin also started the village store that Abby's Aunt Lucy and Uncle Ben now ran.

'Can you manage to get it outside, Abby?' asked Mr Mainbrace, pointing at the Christmas tree.

'I think so, Mr Mayor,' she replied confidently and, finding another mote of Ice Dust to put on the tree, she began to chant.

'Until you're settled in the square,
Christmas tree be light as air.'

The tree and pot rose gently into an upright position and Mr Mainbrace had to grab it before it floated up to the ceiling. He could walk with it now as easily as if he were holding a balloon on a string.

'Hey, look at this, Abby,' said Spike, pointing at an old-fashioned toboggan that had been concealed by the tree.

'May we use this, Mr Mainbrace?' he asked.

'As long as you're careful,' the mayor answered as he manoeuvred the floating tree up the steps. 'I don't want to tell the King and Queen of Lantua that their only son has broken his neck playing with my old sleigh.'

Spike sighed. The mayor had reminded him that in a few days his parents would arrive to spend Christmas in Speller and, glad as he would be to see them, he would once more have to start behaving like a prince.

Spike's homeland was especially important to Light Witches because it was the only known source of Ice Dust left on Earth. At one time, Lantua and its Ice Dust mines had been captured by Wolfbane, the evil Master of Night Witches. He had found a way to mix Ice Dust with toxic waste and other horrible potions to make Black Dust, the vital ingredient of all Night Witch spells. Wolfbane and his cohorts had been on the verge of completely destroying the Light Witches when Abby, Spike and their extraordinary band of friends had finally ousted them and reclaimed Lantua for Spike's family.

Soon after Spike and Abby had first met Captain Starlight and his companion, Benbow the magical albatross, they'd joined forces with Sir Chadwick Street, the Grand Master of the Light Witches, and Hilda who eventually became his wife; and the Great Mandini, the world's greatest conjurer and mind reader. During their titanic struggle with Wolfbane, Abby had proved such an able pupil of magic, Sir Chadwick had allowed her to be made a Light Witch at a very early age.

With Abby seated at the front of the toboggan, Spike gave it a running push and leaped on behind her. The iron-clad runners cut through the fresh snow, gathering more and more speed as they hurtled down the last stretch of lane before the roadway curved into the harbour. Suddenly, the harbour jetty was looming up ahead of them.

Just as they were about to sail off the edge into the freezing sea, Abby pulled hard on the lines that controlled the guiding runners at the front of the sledge. They swung away from the water and plunged into the deep bank of snow that had drifted against the wall of the Speller Tavern.

'That was great,' said Spike, grinning as they emerged from the deep snow. 'Shall we take it to the top of the cliffs and run all the way down through the town?'

Abby sighed, 'I'd like to, Spike, but it would take ages to pull it up there and I've got to do some revision for my Witch examination.'

'You could always use a spell to get it up there,' Spike said innocently.

Abby gave him a push that sent him skidding across the snow. 'You know I'm not allowed to use magic for my own sake, Spike. It's the first rule of the Order of Light Witches.'

'Couldn't you just be doing something for me?' Spike suggested. 'And if you came along as well it would just be to see I didn't get into any trouble.'

Abby shook her head and sat down on one of the bollards that lined the edge of the jetty. Because all of Speller's Sea Witch fleet was on the high seas, the harbour was quite empty of ships.

'No, I couldn't. I'd know I was really doing it for my own amusement,' Abby explained. 'If I were to start making excuses for doing things for myself I'd end up being a Night Witch. They only use their powers for their own sakes. We Light Witches try to help other people with our magic.'

'Doesn't it ever get you down?' asked Spike, sitting on the bollard next to her and taking a book from the pocket of his Atlantis cape. 'It must be like having a fantastic present that you can only let other people play with.'

Abby shrugged and changed the subject. 'What are you reading?'

'It's about the Wild West,' he replied. 'I wish I could go there – it sounds fantastic.'

'Well, I'm going to practise *clouding*,' said Abby.

'What's *clouding*?'

'Watch,' said Abby, pointing to the sky over the cliff-tops and concentrating. The clouds reformed in the shape of a great castle.

'Why, that's our palace in Lantua!' said Spike. 'How do you do that?'

'I just think of the shape,' said Abby, and as they watched, the cloud castle became two white ponies galloping across the sky.

'That's odd,' said Abby, puzzled. 'I wasn't thinking of ponies.'

Spike looked up wistfully. 'Maybe you're reading my mind without realizing,' he said. 'I was just thinking I'd like to be riding in the Wild West.'

It was silent now, everything hushed by the snow, except for the distant cries of the town children playing on the cliff-tops above. Abby and Spike were watching the cloud ponies fading away when there was a sudden plop in the water beside them. Soaring above them was a great white albatross.

'Benbow!' Abby cried excitedly. 'He must have dropped something.'

'Captain Starlight must be close,' said Spike.

Abby looked into the dark water of the harbour to see what had caused the plopping sound. A small round object gleamed on the bottom.

'I wonder what that is?'

'I'll get it,' said Spike, pulling off his Atlantis cape.

Abby laughed to see that, under his cape, Spike was wearing nothing but his swimming trunks. With no regard for the freezing cold, he dived into the icy water. Moments later, he surfaced and threw something round and shiny to Abby.

It was a large silver coin with such a deep dent in it, Abby could not make out any of the images that had once been stamped on each side of it. Above them, Benbow gave a satisfied cry before circling back out to sea.

American Visitors

'The *Ishmael* is on the horizon,' said the Great Mandini as he peered through the brass telescope mounted on the town hall balcony. 'As usual, Captain Starlight is absolutely on time.'

'What else would you expect from the Ancient Mariner?' replied Sir Chadwick Street, shrugging to adjust the extra layer of material on the shoulders of his splendid overcoat. Tall and slender, he was a handsome man with a bold Roman nose dominating his face and, in the chill air, he was looking pinker than usual. His battered tweed hat was pulled casually over his long marmalade-coloured hair and he wore a flowing red polka-dot bow tie with his stylish, fine-cut tweed suit.

Mandini was also slim, but a trifle shorter than Sir Chadwick. He had a pale olive complexion and a thin moustache with carefully waxed ends. Beneath a wide-brimmed black trilby hat his hair was so flat it looked almost as though it had been painted on his head. With his black magician's cape he wore a long red scarf that wound several times around his neck.

Mandini straightened up from crouching over the telescope and with a doubtful expression looked at the clothes he and Sir Chadwick were wearing.

'Do you think we might be dressed a trifle informally to greet such important visitors?' he asked.

Sir Chadwick smiled and shook his head. 'Believe me, Mandini, the plainer the better for American Light Witches.'

'You know best, Chadwick,' said Mandini. 'It's just that I wouldn't wish to give any offence by being too casual in my appearance.'

Sir Chadwick buttoned up his coat. 'Let's go to the jetty and you can test my judgement for yourself when you meet our visitors.'

As they left the town hall, Mr Mainbrace met them on the steps. 'I've lit a modest fire in the visitors' rooms, Sir Chadwick,' he said. 'And I've taken out the comfortable chairs as you instructed. We've put in some wooden ones from the kitchen.'

'Excellent,' Sir Chadwick replied. 'And remember to remind Mrs Mainbrace, no biscuits or cake with the tea. Just plain brown bread and butter – thinly spread.'

'What a strange way to greet important visitors,' muttered Mr Mainbrace as he watched Mandini and Sir Chadwick walking down the freshly cleared path towards the harbour.

As he entered the harbour, Captain Adam Starlight lowered

the mainsail of his ship, the *Ishmael.* He managed the craft single-handed and with perfect skill, as he had learned to do down all the years.

To some, Adam Starlight was a mythical figure, known as the Ancient Mariner. He had begun his life as a boat builder for the American Sea Witches in the port of Bright Town in Massachusetts. Although he was not one of them, the Sea Witches had granted him the life-span of a witch – twenty years for every one year of human life.

When Wolfbane had discovered Black Dust he and his Night Witches built a great fleet of Shark Boats to drive the American and English Sea Witches from the seas. But the Night Witches had never been able to raid Speller itself because over the years the townsfolk had painted their cottages with whitewash mixed with Ice Dust, and pure Ice Dust was deadly to the Night Witches.

But the citizens of Bright Town had taken no such precaution and the Night Witches had destroyed their town. Since its destruction, Captain Starlight had taken his revenge by hunting Night Witches with the great harpoons he had captured from whale hunters.

Although Starlight had no magical abilities, Wolfbane's Night Witch hordes feared him as much as any Light Witch. And no one really knew the extent of the powers of his companion, the great albatross Benbow.

Now, Captain Starlight was drawing *Ishmael* level to the jetty. He threw a line to Benbow who took it in his beak and swooped down to pass it to Spike as Starlight himself looped the aft rope over a bollard.

'Secure forward,' Spike bellowed as he tied the line with the correct loops and knot.

Abby and Spike stepped on to the *Ishmael*.

'Did you have a good voyage, Captain?' Abby asked. 'Where are your passengers?'

Captain Starlight raised a finger to his lips and, pointing to the hatchway, whispered, 'They're composing themselves below. They're not the best of sailors and it's been a hard journey in winter waters.'

'Look what we found, Captain,' Abby said, holding out the dented silver coin. 'We think Benbow dropped it in the harbour.'

Captain Starlight examined the object and scratched the white scar that ran down his jaw. His thick wavy hair was like iron-grey wire and his hands and face were the colour of old oak. He wore a cap, a dark-blue sailor's pea jacket and long sea boots.

Starlight held up the coin. 'I can't see which country this comes from, Abby. But I should hang on to it – it may be lucky.'

Abby slipped the coin into her pocket as the door to the hatchway opened and an extraordinary figure emerged – a tall bony woman who wore a rather grim, frowning expression. She had a long thin nose, sharp grey eyes and tightly-pursed lips. Her pale features looked as though they had been thoroughly scrubbed with a hard brush. Abby had never seen anyone who looked so clean.

But her clothes were the real surprise. They looked as if they had been copied from a history book. A plain white bonnet sat on her straight grey hair. She wore a wide white collar over a long black dress that reached almost to the deck. Shoes with brass buckles just showed as she stopped before them and folded her hands over the white apron she wore over the black dress.

A man followed through the hatchway to stand beside her. His face was rounder and less severe but his expression was just as solemn. He wore a black broad-brimmed hat with a high flat crown and silver hair that touched his shoulders. He also wore a large white collar over his long black broadcloth coat. His trousers were gathered in at his knees over long black stockings, and his shoes, too, bore large brass buckles. He carried a small, flat, polished wooden box with brass hinges.

At that moment, Sir Chadwick and the Great Mandini came on to the jetty and clambered aboard the *Ishmael*. After shaking hands with them, Captain Starlight said, 'Sir Chadwick, Mandini, may I introduce Charity Sycamore, Mistress of the American Order of Light Witches and her husband, Elijah Sycamore?'

'So, Chadwick,' said Charity Sycamore in a strong New England accent, 'still flouting a fancy title? It does thee no credit in our eyes.'

To Spike and Abby's surprise, Sir Chadwick raised his hat and leaned forward to kiss Charity on the cheek. She screwed up her eyes to receive the peck. 'Delightful to see you again, Charity. And you, Elijah. I see the years have not softened your resolve to be disagreeable, Charity.'

'You know each other?' said Mandini, surprised.

Sir Chadwick nodded. 'We're cousins.'

'Second cousins once removed,' said Charity firmly. 'On my father's side, according to the family bible.'

'And that never lies,' said Sir Chadwick.

'May I—' Elijah began but was interrupted by his wife.

'When shall we begin our discussions?' Charity asked. 'We're not here to waste time.'

Sir Chadwick turned to Elijah.

'On behalf of the—' he began again.

'Oh, give it to him, man,' Charity said, taking the box out of her husband's hands. 'This is a present to you from the American Light Witches, Chadwick. It ain't much so don't go making a fuss.'

Sir Chadwick took the box and winked at Elijah who raised his eyes to the sky.

'Thank you, my dear fellow,' said Sir Chadwick. 'On behalf of the English Order of Light Witches, we are humbly grateful for your gift. It shall be placed in our London library for safekeeping.'

Charity sniffed. 'Is that old rapscallion Polartius still in charge of the library? I would not trust him to keep the chickens in my hen house safe.'

Abby and Spike gasped at her words. They knew the wintry figure of Polartius. To describe him as a rapscallion was like saying Captain Starlight was a mere cabin boy.

Sir Chadwick ushered Abby and Spike forward and mischievously used their titles to provoke his cousin. 'Charity, Elijah, may I present Prince Altur, Lord of the Cold Seas, and the Duchess of Lantua, Abby Clover.'

Charity sniffed and looked down at them with a critical expression. 'So, these are the young 'uns who helped bring down Wolfbane and that vile mother of his.'

Charity was referring to the last encounter Abby and Spike had had with Wolfbane. On that occasion, Wolfbane's mother Lucia, an equally vicious Night Witch, had helped her son to kidnap Sir Chadwick's fiancée. The evil pair had transported Hilda into the past, where they were pursued by Abby and her band of friends. They had finally vanquished Wolfbane and his mother by banishing the pair to wander, lost, in the nether world beyond space and time.

'Well, I'm glad to make your acquaintance, children,' Charity said finally. 'I'm just sorry to see thee keeping the company of actors and such like. I take it thou art still fooling around on the stage, Chadwick?'

'I am still actor-manager of the Alhambra Theatre, Charity,' he answered lightly.

She looked at the children again. 'At thy age, thou ought to be looking to thy school books, not traipsing around the world funning away thy time.'

Abby curtsied and Spike gave a formal bow but remained silent.

'Well, there's nothing wrong with their manners. I

doubt if that is thy influence, Chadwick.'

Sir Chadwick put a hand on Spike's shoulder. 'Prince Altur has been deputed by his father the king to speak on behalf of the royal family of Lantua concerning our talks on the Ice Dust trade.'

Charity raised her hands. 'Now I've heard everything. Holding important talks with a boy!' She paused. 'Do I understand thou art married to an actress now, Chadwick? And pray where is thy wife? Gallivanting about on the stage, I suppose.'

'Hilda is due at any moment,' he replied, glancing up at the sky. 'In fact, I do believe this is her now.'

A large flock of birds was flying in close formation over the cliff-tops. As the birds swooped lower, the group standing on the jetty could see they were doves. The flock parted to reveal Hilda, her long fair hair floating about her, descending slowly from their midst until she stood before them on the jetty.

The Evil Indicator

'Charity, Elijah, this is my wife Hilda,' said Chadwick, making more introductions. 'Dearest, this is my second cousin once removed Charity Sycamore and her husband Elijah.'

'I'm delighted to meet you,' said Hilda, shaking hands. 'I've so been looking forward to your visit.'

'Well, she don't look like an actress, Chadwick, I'll say that for her,' said Charity, giving Hilda an appraising stare.

'You must be very cold,' said Hilda, noticing that Charity wore no topcoat. She took off the magnificent cloak of bird feathers she wore and draped it around Charity's shoulders.

'Tush, child,' said Charity, secretly pleased by Hilda's concern. 'We've known harder winters than this in New England.' But Abby noticed Charity's skin was turning an interesting shade of mottled blue.

'Let's go to the town hall,' said Chadwick. 'We have some refreshments waiting.' He turned to Charity and took her arm. 'Nothing fancy, of course.'

As they walked up the hill, Hilda apologized for her

lateness. 'I was rehearsing the pageant you are going to see at Merlin College,' she explained to Charity and Elijah.

'Pageant?' repeated Charity. 'Why would we want to see a pageant? Didn't Chadwick explain to you, we're plain folk?'

'Oh, but it's not like a play,' Hilda said hurriedly. 'It's very educational. Every year at this time, Merlin College re-enacts King Arthur's battle with Charlock the Bad. They actually use Excalibur for the ceremony. It's the only time the sword is taken from its sacred glade.'

'I should like to see that, my dear,' said Elijah with sudden firmness. It will be quite something to tell the folk back home that we've seen Excalibur. And it is part of our heritage, too.'

'I guess so,' said Charity shortly.

'I think she's quite pleased,' Spike whispered to Abby.

When they were all seated in the straight-backed wooden chairs Mr Mainbrace had placed in the town hall apartment, Sir Chadwick threw another log on the fire before turning to the present Elijah had given him. As he lifted the lid, a wonderful arrangement of spheres and arrows, carved from silver and brass, unfolded before them.

'An Evil Indicator!' said Mandini, impressed. 'And the most beautiful one I have ever seen.'

'Early American,' said Elijah with a hint of pride in his voice that earned him a look of mild disapproval from his wife.

'Have you ever seen anything like it, Adam?' said Sir Chadwick, his voice full of admiration.

'Just once,' said Starlight. 'Long ago, in Bright Town.'

'Well, that's enough of that,' said Charity, folding the instrument back into its box before the quivering arrow that surmounted all the others had come to a stop.

Mr and Mrs Mainbrace entered the room with large trays laden with the tea and thinly buttered brown bread. When the cups and plates had been distributed, Mr Mainbrace took a chair. He was to represent the Speller Sea Witches at the meeting.

'It's a pity the children can't try some good American cooking, Charity,' said Sir Chadwick, holding out a plate of brown bread. 'Do you know, they've never tasted blueberry muffins, or carrot cake, or real New England ice-cream.'

'Nor deep apple pie, or chocolate cookies, or angel layer cake,' added Captain Starlight.

'Now, is that a fact?' said Charity, looking at Abby and Spike. 'Well, for your sakes . . .' She clapped her hands three times and the brown bread was transformed into all the delicacies Sir Chadwick and Captain Starlight had mentioned.

'This is just for the children's education, mind,' she added.

There was hardly a crumb left on the plates by the time Charity flashed a look of suspicion at Sir Chadwick, but he was just gazing out of the window with an innocent smile on his face.

The Men at the Ministry of Imagination

When the cups and plates were cleared away, Charity slapped a hand down on the table and said, 'If thy stomach is now satisfied, Chadwick, can we get down to business?'

'As you please, Charity,' Sir Chadwick replied. 'We're all ears.'

'Thou knowest the vexing problem we American Light Witches have,' Charity stated flatly. 'Since the destruction of Bright Town we no longer have our own Sea Witches to bring us Ice Dust. The amount supplied to us by the Speller Sea Witches is pitiful.'

'It's no fault of the Speller Sea Witches,' said Mr Mainbrace. 'You saw the harbour when you arrived. All our ships are on the seas, the crews working as hard as they can. There just aren't enough of us to go around.'

Spike stood up. 'My father, the King of Lantua and the

Cold Seas, wishes you to know that he is happy to supply the American Light Witches with any amount of Ice Dust you desire. He is even prepared to put the royal yacht at your disposal as a means of transporting it.'

'The royal yacht,' said Elijah, hopefully. 'How is it powered?'

'Why, it's a steam yacht,' answered Spike, puzzled. 'It's the very best of its class. It could carry huge amounts of Ice Dust.'

Elijah and Charity exchanged glances, and Elijah shook his head miserably. 'Out of the question,' he said. 'American Light Witches can only work with Ice Dust transported in wooden sailing ships. It is the way it has always been done.'

'So, the problem seems insoluble,' said Sir Chadwick, and a silence fell upon the room.

Finally Charity stood up. 'I shall appeal to the Wizards,' she said.

Sir Chadwick looked thunderstruck. 'But American Light Witches have had nothing to do with the Wizards since America declared its independence,' he said.

'Desperate times call for desperate measures,' Charity replied. 'I shall thank thee for the use of a goose quill, ink and paper, Mr Mainbrace.'

'Certainly,' he answered. 'You will find them laid out ready for you at the writing desk.'

Charity sat down at a table in the corner and wrote a note which she folded once and threw on to the fire.

From her past dealings with Wizards, Abby knew things were never likely to be straightforward when they were involved.

Far away, in a panelled office in another time and place, two tall thin gentlemen wearing high stiff collars, striped trousers and frock coats sat in comfortable leather chairs before a blazing fire. The Permanent Undersecretary of the Ministry of Imagination and his assistant were drinking tea. Outside, snow fell gently from a lemon-coloured sky.

Although the view from the window looked exactly as London had looked in the time of Queen Victoria, this place was actually somewhere quite else. Charity Sycamore's letter had been dispatched to the Wizard World in another dimension, from where the Wizards often took a hand in the affairs of the Light and Night Witches.

The Permanent Undersecretary looked up when Charity's letter appeared in the fire and gave a sigh. 'Oh dear – work. Retrieve that, will you please, old boy?'

The other Wizard casually took the letter out of the flames and handed it to his companion.

As the Undersecretary read Charity's letter he suddenly sat upright. 'By the beard of Merlin!' he exclaimed, astonished. 'This is a letter of appeal from the *American* Mistress of Light Witches. It seems she's visiting Speller.'

'American!' echoed his assistant. 'But surely we have no jurisdiction over American Light Witches since they signed their own declaration of independence?'

The Undersecretary shook his head thoughtfully. 'No, that's not strictly true. I remember the situation well. Charity Sycamore and her followers were a frightful nuisance. Always making appeals and arguing against Wizard Law. You just have to look at the files – they're as thick as an elvish sandwich.'

'So, what happened?'

'Well, when they sided with the colonists and signed their own declaration of independence it was just filed away with a grateful sigh. But the Great Council of Wizards never actually ratified a treaty. So, in the strict letter of Wizard Law, we *are* still responsible.' He groaned. 'Oh, feathered fish and hairy toads! I can see their troublesome arguments starting all over again.'

'What does she actually want?'

'What Light Witches always want – more Ice Dust.'

'Can't we find a way of giving it to them without getting too involved ourselves?'

The Undersecretary took a sip of his tea. 'Hmmm, perhaps we can turn this to our advantage.' He held out a hand. 'Pass me that blue file on the desk, will you, old man?' He opened the documents and studied them.

'Yes,' he said finally. 'Now, let me see . . . there's a bit of trouble brewing in Torgate. Something very odd going on with a waxworks museum.'

'Torgate – isn't that the seaside town along the coast from Speller, where we had the last lot of trouble with Wolfbane?'

The Permanent Undersecretary nodded. 'Perhaps we could tie the new problem in with this request. Maybe there is something to be done.'

He sat thinking for some time and gradually a triumphant smile softened his narrow features, and he explained his intentions to his companion.

'A splendid plan,' said his assistant, 'but risky. Do you think Abby Clover is ready for such a hazardous undertaking? After all, there are great dangers involved and she is very young.'

'I suppose so,' replied the Undersecretary. 'But if there were no dreadful dangers to be faced why would we need Light Witches?'

The Undersecretary went to his desk and scribbled a response to Charity Sycamore's letter. He showed his reply to his companion before throwing it on to the fire. Then, with sighs of contentment, both of them settled back comfortably in their deep leather chairs.

The Great Mandini retrieved the Wizard's reply from the fire in Speller's town hall. Charity took it from him and read aloud:

'To Charity Sycamore, Mistress of the American Light Witches. From the Ministry of Imagination.

Thank you for your recent communication. We are giving your appeal serious consideration and will contact you in due course when the joint standing committee of the Ministry reports on its latest findings. Meanwhile, may we hope that you enjoy your visit.'

'What does that mean?' Spike asked.

Charity screwed up the letter and threw it back into the fire. 'The usual nonsense from the Wizards. They always were worse than useless.'

'Chin up,' said Sir Chadwick soothingly. 'We're all going to Merlin College for the pageant. Perhaps you can consult the Sword of Merlin. It's been known to work wonders in the past.'

Elijah took Charity's hand. 'There may be something in what Chadwick says, wife.'

Charity gave him a weary smile. 'Thou art a great comfort to me, Elijah. I know I have a shrewish tongue. I thank thee for thy patience.' And with those words she rested her head on his shoulder.

Sir Chadwick thought this was a good moment to withdraw and he indicated to the others to follow him. 'Until the morning then, Charity,' he said. 'We'll leave you to rest now.'

When they left the town hall, Spike, Abby, Sir Chadwick, Hilda and the Great Mandini all said goodbye to Captain Starlight, who was returning to his boat, then made for the old lighthouse where Abby lived with her parents. They were all staying there that night, before leaving for Merlin College to celebrate in the pageant.

As they walked up the snow-bound lane leading to the

cliff-top, Hilda explained to Abby and Spike what arrangements had been made for the following day. 'Sir Chadwick, Captain Starlight and Mandini will take Charity and Elijah to Merlin College on the Atlantis Boat,' she began.

'What route will they take?' asked Spike as he stopped to gather a handful of snow.

Hilda thought for a moment. 'Around the coast to the Thames estuary and straight up the river to Oxford, I suppose,' she replied.

'That will take them some time,' said Spike as he threw his snowball at an icicle hanging from the eaves of a cottage. 'They'll have all the locks on the Thames to go through. What about us?'

Before she could answer, a starling suddenly landed on Hilda's shoulder and chirped something softly into her ear. Hilda replied in the same language and the bird flew away.

'Mandini, Chadwick!' she called softly to the two men who were striding on ahead. 'Please come here a moment.'

The two men returned to her side and she whispered, 'Arm yourselves with snowballs. We're about to be ambushed.'

Grinning as if they were boys again, Sir Chadwick and Mandini quickly filled their arms. As they drew abreast with the corner of the next cottage, they saw a gang of town children lying in wait. A furious barrage was exchanged to the sound of splattering snowballs, delighted shouts and bursts of laughter until the vanquished children ran whooping down the lane towards the town square.

A flock of starlings circled around Hilda, chirping happily before they darted away.

'Now, where was I?' she said breathlessly. 'Oh, yes, arrangements. Abby, Spike, I am coming on the train with you both to London. Abby, we will drop you off at the Alhambra Theatre where you will stay overnight in our apartment. Sir Chadwick's man, Shuffle, will be there to look after you. Spike and I will go straight on to Oxford. And the following morning, Polartius will oversee your Witch examination.'

Abby nodded, feeling quite grown up to be on her own in the city. 'I might ask the library elves to join me for some supper.' She spoke so grandly, Spike sprinkled some snow down the collar of her Atlantis cape.

Abby hurled a snowball back at him, before asking Hilda, 'How shall I get to Oxford after the examination?'

'Polartius will take you through one of the Wizard Ways. It shouldn't take long.'

'A lot quicker than going through all those locks in the Atlantis Boat,' said Spike.

They had reached the top of the cliffs now and the last rays of the fading sun gave way to a soft glow of snow light. They paused for a moment and looked down towards the town square. The Christmas tree shone brightly with globes of St Elmo's fire and the church choir began to sing. Joining in, they all trudged through the snow the short distance to the lighthouse, singing at the tops of their voices, *God Rest Ye Merry Gentlemen*.

The Waxworks Exhibition

Before Sir Chadwick departed the following day, he handed Abby the present Elijah Sycamore had given him. 'Just leave it in my apartment until I get back,' he said. 'If you try to give it to Polartius, he'll only insist on giving you receipts and making you sign things. You know what a fusspot he is.'

'I'll put it on the mantelpiece next to your Persian dagger,' she said.

'Splendid. I know you'll do well in your examination, Abby, so don't worry. Try to do a bit of revision tonight but not too much.' He tapped her head. 'You can overstuff this, you know.'

'See you in Oxford,' she said, waving him and Mandini off from the front door of the lighthouse.

In the living room, Abby found Spike reading a copy of the *Torgate Gazette*. 'Hey, listen to this, Abby,' he said. 'There's a new attraction on the pier. A waxworks show. And it's got an alchemist turning base metal into gold.' He shut the paper and said, 'I wouldn't mind seeing that.'

'Really? I'd like to see it too,' said Abby.

'See what?' said Hilda, entering the room with a seagull perched on her shoulder.

'A waxworks on Torgate Pier,' said Spike. 'It's a new attraction.'

Hilda opened a window and spoke to the seagull in a series of explosive squawks before it flew away. 'What an interesting accent the gulls have on this part of the coast,' she murmured to herself as she turned to Abby and Spike. 'Well, why don't we go and have a look at the waxworks before we catch the train to London?'

'Can we really?' said Spike.

'I don't see why not,' answered Hilda. 'Our train doesn't leave Torgate until just after six o'clock. That gives us masses of time.'

In the early afternoon, Hilda, Spike and Abby said their goodbyes to Abby's parents and set out for Speller Station. The Sea Witches had arranged for another fall of snow during the previous night, but the whiteness came to an abrupt end when they emerged from the maze that separated Speller from the outside world.

Beyond the maze, they found cold crisp weather and a gusty wind that shook the bare trees of Darkwood Forest which began on the far side of the Torgate Road.

They strolled to the station and Hilda exchanged a few words with Mr Reef, the stationmaster, who was actually a

Sea Witch and in charge of dispatching Ice Dust to Light Witches all over the country. The train arrived a few minutes later and, after a brief journey, they drew up in Torgate.

As they emerged from the station, Hilda consulted her watch and said, 'Just time for a late lunch before we visit the pier. What would you like to eat?'

'Fish and chips at the Imperial Fried Fish Emporium,' Abby and Spike said together.

'Lead the way,' said Hilda and they set off for the promenade.

Abby and Spike finished their great plates of crispy golden fish and chips and sat back with a sigh. Abby was looking around at the green marble pillars and the engraved glass when a friendly lady in a spotless white overall bustled up to take their empty plates. 'You two looked as if you enjoyed that,' she said, smiling.

'It was just as good as when the Imperial first opened,' said Abby.

The lady laughed. 'That was a bit before your time, my dear,' she said. 'This place has been open more than a hundred years. It says so in a sign on the wall.'

'Oh, yes,' said Abby carefully. 'I meant it was as good as it was on my first visit.'

The lady nodded, and Abby recalled the time she had come to the restaurant with Sir Chadwick Street in an earlier century. But her thoughts evaporated as the waitress gave a sudden cry.

A chip had flown across the room and hit her on the nose. Hilda, Spike and Abby looked to see where it had come from. A party of boys and girls filled the rest of the restaurant – schoolchildren on an outing, Abby guessed.

Most of them were quite well behaved but on one table a boy and girl were throwing chips at each other. Judging by their matching carrot-coloured spiky hair and freckles, they were probably twins.

'Nigel, Mandy, stop that!' But the twins ignored their harassed-looking teacher and continued to throw chips until their plates were cleared.

'I'm so sorry,' said the teacher as she stood behind Hilda to pay the bill at the counter. 'High spirits, you know.'

The lady in the overall nodded in sympathy. 'I wouldn't want your job, my dear,' she replied.

Abby, Spike and Hilda decided to take a stroll around Torgate before they visited the Waxworks Exhibition. Hilda showed them the haberdashery shop she had worked in before she joined Sir Chadwick's Alhambra Theatre Company in 1894.

It had hardly changed at all, Abby thought. Next they went to a large building near the station, which had once been the orphanage where Hilda had spent her early years. It was now the Torgate Museum, and Hilda showed them the dormitory where she had slept as a child.

'Were you unhappy in those days, Hilda?' Spike asked.

Hilda shook her head. 'No, not really,' she answered. 'The people who ran it were very kind.' She looked at her watch. 'We'd better go to the pier. We've just got time before we have to leave for London.'

It was quite dark now but the promenade glittered with lights and the *Torgate Belle*, the great steam train that Abby and Spike had once before taken to Oxford, stood gleaming under a spotlight by the floral clock. Fairy lights were strung along the pier and swayed in the gusty wind as the three of them made for the Waxworks Exhibition.

As they were about to enter, they saw that the children from the Imperial Fish Emporium had joined the queue behind them. Nigel was punching a smaller boy, and Mandy was pulling the hair of the girl next to her.

'I hope that Nigel tries to start something with me,' Spike said softly to Abby as they passed through the turnstile. But the children took another direction once they were inside.

On the whole, Abby and Spike were disappointed by the exhibition. They quite liked the tableau depicting the Death of Nelson and the Conquest of Everest. And they were astonished to find a waxwork of Sir Chadwick Street, playing the role of King Lear. But they thought the Alchemist's Workshop was pretty poor stuff.

The waxwork figure in it was of a vastly fat man dressed in long dusty robes and wearing a large velvet beret on his head. A long straggly beard, fashioned from horse hair, hung to his waist. The figure held one hand out to the viewers and pointed with the other to a table holding an assembly of glass tubes and retorts, through which yellow liquid hissed and bubbled. Behind him was a bookcase holding some large, ragged volumes and a backdrop of cardboard, badly painted to look like a cellar wall. Lights shone from the floor in the vain hope of giving an eerie effect to the sideshow.

Abby and Spike stood contemplating the scene until Spike said, 'I think I preferred your old orphanage, Hilda.'

As they walked away, the party of children arrived to view the Alchemist. Nigel was still punching the smaller boy when the teacher wasn't looking but Mandy was now pinching a different girl.

'Closing time,' a voice proclaimed as Abby, Spike and Hilda left the pavilion. Hilda looked at her watch. They had plenty of time to catch their train.

Inside the Waxworks Exhibition, the teacher was ushering the children away from the Alchemist's tableau. 'Time to go, boys and girls,' she chanted. 'Please form a crocodile outside.'

Most of the children obeyed her but Nigel and Mandy lingered on. Nigel was trying to pull the wax figure's beard when Mandy spotted two large sickly-looking yellow sweets in the hand held out towards her. Nigel saw them too, and each child snatched one from the wax hand and crammed it into their mouth.

Outside in the gusting wind, the teacher was calling forlornly, 'Has anyone seen Nigel and Mandy?'

Bad Pennies Return

Inside the Waxworks Exhibition, the chief attendant and the teacher were searching through all the halls for Nigel and Mandy. Eventually, they stood before the alchemist, having found no sign of the missing children.

'Well, they don't seem to be in here,' said the attendant. 'They'll probably turn up on the pier. You know what kids are.'

'I know what those two are,' said the teacher with some feeling. 'I'd better go and search outside again.'

When the attendant had seen the teacher off the premises he turned off the main light switch, plunging the whole building into darkness. After locking the door behind him he set off home for his tea.

Inside the darkened pavilion a match suddenly flared on the Alchemist's tableau. Reaching out, the wax figure lit a paraffin lamp on the table and drew back his dusty robes. Beneath them, set solid as waxworks, stood Nigel and Mandy, looks of utter astonishment moulded on their faces.

Casting off the robes, the figure removed the beard to

reveal himself as a thin man with sharp white features and slanting yellow eyes that glowed slightly in the dim light.

'Come out, Caspar,' he said softly, and from behind the books on the shelf hopped a large raven.

'Well done, Mr Valentine,' the raven croaked.

'It will be well done if I can get this to work,' said the alchemist as he drew a large star on the floor with a brush dipped in the bubbling yellow liquid seething in the retort beaker. When the star was finished he added symbols of reptiles and scaled birds to each point. Eventually he stood back to admire his work.

'So, Caspar, the last time you saw my wife and son was when Sir Chadwick Street cast them into the nether world by blowing up the spectral carriage in which they rode?'

'Correct,' croaked Caspar. 'As you know, we spirit animals are not governed by Wizard Law, so I was able to return to this world and find you.'

Valentine Cheeseman nodded, took a black robe from a leather bag on the floor and swirled it around his shoulders. It immediately began to sway as though stirred by a wind. Writhing demons, snakes and hideous animals appeared on its surface, as if woven into the material.

Valentine placed the waxen figures of Nigel and Mandy in the centre of the star before taking a tiny fragment of Black Dust from his waistcoat pocket. He threw the speck of dust into the star. A flash of blue light flared briefly, and he began to chant:

'Demons of darkness hear my plea,
Bring my wife and son to me,
Release them from your bonds of space,
Accept these children in their place.'

There was silence . . . then came the sound of a distant howling wind. It grew louder and louder until Valentine had to cover his ears. With a sudden flash of lightning the two children vanished. A moment later, twin columns of black smoke wavered within the star and gradually materialized into the crouching figures of Wolfbane and his mother Lucia.

Caspar gave a croak and flew to sit on Lucia's shoulder.

'Hello, my little black-hearted darling,' she crooned, tickling the raven beneath his beak. 'Did you miss me?' She turned to her husband. 'So, Valentine, you managed to get something right for once.' As she spoke, Wolfbane vigorously exercised his stiff limbs, while totally ignoring his father.

'Is this all the thanks I get,' Valentine complained. 'I rescue you from an appalling fate and you're gladder to see that wretched bird than you are *me*.' And glaring at Wolfbane, he added, 'As for this pitiful excuse for a son, he doesn't even have the decency to say hello – even though he hasn't clapped eyes on me for at least two hundred years.'

'What do you expect?' said Wolfbane coldly. 'You're the man who named me *Snivel* Cheeseman. Have you any idea what it was like to attend an English boarding school with a name like Snivel Cheeseman?'

Valentine gave a shrug. 'I gave you that name to make a man of you. And it worked. Look how far you've gone – Master of the Night Witches. You do honour to the family.'

'What do you care about the family?' said Lucia indignantly. 'You go traipsing off without so much as a farewell. We don't hear a word from you, not even a poison-pen letter. Then you turn up and expect us to fall into your arms.'

'What do you want, Father?' Wolfbane asked. 'You wouldn't have rescued us if there wasn't something in it for you.'

'Well, of all the ungrateful—'

'Oh, do get to the point,' said Lucia.

Valentine reached beneath the waistcoat of his rather greasy suit and searched about for a moment before finding the flea that was irritating him. A shifty smile played on his lips. 'You'll soon alter your tune when you hear what I've done,' he boasted.

Ignoring him now, Lucia reached into her handbag, took out a pocket mirror and began to check her make-up. As always, her appearance was immaculate. She looked as though she was dressed for tea at the Ritz but it was all an illusion. So that she could go about unnoticed, Lucia used something of her own creation called *designer dirt*, which created an effect of freshness. Actually, she was just as grubby as all Night Witches, none of whom could bear to be clean.

'So, what *have* you done?' Wolfbane asked his father, while noticing that he and his mother were still dressed in the Victorian clothes they had been wearing when they became lost in time. He snapped his finger three times and their clothes were transformed to modern dress.

'Thank you, dear,' said Lucia, looking down to admire her stylish black dress and matching string of black pearls. 'I always did favour the French designers. Givenchy, isn't it?'

Wolfbane nodded. 'I had it rinsed in sewer water first.'

Lucia inhaled. 'Ah, there's nothing quite like the scent of a Paris sewer!'

'Will you please pay attention to *me*,' snapped Valentine.

They both glanced casually at him.

'I have found a Black Dust ten thousand times stronger than the one you manufactured with Ice Dust,' he stated.

'Impossible,' replied Wolfbane curtly.

'How do you think I managed to rescue you from being lost in time?'

Wolfbane and his mother began to take notice.

Valentine continued. 'For the last two hundred years I have been searching for a Black Dust that will finally destroy the Light Witches. I have trod the rainforests of the Amazon and the furthest reaches of the Gobi desert. I descended the Volcano of Charaki and climbed the highest—'

'Yes, yes!' interrupted Lucia again. 'So what did you find?'

'This,' he said, taking a small wooden box from his pocket. He opened it and they looked down on the scarlet silk lining. There were a dozen tiny specks of Black Dust nestling in the silk.

'Is that all you've got?' Wolfbane sneered dismissively. 'What is it?'

'Fragments from the armour of Charlock,' said Valentine.

Wolfbane and Lucia said nothing, but Valentine could see that, at last, they were impressed.

Supper with the Elves

On the train from Torgate to London, Abby produced her books from her satchel and revised for her examination with Polartius the following morning. Spike read his book on the Wild West, and Hilda worked on some embroidery she'd had in her handbag. She was sewing Chadwick's initials on some white linen handkerchiefs. The journey passed quickly and they were soon crossing the concourse at Waterloo station.

'Gosh, this station has changed a lot since I was here with Sir Chadwick in Victorian times,' Abby told Spike. 'We took a hansom cab then.'

'Well, it's a taxi cab for us today,' said Hilda, and they walked towards the rank.

'What was the traffic like in those days?' Spike asked.

'It was all pulled by horses,' said Abby, 'but there was still masses of it on the streets.'

Finally they drew up outside the Alhambra Theatre in Shaftesbury Avenue. The rest of Sir Chadwick's company were performing *Cinderella* for the Christmas season. The three of them entered by the stage door and Hilda stopped

for a moment in the wings to watch her own understudy performing the role of the prince.

'She's not as good as you, Hilda,' said Spike in a whisper. 'You really know how to act the part properly.'

'That's a fine compliment, coming from a real prince, Spike,' Hilda replied, smiling. 'I shall treasure it.'

They followed Hilda up the spiral iron staircase to the rooms where she and Sir Chadwick lived when they were in London.

Shuffle, Sir Chadwick's valet, was waiting to greet them.

'Would you care for any refreshments, my lady?' he asked in his usual gravely courteous manner.

'No thank you, Shuffle,' said Hilda. 'Spike and I are going immediately to Merlin College by the Wizard Ways. I've still got lots of work to do for the pageant tomorrow. As you know, Abby is staying the night here. She will follow us after her examination tomorrow morning.'

'And how will you be going up to Oxford, miss?' he asked Abby.

'Polartius will take me by the Wizard Ways too,' said Abby.

Putting a hand on Spike's shoulder, Hilda said, 'We must get off now, Abby. We'll see you tomorrow. Good luck with the exam.'

'Thanks,' said Abby. 'I'll just unpack my night things before I go down to see Polartius—' She stopped. 'Oh, but they're performing on stage. How will I get down to the library?'

Hilda smiled. 'We've installed an alternative way,' she said, 'so we can use it when the stage is occupied.'

She opened a cupboard on the landing and ushered Spike in before she joined him. 'When you're ready, just stand in here and say, *Kavispol*!'

With that, Spike and Hilda vanished from sight. Abby knew they were now descending far beneath the earth to where Polartius, keeper of the great Light Witch Library, dwelled.

Abby found Shuffle dusting in the living room. It was much the same as it had been when Abby first saw Sir Chadwick's quarters, but then it had been a bachelor's establishment.

The same odds and ends of old theatrical posters and playbills hung on the walls and other stage memorabilia cluttered the room. Even the bust of Napoleon was still on its familiar stand but Abby could detect Hilda's touch in the new upholstery on two of the easy chairs and the curtains had been replaced with brighter material.

Abby placed the present from Charity and Elijah Sycamore on the mantelpiece next to the Persian dagger, as she had promised Sir Chadwick.

'Would you mind if I invited Wooty and his friends to supper this evening, Shuffle?' she asked.

'I should be delighted, miss,' he replied. 'It is always rewarding to cook for the little gentlemen. They have such hearty appetites.'

'What would you suggest we give them?'

'I took the liberty of anticipating your wishes, miss. I have prepared a steak and kidney pudding in the way I know the elves favour. And there will be a generous fruit trifle to follow.'

'Oh, good,' said Abby. 'And how do the elves favour their steak and kidney pudding?'

'In enormous helpings, miss.'

Abby grinned. 'I can see why Sir Chadwick and Lady Street treasure you, Shuffle.'

'I endeavour to give satisfaction, miss,' he replied, allowing himself the ghost of a smile.

Abby returned the smile and said, 'I'm just going to pop down and say hello to Polartius.'

'Supper will be ready in half an hour, miss.'

'We shall be on time,' Abby answered and she went to the cupboard on the landing.

At the command *'Kavispol!'* it was as if the floor had opened beneath her feet and she plunged down at a giddying speed. After a time, she felt the contraption slowing down.

When it had stopped, Abby stepped out into the vast chamber that housed the Light Witch library. Great shelves reached up to the vaulted ceiling and stretched away as far as the eye could see. Abby saw Polartius seated as usual at his high desk in the centre of the room, scratching away with a quill pen. His silver hair lay in coiled pools on the stone-flagged floor. When she stood before him, he spoke without looking up from his writing. 'So, Abby Clover, are you ready for your examination in the morning?'

'I won't know until I see the questions, Polartius,' she answered brightly.

The ancient man looked at her over his wire-rimmed spectacles and gave a wintry smile. 'Quite right. I see my instructions in clear thinking have been understood.'

He was referring to the lessons he posted to her each week. As Abby had got to know the librarian better she felt less in awe of him. She had begun to suspect that beneath his crusty exterior he was less grumpy than he liked people to imagine.

On a sudden impulse, Abby said, 'Polartius, why do you like to give the impression you are annoyed with everybody?'

He laid down his quill and removed his spectacles before he replied. 'Look around you,' he said in a gentler voice than usual. 'This is the greatest library in the history of the world. Everything is here and in its proper place – well, most of the time. The trouble is, Light Witches are a scatterbrained lot. Oh, I know they mean well and they tend to be generous and kind. But if I didn't give them an occasional tongue-lashing they would never bring their books back. It's the only way to keep them on their toes.'

Abby felt a little sorry for Polartius. It must be a lonely life down here, she thought. 'Would you care to come to supper tonight?' she asked. 'Shuffle is cooking steak and kidney pudding for the elves. I'm just going to invite them.'

'That's most kind of you, my dear,' he replied. 'But I'm afraid I have another engagement at my club. I am grateful for the thought though.'

'I'll go and ask the elves then,' said Abby and she walked to a section of one of the bookcases that swung back at her push to reveal a panelled room in which a log fire blazed. Elves were scattered about the room, some lounging in leather armchairs reading, others leaning over various board games. Two in shirtsleeves were playing a fast and furious game of Ping-Pong at a tiny table. One sat in a corner practising on a little trombone. They all looked towards her when she entered, and called out greetings.

These were the town elves, who helped Polartius in the library. They wore the clothes of Victorian gentlemen: top hats, frock coats, high stiff collars and striped trousers. Abby also knew the elves who lived in Darkwood Forest and dressed in a more rustic fashion.

'I've come to invite you to supper, gentlemen,' she said.

'Oh, good,' said Wooty, the chief elf. 'We wondered why Shuffle was out buying steak and kidney this morning. We hoped you'd ask us to supper, so we only had a light tea.'

'Just four muffins each,' said another elf. 'I'm starving.'

'Well, you've just got time to wash your hands. Shuffle is nearly ready to serve,' said Abby.

Back upstairs in Sir Chadwick's dining room, Abby sat at the head of the table, looking down at the rows of eager elves. Shuffle had put a pile of books on each of their chairs so they could reach the table. Each elf had a napkin tucked into his collar. The door to the kitchen swung open and Shuffle entered bearing a vast steak and kidney pudding. A great sigh of pleasure rose from Abby's guests and there was little conversation until prodigious portions had been consumed.

Abby had told them about Charity and Elijah Sycamore and showed them the Evil Indicator on the mantelpiece. When they were ready to talk, Abby asked, 'Do any elves live in America?'

Wooty answered her. 'They used to but they all seem to have vanished. At least, we've not heard from them in hundreds of years.'

This started an animated conversation about elves around the world. Later, when the table was cleared, the elves played a quiz game with Abby. In fact, it was all sorts of questions about the subjects she was going to take in her examination in the morning.

'You've done jolly well,' Wooty said finally, when Abby had let out a small yawn. 'Just one more question.'

'Go on,' said Abby.

'Do you know the verse that fetcher elves use to find the source of precious metals?'

Abby shook her head.

'It goes like this,' said Wooty, and he recited:

'Metal, metal from the ground,
Take us where you first were found.'

'But in place of the word *metal* you have to name the kind of metal you're looking for,' he explained.

Abby repeated the verse. 'I shall remember it now,' she said.

The elves gave their thanks to Abby and Shuffle, said their farewells and departed through the cupboard, soon after which Abby said goodnight to Shuffle and went up to bed.

She liked the little room where she always slept when she was in London. The walls were covered with rose-patterned wallpaper and there was a gleaming brass bedstead to which Hilda had added a beautiful patchwork counterpane. The room was quite cool, but Shuffle had put an old-fashioned stone hot-water bottle in the bed earlier so she was very snug.

About an hour after she had gone to sleep, there was a violent storm to the south. Jagged bolts of lightning slashed across the sky and thunder crashed like great guns firing in the distance. It did not wake Abby but on the mantelpiece in the darkened living room the Evil Indicator suddenly sprang to life, the arrow pointing towards the heart of the storm.

Into the Wizard Ways

The following morning, Shuffle persuaded a nervous Abby to have a light breakfast of boiled egg and toast. He wished her good luck, and she entered the cupboard to descend to the library. As she came into its great chamber, she saw there was a small table set before Polartius's desk. He looked up and Abby noticed a clock with a loud tick was suspended in the air. The large hand showed that there was still a minute to go before nine-thirty.

'Sit down,' Polartius said in a kindly voice. 'The examination is in two parts,' he explained. 'The first part consists of written questions. The second part will be your spoken answers to my questions. Is that clear?'

'Quite clear, thank you,' Abby replied, and when she took her seat the examination paper appeared on the table top. There were spaces beneath each question where she was to write her answers. Abby took a deep breath and began to read. After a few minutes she gave a sigh of relief. She could remember all the answers!

For the next half an hour the library was so silent all

that could be heard was the ticking of the great clock suspended over her head.

Finally, Abby laid down her pen and stood up to place her completed paper before Polartius, who was reading a large leather-bound book.

'Finished already?' he said, raising his eyebrows. 'You may take another half an hour if you wish.'

'No, thank you,' said Abby.

Polartius quickly read through her answers, making notes with his own quill pen. Finally, he pushed the paper aside. 'Take your seat again,' he instructed. Then he continued. 'How many Light Witches does it take to form a Light Witch Will circle?'

'A minimum of three.'

'When, why, and who discovered the Light Witch art of *tobbing*?'

'Pansy Applebloom, in 1631, when she was being chased by a Night Witch's cat. Pansy's escape route was cut off by a fast-flowing stream and she wished she was on the other side of it. A moment later, she found herself on the opposite bank.'

'Where did Ice Dust come from before the source in Lantua was discovered?'

'Two mines, five miles from the North Pole, and on four of the volcanic islands of Tiptu in the Pacific Ocean.'

'Name three ways a Light Witch can tell if a Night Witch is in the vicinity.'

'White flowers, such as Michaelmas daisies and snowdrops, will take on a faint yellow tinge. Hens will stop laying eggs, and cows give sour milk. Or by using an Evil Indicator. And—'

'That's enough,' Polartius interrupted. 'What is the fetcher-elf verse for locating the origin of metals?'

Abby smiled, and recited:

'Metal, metal from the ground,
Take us where you first were found.'

Abby looked up at Polartius and saw that he was actually smiling.

'Now for the last part,' he said, reaching up and waving his hand casually over Abby's head. A ball of white mist formed, about the size of a large armchair.

'I want you to cloud something for me,' he said. 'Make it as complicated as you like.'

Abby thought for a few seconds and then concentrated. Gradually, the mist formed into the intricate shape of the Evil Indicator that now stood on Sir Chadwick's mantelpiece. All the complicated cogs, spheres and arrows were quite clearly defined.

'Great dragon's teeth!' Polartius exclaimed. 'An Evil Indicator. What a fine piece of work. Where did you see that? I thought I had all the best examples in the ancient artifacts section of the library.'

Abby explained about Charity and Elijah's gift being in Sir Chadwick's apartment and, as they spoke, the arrows on the Evil Indicator Abby had clouded began to quiver and point south.

'Did you make it do that?' Polartius asked.

'No, Polartius,' Abby replied.

The ancient man looked thoughtful for a moment, before his brow cleared. 'I'm delighted to tell you that you have gained full marks in your examination, Abby Clover. These results are excellent. You can justifiably feel proud.'

There was a sudden round of applause and Abby saw Wooty and the rest of the elves clapping enthusiastically behind her. They had obviously heard Polartius's little speech. She noticed something different about them. Instead of their usual top hats, frock coats and striped trousers, the elves were wearing other outfits. Some were in sports jackets and brown trilby hats, others wore striped blazers and straw boaters. They each had a little suitcase with them.

'Aren't you ready yet, Abby?' asked Wooty. 'We're all coming with you to the pageant at Merlin College.'

'Go and collect your things, Abby,' said Polartius. 'We're leaving by the Wizard Ways in a few minutes.'

As Abby was about to board the lift, Polartius added, 'Oh, and bring the Evil Indicator with you. I'd like to have a good look at it.'

She returned a few minutes later, wearing her Atlantis cape.

'Come over here,' Polartius instructed and she stood with him and the elves in a tight group.

'Which Wizard Way are we using, Polartius?' Wooty asked.

'How many are there?' asked Abby.

Polartius looked down. 'Oh, of course, you haven't seen all the Wizard Ways have, you, Abby?'

'I once saw one of the tunnels,' she answered.

Polartius nodded. 'Well, as you've done so well in the examination I'll show you some of them.' As he spoke, the section of stone-flagged floor they were standing on slowly began to sink and Abby found herself descending into a wide shaft hewn through rock. Eventually they came to a stop in a great cavern paved with cobblestones. The walls and massive vaulted ceiling were lined with dark-red bricks. The cavern was illuminated by hundreds of flickering gas lamps.

'Step off for a moment,' said Polartius.

Abby followed him and saw they stood at a great junction. From the central cavern smaller tunnels led off in all directions. An old-fashioned penny-farthing bicycle was leaning against a vast lamppost set in the middle of the cavern.

'This Wizard Way was renovated in 1882,' he said. 'That's when the gas lights were installed. It's the Wizard Way I make most use of.' Polartius pointed at the penny-farthing. 'I try to keep fit by riding my bicycle whenever possible.'

Abby stared about her in wonder, until Polartius said, 'Come along, back to the elevator.'

They stepped aboard and descended further through the rock shaft.

Then came a roaring sound, almost like a train approaching through a tunnel. The elevator stopped again and all was blackness.

Polartius produced a lantern from beneath his coat and lit it with a match. The light grew bright enough to reveal the edge of another mighty cavern, but this one was roughly hewn from the rock.

Before them was a collection of small rowing boats bobbing gently on a lagoon that stretched away into darkness. The roaring was louder than ever. Polartius took Abby's hand and they stepped on to a causeway that was raised above the lagoon. They walked for a few minutes until they came to an embankment. Here the lagoon poured over a massive weir and the roaring torrent divided to rush into various tunnels.

'This is the Water Way,' Polartius shouted above the roar. 'You must be a good sailor to use the Wizard Water Way.'

Abby nodded and was glad when they turned back. There was something threatening about the dark turmoil of the raging underground rivers.

They descended once again and gradually it began to grow lighter, which surprised Abby as they were now so deep beneath the earth. The next cavern they entered seemed to be filled with sunlight. The walls were pale blue and the floor covered with a layer of white sand. The effect was somewhat like a vast seaside beach.

At intervals along the great strand stood large gaily painted contraptions like flat-bottomed boats fitted with masts and large wheels.

Polartius saw how intrigued Abby was by her new surroundings. 'Legend has it that the Wizards made this Way so they could come here for their holidays,' he said. 'There are little shafts with thousands of tiny mirrors all the way to the surface. That's how the daylight is reflected down here.'

Wooty and the elves quickly selected one of the contraptions. They swarmed on to the deck and Wooty held out a hand. 'Come aboard and take a seat, Abby,' he said.

She and Polartius sat in canvas chairs before the main

mast and watched as the elves made the craft ready. Soon its sails were unfurled and, as they descended, Abby felt a warm breeze on her cheeks. The jolly little craft was bowling across the sandy surface of the cavern at quite an impressive speed. As they gathered even more momentum, Wooty shouted, 'Second tunnel on the left for Merlin College, Oxford, helmsman.'

The elf at the rudder steered into the opening Wooty had indicated and the wind grew even stronger as the walls closed around them.

To Abby's astonishment, the walls of the tunnel were painted with scenery. Mountains and lakes flashed past, rolling countryside and seaside resorts. They seemed to enter a wood and the wind died down, the sails slackened, and the machine came to a halt.

Abby suddenly realized they had emerged into a real wood. In the distance, they could hear people talking. They disembarked and Polartius led her through the trees and on to the lawn by the lake in the grounds of Merlin College. Everything was white with frost.

The Secret of Charlock's Tomb

After Abby, Polartius and the elves had left the library there was a long deep silence. Some time later, the stillness was broken by the sound of an insistent tapping. Eventually, one of the stones that lined the walls fell into the great chamber and Caspar the raven fluttered through the hole. Four more of the stones were heaved out, and Wolfbane, Lucia and Valentine crawled through the gap. They each carried a pickaxe.

'Help me replace the stones,' Valentine instructed.

Reluctantly, Wolfbane and his mother stooped to do the work.

'Why can't we just leave it?' Lucia asked peevishly.

'Because we might want to come this way again,' Valentine snarled. 'Just do as I say. I've done this before, you know.'

When they were finished, Valentine stood by Polartius's desk and said, 'Now, let me get my bearings.'

'Is there more digging to do?' complained Lucia.

Valentine shook his head as he reached into his pocket

for a slip of paper. He glanced down, pointed to a blank wall and chanted:

'Unbind the tomb at my request,
Let Charlock's grave fulfil my quest.'

A portion of the wall trembled for a moment, before it dissolved to reveal the arched entrance to a tunnel. Valentine took a powerful torch from his pocket and led the way. The tunnel opened out into a plain stone chamber as large as a church. A huge square block of black marble lay at its centre. Inscribed on the side were letters carved in an ancient language. Wolfbane took the torch from his father's hand and studied the inscription.

'I don't recognize the language,' he said.

'You never were any good with languages,' said his father. 'It's what the ancient Britons spoke. Allow me to translate.' He took back the torch and began to read:

'Within lie the remains of King Charlock the Bad
He who ruled over the Celtic tribes of the west.
So evil were his ways the people he oppressed
Cried a river of tears in which he forged his armour.
Slain by our liberator, King Arthur, in the battle of Avon.'

Lucia looked dreamy-eyed. 'King Charlock,' she said, 'he always was a favourite of mine. Imagine causing a river of tears.'

'I think they were only talking poetically, my dear,' said Valentine. He led them to the side of the block, where a great jagged hole had been gouged through the marble. Inside, in the gloom, a suit of black armour lay on a stone plinth, and from somewhere came a distant sound of wailing as if thousands of people were weeping.

'What's that?' said Lucia.

'It seems to come from the armour,' Wolfbane said. 'Odd, isn't it?'

'Just think!' said Valentine. 'The Light Witches have kept the remains hidden here for over a thousand years.'

'So, where's the Black Dust?' asked Wolfbane.

Valentine rapped on the breastplate of the armour with his knuckles. 'It comes from here. The armour of King Charlock is pure, forged evil. Every piece of it was paid for in fear, misery and death.'

'Why did you only take so little?' asked Lucia.

'You try breaking off a piece,' he replied.

Wolfbane took a mighty swing with his pickaxe. The spiked end bounced off with a dull thud and left not the slightest sign of a blow on the surface of the armour.

'It is strong enough to resist the most powerful diamond cutters in the world,' said Valentine. 'I know, I've tried. I've been breaking in here regularly over the last two years.'

'So how did you gather the fragments you do have?' asked Lucia.

Valentine removed the helmet and breastplate, revealing the skull and part of the skeleton beneath. 'See here,' he said, poking a finger through a large slashed hole in the breastplate. 'This is where Excalibur cut through the armour. I reasoned that fragments must have become embedded in Charlock's body. I was right. I found where they had dropped away after the flesh had turned to dust.' He picked up the helmet. 'Arthur killed Charlock with thrusts to his body and blows to the helmet. What does that tell you?'

Lucia and Wolfbane looked puzzled. Then Wolfbane began to smile. 'That Excalibur can cut through Charlock's armour!'

'Exactly,' said Valentine triumphantly. 'All we have to do now is to steal the Sword of Merlin and use it to manufacture the most powerful Black Dust in history by cutting the armour up into tiny pieces.'

Valentine produced some large sacks from under his coat. 'Help me put the pieces into these,' he instructed.

A few minutes later, carrying the sacks containing Charlock's armour, Valentine, Wolfbane and Lucia re-entered the library and located the section of floor that descended to the Wizard Ways. When they reached the Water Way, they alighted and Valentine hurried them across the causeway to the river's edge.

He clapped three times and the sinister black shape of a Shark Boat rose to the surface of the torrent.

Before they climbed aboard, Wolfbane and Valentine fixed one of the gauntlets of King Charlock's armour to the prow of their ship.

'That should take care of the Atlantis Boat,' said Wolfbane, his slanted yellow eyes blazing malevolently in anticipation.

Beneath the Lake

There was quite a crowd beside the lake at Merlin College when Abby, Polartius and the elves emerged from the wood. Dr Gomble, the Master of Merlin College and the rest of the dons, dressed in their splendid academic robes of scarlet satin, were clustered around Charity and Elijah Sycamore.

Hilda was the first to notice the new arrivals. 'Look, Chadwick,' she said. 'Here's Abby and the others.'

Sir Chadwick and Mandini had been explaining to Captain Starlight that although Merlin was the oldest of the Oxford Colleges, none of the other academic establishments in the city knew of its existence.

Dr Gomble now hailed them. 'Just in time for some founder's punch, Polartius, and there is some crab-apple wine for Abby Clover and our Elfin friends.' He took Polartius's arm. 'I don't think you've met the Mistress of the American Light Witches, Charity Sycamore and her husband, Elijah.'

'On the contrary,' said Polartius, 'I've met Charity several times across the centuries.' He shook hands. 'I'm delighted to see that you American Light Witches still value the standards of the past,' he said, admiring their clothes. 'No change in fashion for four hundred years. A sentiment after my own heart. If only English Light Witches could show such admirable conformity.'

Charity looked bemused. 'I see thy tongue has not lost its way with silver words, Polartius.'

'No, Charity,' said Polartius. 'Nor yours its cutting edge.'

'Polartius is keeper of the second key to the glade where we keep the Sword of Merlin,' said Dr Gomble, changing the subject. 'In the rehearsal, which we shall see in a moment, the sword will be a wooden one. But the real Excalibur will be used in the proper performance this evening.'

Then Dr Gomble had a special word for Abby. 'And how did your examination go, young lady?' he said with a smile.

'She gained top marks,' said Polartius gruffly.

'Well done,' said Hilda and Sir Chadwick.

'Thank you,' said Abby, a little embarrassed by all the attention. 'Is Spike here?'

'He's on the other side of the lake with Benbow,' said Captain Starlight.

'You ought to put on your Atlantis cape, Abby,' said Hilda. 'It's quite cold out here.'

Abby took it from her satchel and the garment wound itself about her snugly. She also found the Evil Indicator and handed it to Sir Chadwick. 'Polartius thought it would be a good idea to bring this with us, Sir Chadwick,' she said.

'Oh, splendid,' he replied. 'Now I can show it to Dr Gomble.'

Leaving the Merlin College grandees and their distinguished guests, Abby went to look for Spike. She grinned with the familiar thrill of pleasure she always felt at the sight of the Atlantis Boat. It was now moored in the lake beside the gathering on the lawn. The sleek little craft glowed silver in the bright sunlight, its body shining with opalescent scales. To Abby, its cabin looked exactly like the shell of a giant turtle.

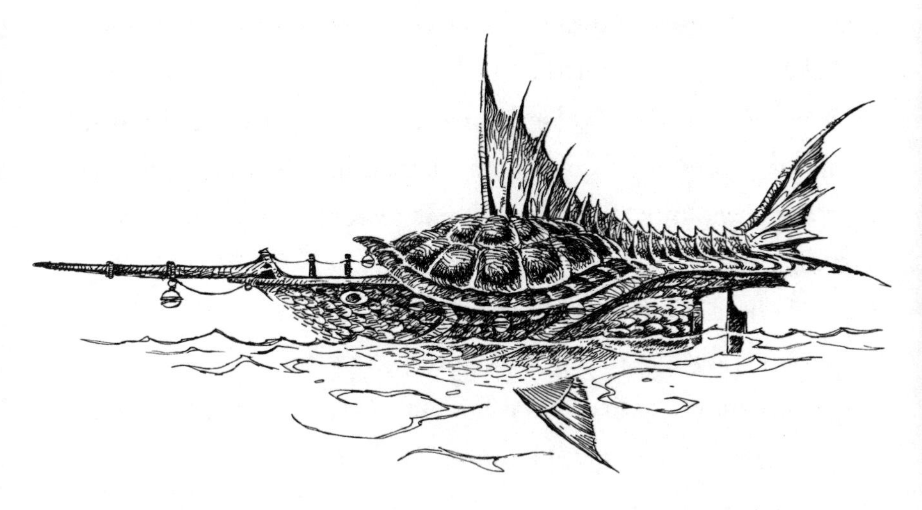

'Hello, Boat,' Abby said, and the craft bobbed in greeting on the still water.

'Abby, Abby!' she heard Spike call from the far side of the lake. He was standing on a high branch of a mighty cedar tree that grew close to the lake's edge. Despite the sharp cold, he was wearing only his swimming trunks.

'Watch,' he shouted, launching himself into a dive. Just before he entered the water, Benbow swooped down and caught his ankles, flew high into the air, and dropped him so that he knifed down into the middle of the lake.

'Tell Spike to get dressed now, Abby,' Hilda told her. 'The rehearsal for the pageant will start quite soon.'

Abby waved and circled the lake to stand by the cedar tree. After quite a long time, Spike surfaced and swam to where she stood.

Abby gave him Hilda's message and he began to towel himself with his own Atlantis cape. No matter how wet or dirty they made the capes, they only needed to give them a shake and it was as if they had just been freshly laundered. When he was dry, Spike flapped his cape quickly and put it on. It immediately became dark blue, which was his favourite colour. Abby's cape was as red as the fisherman's smock she usually wore when the weather was fine.

'Where has Benbow gone?' Abby asked.

Spike shrugged. 'I don't know. He's been a bit restless this morning, as if he was looking for something. By the way, how did the examination go?'

'I passed.'

Spike nodded. 'I knew you would.' He waved his arms to indicate all of Merlin College. 'Does it seem odd that you'll be coming here one day?'

Looking around at the grounds, Abby smiled and shook her head. 'No, not really.' Bright sunlight shone on the worn stones of the ancient college buildings and the frost glistened on the trees and lawn like icing on a cake. A light wind rippled the blue-green surface of the lake. Abby thought it looked lovely.

'There's some jolly interesting things at the bottom of the lake,' said Spike.

'What kind of things,' asked Abby.

'All sorts of tunnels. There's a tributary from the lake that leads to a great raging underground torrent.'

'That will be the Wizard Water Way. Polartius showed me part of that,' said Abby.

'But there's a lot more,' Spike continued. 'There's a complete maze of streams and rivers. Two of them lead to the magic glade where they keep Excalibur.'

'Two?' said Abby.

Spike nodded. 'One tunnel is wide enough for a boat to go through. It winds about a great deal and seems to go in a circle for a time.'

'You saw it?'

Spike nodded. 'I swam down it and came up in a stream next to the glade. But there's another smaller underwater passage that leads directly to the stream in the glade. That's quite a short distance but it's only wide enough to swim through.'

'I shouldn't mention that to anyone else, Spike. I expect it's forbidden,' said Abby.

'Yes, probably,' said Spike. 'Most things that are fun to do usually are.'

On the other side of the lake, there was a sudden flurry of interest. Sir Chadwick had unfolded the Evil Indicator to demonstrate it to Dr Gomble and the college dons, when the arrow suddenly swung wildly towards the south and began to quiver violently.

'Night Witches!' Charity Sycamore cried out in alarm. 'And they're very close.'

Sir Chadwick took command. 'Charge your wands,' he commanded. 'We'll fight them here in the open. Form a circle.'

Captain Starlight ran to the Atlantis Boat and took his harpoon from the cabin.

'How long do we have?' Dr Gomble shouted, producing his own wand from the folds of his academic gown.

'Any time now,' said Elijah Sycamore, holding out his wand. 'May I trouble you for a portion of Ice Dust, friend?'

Along with his harpoon, Captain Starlight had brought a large bag of Ice Dust from the Atlantis Boat. He poured a stream of it into the handle of Elijah and Charity's wands before immersing the blade of his harpoon in the bag. All about them the Light Witches formed a circle and stood facing outwards with the elves in the middle.

'Abby, Spike!' shouted Hilda. 'Quickly, get back here inside our circle.'

But before they could move, the surface of the lake boiled up and the Shark Boat broke the surface. Suddenly, the sky was filled with Night Witches, their flapping black cloaks darkening the sun.

Victory for Wolfbane

Too late to reach the protection of the Light Witch circle, Abby and Spike crouched down to hide in the reeds that fringed the lake. They watched as the Night Witches launched their attack. Although outnumbered by at least four to one, the Light Witches more than held their own as the attackers bore down on them screaming their hideous war cries.

Night Witch wands charged with Dirt Dust clashed with Light Witch wands in flashes of sparks and puffs of yellowish-black smoke. As it drifted across the lake, Abby and Spike caught the odour. It smelt like old cabbage water and rotten eggs.

'Dr Gomble is a fine fighter,' exclaimed Spike as he watched the Master of Merlin spin and swirl in the fray, and sounding surprised that someone so fat could move with such nimble ease.

'Look at Charity and Elijah,' said Abby, as the two fought shoulder to shoulder, striking down a particularly ferocious charge of five Night Witches.

'Remember Bright Town!' Captain Starlight roared and

swung his harpoon, felling three Night Witches with one blow.

'I think we may be winning,' said Abby, as the Night Witch attack seemed to falter. The first rank was holding back, wary now of coming too close to the valiant circle.

Abby and Spike saw danger coming from another direction. The Shark Boat had thrust its bow on to the lake's embankment. The turret flew open and Caspar fluttered out, closely followed by three dark figures.

'Wolfbane!' Abby and Spike both gasped in horrified voices.

The three Cheesemans leaped to the bank and charged towards the Light Witch circle, Wolfbane shouting, 'Make way, you cowardly scum!' as he shouldered aside his now reluctant Night Witches.

The ranks parted to let them pass. Wolfbane, Lucia and Valentine cut through the Light Witch wands as if they were made of snow and their own were red-hot pokers.

Under this fresh onslaught with superior weapons, the Light Witch circle broke. Dr Gomble and the dons were the first to fall, then Charity and Elijah. Polartius tried to protect the elves but Wolfbane swung his wand over them and, as one, they all fell to the ground.

It was clear to Abby and Spike that Wolfbane, Lucia and Valentine possessed some new and terrible force that rendered the Light Witch wands virtually powerless against them.

'Find the keys!' Valentine shouted at Wolfbane and

Lucia, who were about to attack Sir Chadwick, Hilda, the Great Mandini and Captain Starlight. 'Forget them,' he said with a dismissive flick of his hand. He bent down to search through Dr Gomble's clothes while Lucia tore open Polartius's shirt.

Sir Chadwick, Hilda, the Great Mandini and Captain Starlight were standing shoulder to shoulder. The other Night Witches were clearly reluctant to fight them.

'To the Atlantis Boat,' Sir Chadwick ordered and the group quickly retreated to the water's edge. 'Abby, Spike!' he shouted. 'Where are you?'

Abby and Spike stood up. Wolfbane was staring across the lake at them. He raised his newly terrible wand in their direction but before he could use it, Spike seized Abby's hand and plunged them both into the lake.

Helpless, Captain Starlight and Sir Chadwick watched it happening, until the Great Mandini shouted, 'We must go, Chadwick. We can't rescue them if we're all dead.'

Reluctantly, Starlight and Sir Chadwick entered the Atlantis Boat and it immediately sank beneath the surface of the lake.

Saving the Sword of Merlin

Clutching Abby's hand, Spike struck out underwater towards where Wolfbane had last been standing. Abby had been holding her breath so long, it felt as though her lungs would burst.

Finally, Spike swam to the surface and they hid, heads just above the water at the side of the lake. Spike gently parted the reeds. Wolfbane had retreated from the lake's edge and was now looking down, gloating at the bodies of the fallen Light Witches.

'I knew Wolfbane wouldn't come too near the lake,' Spike whispered.

'Why?' Abby asked softly.

'The water is incredibly pure,' he replied.

'I suppose to a Night Witch it must be like some deadly acid.' Abby replied, knowing how Night Witches dreaded anything even moderately clean. To them, a hot bath was unspeakable torture.

As they watched, Wolfbane raised his wand above the

still forms lying at his feet and chanted:

'Light Witch and Elf now feel my hate,
To turn to wax shall be your fate,
When comes the sun you then shall melt,
And know the blow Wolfbane has dealt.'

'Come on,' shouted Valentine. 'We must get Excalibur.'

Wolfbane looked about at his own rabble of Night Witches. 'Be gone until I call you again,' he shouted at the few still scattered about the college grounds. 'And take your dead with you.'

The Night Witches seized their casualties and fluttered away into the sky as Wolfbane hurried to the doorway where Valentine and Lucia were trying to turn the keys they had seized from Dr Gomble and Polartius. It was taking them some time. Abby was grateful the locks were always so stiff. Raising herself slightly from the water she chanted:

'Weather know my Sea Witch ways,
See that winter in this garden stays,
Spring shall come when I return,
Wolfbane's vengeance you shall spurn.'

They heard the first of the keys turning in its lock.

'Hurry, Spike,' Abby whispered. 'We must get to Excalibur.'

'Take a deep breath,' Spike instructed and, clasping her hand, he plunged once again beneath the surface of the lake.

The water turned a darker shade of blue-green as they swam deeper and deeper. Abby could see interesting shapes scattered among the tangle of weeds on the lake-bed. There were great iron-bound chests, ancient statues and even the wreck of a small boat. She wished she could explore but that would have to wait.

Spike struck out strongly with his one free hand and soon a narrow gap appeared in the lake wall. It was not wide enough for them to swim side by side, but Spike pushed Abby through first and followed.

Abby had only done a dozen strokes through the narrow passageway when she burst into a flowing stream. She could see light above her.

They broke the surface together, gasped in some deep breaths, and swam to the side of the stream, where they scrambled on to a grassy bank. There was no sign of winter weather here. It was a perfect summer day.

'Over there,' called Spike and they pushed their way through a bank of long grass to stand in the sacred glade. Abby recognized the place at once. Before them stood the great granite boulder in which Excalibur was embedded.

Almost immediately, they heard curses and the sound of the Night Witches crashing through the undergrowth nearby.

Abby did not pause: she ran forward and seized the

handle of the great sword. She expected to have to pull very hard but Excalibur swung free from the granite boulder as easily as if it were a willow wand thrust into a sand bank. To her surprise, she found she could quite comfortably hold the gleaming blade in one hand, although the great sword was almost as long as she was tall.

Wolfbane was the first to crash through into the clearing, immediately followed by Valentine and Lucia who stood either side of him.

'Abby Clover!' he snarled and, pointing his wand, said with fearful loathing:

'Rats eat your flesh and gnaw your bones,
Let your eyeballs turn to stones.'

A flash of oily smoke erupted from the tip of his wand and hurtled like a bullet towards Abby, but she parried it with Excalibur, deflecting it into the ground.

'Attack the boy!' Wolfbane screamed.

Lucia and Valentine levelled their wands at Spike.

'Into the river, Spike,' Abby yelled, just managing to deflect more missiles as they ran for the embankment.

Wolfbane, Valentine and Lucia pursued them. Wolfbane shouted a spell and a thick barrier of vicious brambles sprung up before Abby and Spike. It was strong as steel cables with razor-sharp thorns glinting in the sunlight.

With one sweep of the great sword, Abby sliced through it.

They reached the embankment and Abby almost sobbed with relief when she saw the Atlantis Boat bob up to the surface.

'Abby, Spike!' Starlight shouted as he opened the hatch. They leaped from the riverbank straight through the hatchway. Starlight slammed it shut and the Atlantis Boat dived beneath the surface of the river.

Sir Chadwick was at the controls, watching their progress through the great crystal ball they used to see below the surface.

'We're entering an underground tunnel,' he informed them.

'That will be one of the Wizard Water Ways,' said Starlight.

'It's quite narrow,' said Sir Chadwick. 'Not much room to manoeuvre.'

Abby and Spike slumped down on one of the padded benches and Abby laid Excalibur on the chart table.

'You did well to save this, Abby,' said Mandini, looking at the great sword.

'Did you see what happened to Charity, Elijah and the others at Merlin?' Hilda asked.

Abby nodded, still slightly out of breath. 'Wolfbane turned them to wax.'

'To wax!' Mandini exclaimed.

'So they would melt in the sun while they were still alive,' said Spike. 'But Abby put a spell on the gardens to keep them cold until she returns.'

'It was all I could think of to do,' she said. 'I hope it works.'

'What could Wolfbane be using?' said Sir Chadwick, puzzled. 'The Ice Dust in our wands had *almost* no effect on his weapons. Whatever they've got, it's incredibly powerful.'

'I don't know,' said Abby. 'But he was most anxious to get his hands on Excalibur. Or, at least, the man who was with him was. It was someone I've never seen before.'

'I have,' said Sir Chadwick grimly. 'That was Valentine Cheeseman. Husband of Lucia and father of Wolfbane.'

'Wolfbane's father!' said Spike. 'I thought they looked alike.'

'And each one as evil as the other,' said Mandini.

'Did either of you see Benbow?' asked Captain Starlight.

'I did,' said Spike. 'Just before we dived under I saw him chasing Caspar high above the college grounds.'

'He'll turn up again,' said Starlight.

Looking relieved, Abby said, 'Well, I'm jolly glad to be safely aboard the Atlantis Bo—'

A tremendous crash at the back of the craft suddenly thrust the Atlantis Boat forward. Everyone who wasn't seated was thrown to the floor.

Sir Chadwick scrambled to his feet, quickly regained the controls and opened the throttle wider. 'Great trolls and goblins!' he gasped. 'What was that?'

'I'm focusing the crystal to the rear,' reported Captain Starlight, staying coolly in control.

'Bad trouble!' The Great Mandini spoke softly as the crystal cleared to reveal Wolfbane's Shark Boat close behind them.

'What's that attached to their prow?' asked Hilda, peering into the crystal.

Mandini looked closer. 'It appears to be a gauntlet from a suit of armour.' Then he shouted, 'Hang on, everybody, they're about to ram us again.'

Once more, the Shark Boat thrust forward and smashed its gauntletted prow into the Atlantis Boat.

'Can't we go any faster?' cried Mandini as the Shark Boat rammed them again. Leaks began to spring in the seams of the little craft.

'I think one of the engines may be damaged,' said Starlight as they hurtled on through the underground river.

Suddenly, the lights failed and they were plunged into darkness just as they took another massive blow.

'We must escape somehow,' Sir Chadwick cried out.

Without thinking, Abby took the handle of Excalibur and, remembering the dented silver coin in the pocket of her Atlantis cape, she took it in her other hand and muttered quietly:

'Silver, silver from the ground,
Take us where you first were found.'

Suddenly, a great surge of power coursed through Excalibur, as if the sword had come to life in Abby's hand. One great flash illuminated the Atlantis Boat's cabin for less than a second, then there was only perfect blackness.

They could all feel themselves hurtling towards some unknown destination. There was no longer any buffeting from the river's current, just the sensation of rushing through time and space. Finally, they realized they had come to a halt. The Atlantis Boat was at rest. But where? They were not on water and the boat had tilted over on its port side.

A Strange Destination

On board the Atlantis Boat they could see nothing in the crystal to tell them where they might be – all was blackness. One pale emergency light still shone in the cabin.

'Is everyone all right?' Sir Chadwick enquired, and was relieved to hear there were no injuries.

'How are you, Boat?' asked Abby.

The Atlantis Boat answered in a soothing voice. 'I have sustained some damage but I will repair myself in a short time. Thank you for your concern.'

'Are you able to turn on your floodlights?' asked Captain Starlight.

'It will be some time before I am able to perform that function,' replied the boat.

'I'll get the St Elmo lamps,' said Starlight, taking some glowing globes of glass from a locker.

'Does anyone have any Ice Dust?' asked Sir Chadwick. 'My wand is quite empty.'

The others all shook their heads. 'We used it all in the fight at the lake, Chadwick,' said Mandini.

'There's no more on board the boat,' said Starlight.

'I think we'd better go and take a look outside,' said Sir Chadwick, opening the hatch and leading the way.

'Shall I bring Excalibur?' Abby asked as she was about to follow the others.

Sir Chadwick paused and thought for a moment before shaking his head. 'No. Better leave it on board for safekeeping,' he replied.

The light from their lamps revealed that the Atlantis Boat was facing the end of a narrow tunnel roughly cut through earth and rock. They examined the damage and Starlight said, 'It looks as if holes have been punched in it with a powerful fist.'

'We seem to be in some sort of mine,' said Mandini, studying the walls. 'You see, there are wooden pit props here,' he added.

'I think this shaft may have been abandoned,' said Abby, looking at the blank wall of earth close to the prow of the Atlantis Boat.

'Why do you say that?' asked Spike.

'I don't know,' she answered. 'It just has that feeling houses have when people no longer live in them.'

'You're right, child,' said Sir Chadwick. 'That's Light Witch instinct. I feel it too. Let's go back along the tunnel,' he said. 'Perhaps other parts of the mine will still be active.'

In single file, they followed Sir Chadwick until he stopped abruptly. They crowded forward to see three points of light fizzing towards the wall of the tunnel a few paces ahead of them.

After a moment, it dawned on Captain Starlight what they were.

'Dynamite!' he shouted. 'Run for your lives.'

They dashed forward, passed the fizzing dynamite, and stumbled along the tunnel until they heard a voice call out from a shallow inlet in the wall.

They all crammed in beside three crouching men, who looked astonished by their sudden arrival. The men wore rough clothes and helmets with flickering lamps attached. There was a shattering explosion. The ground quaked for a few moments and the walls around them trembled. Abby felt as if a great hand had given her entire body a mighty shove. The air instantly filled with choking dust.

As the dust began to settle it left a haze in the air, like fog on an autumn morning. The miners were talking excitedly in a language Abby had not heard before.

'Can you read their minds, Mandini?' Sir Chadwick asked.

The magician shook his head. 'I'm afraid their thoughts are too wild and random for me to comprehend at the moment,' he replied with a shrug.

'I seem to recognize a few words of their language but it will take some minutes for me to remember enough of the grammar,' said Sir Chadwick.

Hilda spotted that one of the men was carrying a bird-cage with a canary in it. She chirruped a few sentences and the canary chattered away to her. She translated as the bird answered her questions.

'The miners are Polish,' she said, 'but from a part of Poland where they speak a lot of German.'

'So, are we in Poland?' asked Sir Chadwick.

'I'm afraid the bird doesn't know exactly where it is,' said Hilda. 'The men were coal miners in Poland but they left and went on a long voyage that took several weeks.'

'So, all we know is that this isn't a coal mine and we're a long way from Poland,' said Spike.

'Come, come,' one of the miners now said in English and tugged Sir Chadwick by the arm.

'We should go and check on the Atlantis Boat,' he answered.

But to their dismay, when they stepped out of the inlet, they saw that the part of the tunnel where the Atlantis Boat rested was now sealed off, and it was clear to them that the miners were preparing to dig a new shaft in quite another direction.

'Come, come,' the miner repeated.

Reluctantly, they followed the three men. There were rail tracks in this part of the mine and wagons for transporting the rubble that had been dug out. After walking for some time they reached a part of the mine where the tunnel was of much larger proportions. There was also the cage and machinery of a lift. The miners made signs for them to enter the cage. One pulled a rope and high above them they heard a bell ring. The machinery clanked into action and the cage ascended.

When they reached the surface, they found themselves in a building that housed a steam engine which operated the lift. When they alighted, an angry red-faced man with a wide moustache was standing next to the cage.

'What in the name of Hades were you folks doing down there?' he shouted in English as the miners grouped about him. 'I'm the foreman of this mine. Don't you know you're trespassing?'

'I do apologise,' said Sir Chadwick, smoothly. 'On behalf of myself and my colleagues, please accept our sincere regrets for any inconvenience we may have caused.'

Before the foreman could think how to respond to such uncommon courtesy, Mandini waved a hand in front of the bewildered men. 'You will all forget you have ever seen us,' he intoned.

'Shouldn't you have said that in Polish as well?' asked Spike.

'The language of magic is universal,' replied Mandini, as Sir Chadwick led the party from the rough wooden building.

Once outside, they stood in dazzling sunshine, blinking at the astonishing scene before them.

A View of Silver Springs

The mine from which they had just emerged had been sunk in the middle of a town's main street. It was obvious at a glance that they were somewhere in the Wild West of America at a time when pioneers were still settling on the land. The street was lined mostly with wooden buildings. Some were weathered-looking and basic, with corrugated iron roofs. Other more substantial ones looked brand new. Clearly, much of the town had only been built in the last few years. Buildings were actually being constructed as they stood, taking it all in. Workmen bustled about vacant lots, sawing and hammering timbers, erecting frames for new buildings.

Facing them across the street was a large general store, its windows filled with pots, pans, ropes, saddles, boots, hats and guns. Barrels and sacks of goods were stacked outside it on the sidewalk. Next door was a newspaper office. Through its window they could see a printing machine. There was a barber's shop. One sign proclaimed

Land Registration Office. And the biggest building of all, which was four storeys high, displayed a large sign with the name *Silver Springs Saloon* written in flowery lettering over its imposing verandah.

Most of the buildings along the main street had wide covered verandahs that cast deep shade over the people on them. The surface of the street was thick with a powdery reddish dust that rose in continuous clouds around the hooves of the horses. A small herd of cattle, flanked by two cowboys, raised even more dust as it passed.

The little town was busy. People thronged the sidewalks. A few wore city clothes, but most were dressed in western outfits. They all stared with undisguised curiosity at the strangers who had appeared in their main street.

'I wonder why they are so interested in us,' Sir Chadwick pondered. 'We look no more colourful than they do.'

'I think it may be me, dearest,' Hilda said. 'My clothes

must look rather odd in this time and place. Gentlemen seem to wear all sorts of clothing, but look at the ladies.'

Most of the women who were walking in the main street were wearing long dark frocks and bonnets. A few, more splendid in bustles and fancy feathered hats, carried parasols against the fierce glare of the sun.

The dress Hilda wore was much shorter than any other in sight. Everyone seemed to be staring at her ankles and there were some grim expressions of disapproval from certain ladies.

Mandini swept off his long magician's cloak and draped it about Hilda's shoulders. As he was much taller than Hilda it reached to the ground, enveloping her entire body.

'Thank you, Mandini,' she said gratefully. 'I feel much less conspicuous now.'

'How on earth did we get here?' asked Captain Starlight.

'I think I know,' said Abby.

'What exactly did you do to bring us here, Abby?' asked Sir Chadwick.

Abby thought for a moment. 'I was holding Excalibur in my hand,' she answered. 'Then I took hold of the coin in my pocket—' She stopped and looked down at her clothes in surprise. Her Atlantis cape had changed completely. It had transformed itself into a red shirt, a fringed leather waistcoat, a buckskin skirt and leather cowgirl boots. She felt something on her head and reached up to take off a wide-brimmed hat with a silver band.

Spike's Atlantis cape had also transformed itself. He was wearing wild-west clothes, too, but his trousers and shirt were in his favourite shade of blue.

From a pocket in her buckskin skirt Abby withdrew the coin and was astonished to see it was no longer dented!

Sir Chadwick took it from her, and Captain Starlight, Hilda and Mandini crowded around to look at the coin.

'A silver dollar, minted in 1886,' he said softly, reading the date aloud. 'What chant did you use, Abby?'

'The fetcher elves' chant,' she replied, and recited:

'Silver, silver in the ground,
Take us where you first were found.'

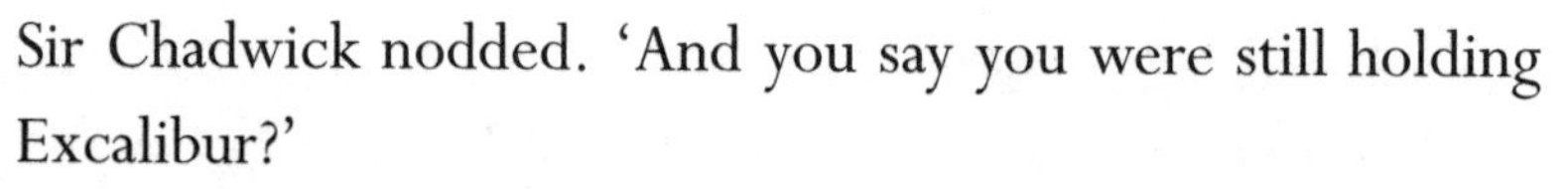

Sir Chadwick nodded. 'And you say you were still holding Excalibur?'

'Yes,' said Abby.

'That explains it,' he continued. 'The sword must have intensified the spell; made it so powerful, in fact, it was enough to transport the Atlantis Boat and all of us to the mine from which the silver for this coin was taken.'

'Well, no matter how it came about, we're very grateful, Abby,' said Hilda.

'Yes,' said Starlight. 'One more blow from that Shark Boat and we could have been done for.'

Sir Chadwick nodded approvingly. 'A good job for us all that you pay such close attention to your lessons, child.'

Abby thanked him for the compliment, but something still concerned her. 'My parents will be awfully worried if we get stuck in the past, Sir Chadwick. I hope we'll get home in time for Christmas.'

He smiled reassuringly. 'Once we find the Atlantis Boat, we shall ask it to take us back to whatever exact time suits us. I don't expect your parents will miss you at all.'

Only Mandini looked anxious. 'Won't Wolfbane be able to track us through time, Chadwick?' he asked. 'He's fiendishly clever. Perhaps he'll get to the Atlantis Boat and Excalibur before we can.'

Mandini's words caused the friends to pause uncomfortably, for a moment. Sir Chadwick stooped down and took a handful of dusty red soil. He blew gently on it, closed his hand and, pointing across the street, said, *'Balaki!'*

A rather self-important-looking man strolling along the opposite side of the street looked up astonished as his hat rose from his head and turned over three times before depositing itself back on his head. The man snatched off the hat, examined it, puzzled, then walked on with rather less self-assurance.

'What are you doing, dearest?' asked Hilda.

Sir Chadwick smiled. 'Do you all have a feeling of well-being?' he asked.

'Actually, I feel tiptop,' said Mandini, and the others agreed.

'It's the soil around here,' said Sir Chadwick. 'It's not an unknown phenomenon in other parts of the world.'

'What is, dearest?' asked Hilda, with just a hint of impatience.

'There's Ice Dust in the ground. Just the tiniest traces, probably left over from deposits in the ancient past. Not in sufficient quantities for us to use but enough to stop a Night Witch from detecting the Atlantis Boat.'

'But will it be enough to stop him detecting us?' asked Spike.

Sir Chadwick shook his head. 'Nothing is ever perfect in life, my boy.'

'What are we going to do now, Chadwick?' Hilda asked.

He smiled confidently. 'I think we shall take stock of our surroundings and establish the exact date before we act. We should be able to find that information in the newspaper office,' he replied. To Abby and Spike he said, 'Remember to look both ways before you cross the road. Americans drive on the other side to us, you know.'

'They just seem to gallop about on any old side,' Spike said to Abby as they all made their way through the wagons, buggies, horses and cattle that crowded the dusty narrow street.

They found the front page of the latest edition of the *Silver Springs Recorder* hanging in the window of the newspaper office. Sir Chadwick read the date aloud. 'It's the fourth of July, 1886.'

'Independence Day,' said Captain Starlight.

'By the beard of Merlin, so it is,' exclaimed Sir Chadwick. 'I think I'd like to see more of the lie of the land,' he said, looking down the main street.

Abby pointed to a staircase on the outside of the Silver Springs Hotel which led to a balcony fringing its shingled roof. 'We could go up there and look over the countryside,' she said.

'Excellent idea,' he replied.

A few minutes later, Sir Chadwick, Hilda, Captain Starlight, Mandini, Spike and Abby were standing on a rampart that ran around the roof of the entire building.

The air was extraordinarily clear once they were high above the dusty street. The only clouds in the sky wreathed a distant range of mountains to the west, which were sharply in focus even though they were many miles away. From their vantage point they could examine all of the landscape stretched about them.

The town stood at the mouth of a long, wide valley. At each side of the valley the land rose up and levelled off in flat desert plains that were dotted with tall cacti. From the distant mountains a single river meandered across the valley. They could see where other rivers must have flowed from the mountains, criss-crossing the valley, but they all appeared to have run dry.

'Look,' Spike said to Abby, pointing, 'a stream must have once flowed along there, next to the town.'

The course of the river had obviously run parallel to the main street, which was really all the town consisted of, apart from a few barns, corrals and outbuildings to the rear of the shops, saloons and houses. On the eastern end of the little town was a small oasis of greenery. In it stood one large house surrounded by trees and even a large lawn. The rest of the town appeared to be as dry as the desert.

'Where do you think Silver Springs is in America, Captain Starlight?' Abby asked.

'Somewhere in Arizona would be my guess,' he replied. 'There were little mining towns like this all over the southwest in the nineteenth century. A few became big cities; others became ghost towns when the silver or gold ran out.'

As they continued looking down on the main street, they could see that the mine they had just come from was not the only shaft in Silver Springs. There was another one close by but it was boarded up and looked abandoned. A collection of rickety shacks and tents at the west end of town were scattered about a large corral, where the main street petered out into the surrounding countryside.

Suddenly, there was a rattle of explosions that sounded like fireworks. 'Fourth of July celebrations, I suppose,' said Mandini.

But it wasn't fireworks. They looked down to see two men backing out of a saloon across the street. Each held a pistol and was firing back through the swinging doors. Two figures followed them out, rapidly returning the gunfire.

The crowds on the street and sidewalks below scattered to take cover. In a moment the street was deserted except for the four men shooting at each other.

It was all over in a minute. The two men who had fled from the saloon lay in the dust. Laughing, the two who had shot them holstered their pistols and returned to the saloon. Almost immediately, the crowds returned to the street and resumed their business as if nothing had happened. A few minutes later, two men in a splendid horse-drawn hearse pulled up and lifted the bodies into the back before driving away.

'Perhaps that's the way they like to celebrate the fourth of July in Silver Springs,' said Spike dryly.

Sir Chadwick turned away from the scene below and said, 'I think we'd better review the situation. Would you like to summarize our position, Mandini?'

'As you wish, Chadwick,' he replied. 'We have been transported to Arizona in the year 1886. The Atlantis Boat is sealed several hundred metres below the earth in the abandoned tunnel of a silver mine. Excalibur, the most powerful and precious heirloom the Light Witches possess, is on board. We have no Ice Dust and no weapons to protect ourselves in a clearly lawless town, and we can expect Wolfbane to pursue us at some point. We also have no money.'

'Would anyone like to add anything?' asked Sir Chadwick.

'I have a silver dollar,' said Abby.

'And we have our strength, our wits and our talent,' said Sir Chadwick with sudden enthusiasm. He waved around him. 'That is all the people of this great republic had when they came as pioneers into the wilderness. Are we any less than them?'

'Are we going to be pioneers?' asked Spike.

'Certainly not,' replied Sir Chadwick. 'We shall do what all Light Witches do when they are in trouble.'

'What's that?' said Spike.

'Tell him, Abby,' said Sir Chadwick.

'Head for the nearest theatre,' said Abby.

'Correct, child,' said Sir Chadwick.

'Will there be a theatre here?' asked Spike doubtfully.

'Almost certainly,' replied Sir Chadwick. 'There were theatres all over the wild west. It was the favourite form of entertainment.'

'I would have thought it was shooting each other,' said Spike, but Sir Chadwick ignored him and, striking a dramatic pose against the skyline, pointed to the staircase, declaiming:

'March on bravely! Let us to't, pell mell –
If not to heaven, then hand in hand to hell.'

The others followed him down the stairs, with Spike and Abby at the rear.

'I'm not so sure about that last part,' Spike whispered to her.

'Don't worry, he's only quoting from Shakespeare again,' Abby replied with a grin.

Some Prominent Citizens of Silver Springs

Sir Chadwick and Hilda led them all back out on to the narrow sidewalk, and as they were passing the doorway of a rather grand establishment built of brick and white stone, another fusillade of shots sent them rushing for cover.

Sir Chadwick and Hilda swept Abby and Spike into the open doorway, and were quickly followed by Starlight and Mandini. They found themselves standing in a gloomy interior, peering out at the sunlit street.

A huge bearded man dressed in tatty buckskins, who appeared to be very drunk, stood swaying in the middle of the main street, randomly firing two pistols and causing the citizens to scatter and take cover.

'Part bobcat, part rattlesnake, that's me,' he roared defiantly. 'When I want a fight, cougars move to the next county. I can wrestle with bears, eat cactus and spit bullets.' He fired the pistols again. 'Who dares to fight The Kentucky Kid?'

'What a dreadful braggart,' said Sir Chadwick. 'I'll go and have a word with him.'

'You have no Ice Dust,' Mandini warned him.

'Hmmm, perhaps not, then,' said Sir Chadwick.

Abby had an idea. She could see that behind the wild figure, a mule was hitched to a rail. The mule had its head turned, watching the man balefully. Abby took the silver dollar from her pocket and reaching forward, held it in a thin stream of bright sunlight that cut through the shadows, reflecting the sun into the raging man's eyes.

He staggered backwards to avoid the blinding light. The moment he was close enough, the mule lashed out with its back legs. The Kentucky Kid soared through the air to land in a crumpled heap in the dust with all the fight knocked out of him.

'That was clever,' Spike said, impressed. 'You couldn't have done better with a spell.'

'Can I help you, ladies and gentlemen?' asked a high-pitched voice behind them. They swung around in alarm, blinking until their eyes adjusted to the gloom of the interior. They were in a bank.

A man stood there, obviously waiting for them to answer. Dressed in black, he was quite thin except for a protruding stomach that swelled his waistcoat and drew attention to his heavy gold watch chain. He wasn't very tall but he nonetheless seemed to be looking down at them through a pair of silver-framed spectacles that rested on the bridge of his nose. His face was unlined and his high-domed forehead was accentuated by a fringe of white hair that grew down into substantial side whiskers. Abby could see he considered himself someone of importance.

'We require no help at the moment,' Sir Chadwick replied easily, 'but that may change in the near future, sir.'

'Allow me to introduce myself,' said the man in black. 'I am Homer P. Stout and I own this establishment, the Bank of Silver Springs.'

Sir Chadwick inclined his head. 'And I am Sir Chadwick

Street, this is my wife Lady Street, my companions Captain Adam Starlight and the Great Mandini.' Pointing to Abby and Spike, he added, 'The children have titles too – but we just call them Abby and Spike.'

Homer P. Stout's attitude underwent a sudden change. 'Delighted to make your acquaintance, Sir Chadwick,' he smiled. 'And may I say it's a pleasure to see people of your cut and calibre moving into Silver Springs. With children too. It shows faith in the future, sir, it certainly does. That is what this territory needs, faith in the future . . . and perhaps the hanging of one or two of the rascals who provide the lawless element here in town.'

There was a slight cough which drew their attention to another man who was standing behind the counter. He was even thinner than Homer P. Stout. His lank blonde hair flopped down on either side of his bony forehead, emphasizing his narrow face and the largest Adam's apple Abby had ever seen, bobbing above his high starched collar. Like Mr Stout, he was dressed in black but his suit was definitely of an inferior quality.

'May I introduce my assistant and chief cashier, Hiram Prune.'

'Delighted, sir,' said Sir Chadwick, and the others nodded.

'I'm surprised to see such a swell establishment this far west,' said Captain Starlight. 'You must have had to freight the stone and bricks a long haul.'

'It was worth every cent,' said Mr Stout. 'People like to

know their cash is safe. There's a lot of money in this town. Last year alone, they took three million dollars' worth of silver out of the mine.'

'I imagine robbers would think twice when they saw the bars on your windows, Mr Stout,' said Abby.

'Those bars are nothing, little lady,' replied Mr Stout. 'Just take a look at the safe back there.'

Behind Hiram Prune was a massive steel vault that filled the entire rear wall of the bank. Its hugely thick door had two great locks with keyholes large enough for Abby to put a hand inside.

'It took two teams of thirty-two mules to haul that from the railhead,' said Mr Stout proudly. 'This is the finest safe west of St Louis.'

'Splendid,' said Sir Chadwick. 'We know where to come when we have funds that need protecting. Now, if you would be so kind, Mr Stout, could you tell us if there is a theatrical company in town?'

Homer P. Stout stroked his chin while he considered the question. 'Well, there is and there isn't,' he said finally. 'There is certainly a building, but I think the theatre company has gone out of business. I saw most of them leaving on the stagecoach to Tucson this morning. The theatre building is along the way, just beyond the blacksmith's shop and the livery stable.'

Sir Chadwick tipped his hat. 'Until we meet again, Mr Stout.'

* * *

Another volley of shots greeted them as they left the bank, this time from inside one of the many saloons, but at least there was no shooting actually on the street. However, there was a raucous fist fight raging in the dust between a group of miners and several cowboys. One of the cowboys was knocked sprawling at Hilda's feet. The cowboy leaped up and swept off his hat in a deep bow to Hilda. 'Please forgive me, ma'am,' he said before diving back into the fray.

They hurried on towards the only other building in Silver Springs that wasn't constructed of wood. It was the blacksmith's shop and was made of sun-baked mud. Captain Starlight slapped the wall as they stopped to watch a great bear of a man hammering a length of red-hot metal on the anvil that was set up outside.

'*Adobe*,' that what the Mexicans call this method of building. I've seen whole villages built like this,' said Starlight. Looking down at a box of old horseshoes by the door, he added, 'Would you spare me a few of these, friend?'

The blacksmith, who had stopped hammering and was now plunging the hot metal rod into a trough of cooling water, replied cheerfully, 'Help yourself.'

Captain Starlight took four horseshoes and tucked them into his belt, winking at Spike and Abby. 'Horseshoes are supposed to be lucky,' he said as Sir Chadwick led them on.

At last they came to the theatre, a handsome-looking building constructed of wood. It rose two storeys above a wide porticoed entrance that was flanked with pillars. Surmounting the whole structure was a copper dome glinting in the sunlight.

They entered, passed the box office and went on through large doors to stand in the dim interior. There was just enough light coming from a grand chandelier hanging over the stalls to reveal a surprisingly splendid decor.

Two tiers of boxes stood on each side of the stage and a single gallery swept in a semi-circle above the stalls. The seating was upholstered in rose velvet and the lavishly plush carpet was royal blue, piped in gold.

'I must say, this is more splendid than I expected,' said Sir Chadwick as he led the party down through the centre aisle to stand before the orchestra pit.

They heard voices arguing, then two men and a woman came on to the stage. The younger of the men had one arm in a sling. The older man was portly but he stood erect with his head of flowing silver hair held high. A large moustache curled to meet his side whiskers.

'Ruined, I tell you – I'm ruined,' said the slim younger man, clutching a curtain with his free arm and lowering his head of dark curls.

'Don't give in to despair, my boy,' said the older man. 'You still have a great career ahead of you.'

'Please listen to him, Quincy,' said the young woman, whose hair was as dark and curly as the young man's, and her eyes the same shade of light brown. She tugged gently at his arm in the sling. 'I know we can overcome this dreadful adversity.'

But the young man pulled free and buried his face deeper into the curtain. 'What have I got to offer you now, sister, but poverty and dishonour?'

'Poverty, maybe,' the young woman replied, 'but dishonour – never!'

'They're overacting a bit, don't you think?' Spike whispered to Abby. 'Sir Chadwick is far more realistic on the stage than they are.'

As the actors fell silent, Sir Chadwick cleared his throat and the three on stage swung their gaze down towards the intruders.

'I'm so sorry to interrupt your rehearsal,' said Sir Chadwick.

'*Rehearsal*, sir?' replied the younger man in a hollow voice. 'This is no rehearsal. This is real life!' He peered down at the group of strangers in the stalls. 'Who are you?' he demanded. 'More riffraff sent by Stoneheart to persecute us, I suppose.'

Sir Chadwick quickly climbed the steps to the stage and the others followed. 'I can assure you, sir, I have only your best interests at heart,' he began, and bowed, at the same time sweeping off his hat with an elegant flourish. 'My name is Sir Chadwick Street. I am actor-manager of the Alhambra Theatre, Shaftesbury Avenue, London.'

'Sir Chadwick Street!' repeated the young man, incredulous. 'But your fame proceeds you, sir. I have read ecstatic accounts of your performances, both as Richard III and King Lear.'

'You honour me,' replied Sir Chadwick, with a modest smile. He made a sweeping motion to include the others. 'This is my wife Lady Street, known in London, where she also graces the stage, as Hilda Bluebell. My friends: Captain Adam Starlight, a seafaring gentleman; the Great Mandini, master of magic and illusion; and last but not least, Spike and Abby. They may be young but they are supreme companions in any adventure.'

'Sir Chadwick,' said the young man, 'I am delighted to make your acquaintance and that of your companions, but I fear you have called on us in sorry times. Due to peculiar circumstances, I must beg you to leave our theatre or your very lives may be forfeit.'

Sir Chadwick drew himself up. 'We are not the kind of people who flinch from danger. Tell us your problem, sir. You will find us very resourceful.'

'Problem!' repeated the young man bitterly. 'I can sum up my problem in one word: Stoneheart! The villain who blights our lives. A vicious tyrant who seeks to force his will upon free people and bend them to his base desires.'

'Exactly *how* does he force his will upon you?' asked Sir Chadwick.

'I can tell you,' said the older man in a deep booming voice. 'He is a serpent, with a tongue so forked, all words he speaks are twisted to a baser meaning.'

'True, true,' said the young man and woman, gazing in admiration at the older figure.

'Was he quoting Shakespeare?' whispered Mandini,

puzzled. 'I've no idea what he's talking about.'

Sir Chadwick shook his head and whispered back, 'It's just a manner of speech some older actors acquire.'

He tried again, this time addressing the young woman. 'This chap, Stoneheart, how did he do you wrong, precisely?'

She laid the back of her wrist on her brow before moaning, 'He has made the golden pleasures of our carefree days a mockery.'

Sir Chadwick could see he was getting nowhere. He whispered to Mandini, 'Do you think you can get them to give me their full attention, old boy? I would like some specific answers.'

Mandini nodded, and with a flourish snapped his fingers in the air. A pure white dove flew from his empty hand. Open-mouthed, the three watched as it circled above the stalls, flew back to perch on his shoulder and vanished! Mandini snapped his fingers again and the three people watched carefully as he passed his flickering fingers before their eyes.

'Be calm and answer Sir Chadwick's questions as fully as possible,' he said in a soothing voice.

The Master of Light Witches nodded his thanks and spoke again to the young man. 'First, tell me your names and the exact nature of the misfortune you suffer.'

The young man replied now in a calmer voice, 'My name is Quincy Flowerdale and this is my theatre. What you see before you, Sir Chadwick, is what remains of my company. Miss Laura Paradine, here, is my sister but uses the name Paradine in her theatrical career. And this is Oscar Wilkington Fitzroy, an actor of international renown.'

Miss Paradine curtsied and Mr Fitzroy gave a stately bow as Quincy Flowerdale continued. 'I came to Silver Springs as a prospector and discovered the first silver mine, which thrived. With the profits I built this theatre in pursuance of my real dream, which was to bring the great plays of the world to the west.'

'A commendable ambition, Mr Flowerdale,' said Sir Chadwick. 'And how did your plans go awry?'

'There is a villain here in Silver Springs, sir – a reptile nestling in the bosom of our fair city. His name is Bart Stoneheart.' Flowerdale gave a shudder of revulsion as he uttered the name. But he reset his shoulders, as if he had overcome some great adversity, and continued. 'My silver mine prospered and the theatre thrived. Then one day Stoneheart came like a snake out of the desert and built the Silver Springs Saloon on the main street.' Flowerdale rolled his eyes to the ceiling. 'That was my downfall. I gambled most of my fortune away, but I did not care. My silver mine continued to thrive and the theatre played to packed houses. It did not make a great deal of money but it paid its own expenses.' He slapped his forehead. 'What a fool I was.'

'Go on,' encouraged Sir Chadwick gently.

'The seam in my silver mine ran out,' Flowerdale said bleakly. 'Meanwhile, Stoneheart had opened another shaft next to mine. His prospered. I went on paying the miners I employed until I had nothing left. I was forced to close down the mine and scratch along with the tiny income from the theatre. But I was determined that the theatre would not fail. We made economies. I even turned our home into a boarding house.'

'So, what has caused your latest misfortune?' asked Abby.

Flowerdale gave a grim smile. 'Bart Stoneheart became intoxicated with power. The richer he became, the more outrageous was his behaviour. When this town was first settled, the valley beyond it was fertile – a lush green haven for settlers. But the rivers dried up and Stoneheart was able to buy the land cheaply, all but the few farms and ranches that lie next to the one remaining river. He has a gang of desperadoes, each one a crack shot. Stoneheart himself is an expert with his six-shooters.'

'Is there no sheriff here?' asked Starlight.

Flowerdale shook his head. 'Every time the town appointed one he was assassinated by Stoneheart's men.'

'Why did the rest of your company decide to leave this morning?' asked Hilda.

Flowerdale drew himself up to his full height and spoke in a quiet voice charged with emotion. 'Last night, the company was performing *Romeo and Juliet* by William Shakespeare. It was the first time we had included the play in our repertoire and a great many in the auditorium were deeply moved.'

He stopped and sighed.

'Go on,' said Sir Chadwick.

'During the interval, when the audience had retired to the bar for refreshments, Mrs Stout, the wife of our banker and a lady of some refinement, was talking about both Romeo and Juliet dying at the end of the play.'

'Yes,' said Sir Chadwick.

'Bart Stoneheart overheard and made several substantial wagers with people in the bar that the play would have a happy ending. Then he came backstage and instructed me to change the play so that the lovers would live happily ever after!'

'Unthinkable!' Sir Chadwick interjected angrily.

'Exactly,' said Flowerdale. 'I told him that such an outrageous change to the plot was out of the question, and he returned to his box.'

'What happened next?' asked Mandini.

'We finished the play as it was written, and Bart Stoneheart shot me.'

'Shot you!' Hilda and Sir Chadwick both exclaimed.

Flowerdale nodded. 'Then, standing in his box, Stoneheart warned the other actors that in future all plays would be performed to his liking, and he would shoot any actor whose performance displeased him.'

He sighed again. 'I'm afraid the rest of the company were not made of the same stuff as my sister and Mr Fitzroy. They left on the stagecoach this morning. Even if we wished to defy Stoneheart, there are no longer enough of us here.'

Sir Chadwick raised a hand. 'Despair not, my fellow Thespians. I place myself and my companions at your disposal.'

Flowerdale looked up, sudden hope in his eyes. 'You mean you are prepared to risk the wrath of Bart Stoneheart?'

'Now and forever!' proclaimed Sir Chadwick, his voice ringing out to the furthest seats in the gallery above.

16

Wolfbane Makes His Plans

Trapped! On board the Shark Boat, Wolfbane paced up and down, seething with frustration. All day, since they'd overcome the defenders of Merlin College but failed to capture Excalibur, snow had been falling. Valentine and Lucia stared hopelessly out of a porthole at the thick white blanket of ghastliness. Night Witches could not bear the touch of anything so pure as fresh snow.

'I'm sure it's the work of that blasted child, Abby Clover,' snarled Wolfbane. 'I've never known such a powerful Light Witch spell.'

'Just make it go away,' Lucia demanded imperiously.

Valentine shook his head. 'And use more of the Black Dust we have? Be sensible, woman.'

'Just use a speck,' she pleaded, 'for *my* sake.'

'He's right, we can't afford even a speck,' replied Wolfbane.

Lucia's attitude changed again. 'This is what I get for

marrying beneath me,' she said, contemptuous now. 'I should have known better than to marry someone called *Cheeseman*.'

'Beneath you!' repeated Valentine, incredulous. 'Must I remind you that you were living on turnips and rats' heads when I plucked you from that job as a scullery maid and made you my bride?'

'I was *not* a scullery maid,' said Lucia haughtily. 'You know very well I was working undercover. The Duke of Gunford had hired me to poison his cousin.'

Wolfbane rolled his eyes in exasperation. 'For Satan's sake stop this futile bickering. We have to overcome Abby Clover's spell.'

'The boy's right. That child is a power to be reckoned with. You should have killed her when you had the chance,' Valentine said, addressing Lucia.

'Don't you think we've *tried* to kill her?' Wolfbane sighed. 'And *don't* call me a *boy*.'

'What should I call you?' said his father sarcastically. 'Would you prefer *Snivel*?'

'*Wolfbane*, if you must – but my correct title is *Master*.'

'Well, *Master* Wolfbane, what do you think we should do now? We can't stay on this boat forever.'

'I'm well aware of that,' said Wolfbane. 'Just give me time to think.'

Valentine nodded. Turning from the porthole he looked about the Shark Boat's interior. Everything was black except where patches of green slime coated some of the surfaces. There was a sticky sludge on the floor that smelt like scrapings from a sewer outlet.

Valentine took a deep breath. 'At least the air is breathable in here,' he said. It looks disgustingly fresh outside.'

'Mother!' Wolfbane commanded suddenly. 'You'll find some emergency fine-weather gear in the locker behind you. Be so kind as to break it out.'

Lucia sullenly did as he asked. Most places Night Witches ventured into were polluted enough to be pleasant for them. But occasionally they encountered a particularly clear day when the air was was so clean that it was, for them, a health hazard.

Lucia handed out the fine-weather gear. 'Nose blockers,' she said crisply. Wolfbane and Valentine each took two black plugs from her outstretched hand and fitted them into their nostrils.

'How long will they last?' asked Valentine.

'They're the latest design,' answered Wolfbane. 'They have a lifespan of twenty years.'

'The marvels of the modern world!' sighed Valentine. 'When I was young we had to stuff our noses with the dusty fluff from under beds – and it wasn't all that effective.'

Lucia passed them each a set of greasy overalls, high boots and wide-brimmed hats.

Valentine held his up. 'Nothing new about these,' he said.

'We got them as a job lot from a Victorian sewage

farm,' said Wolfbane. 'We tried all sorts of modern stuff but nothing touched the Night Witch foulness standard of these. The Victorians certainly knew how to make sewage.'

'Right,' Wolfbane said crisply, when they had all put on their emergency gear. 'Follow me, and don't hang about.'

He opened the hatch, stepped from the deck on to the snow-covered lawn and hurried towards the college buildings.

In the main quadrangle, he paused for a moment to get his bearings.

'What are you looking for?' asked Valentine.

'The rooms of my old Wizard Physics tutor,' he replied. 'If I remember correctly, Professor Newton Mars lived on that staircase.' He led them into one of the ancient buildings and up some narrow twisting stairs.

'This is it,' said Wolfbane, entering a pleasant, book-lined sitting room. 'Come in here, it's the bathroom,' said Wolfbane, opening another door, sure of his location now.

'*Bathroom!*' exclaimed both Lucia and Valentine suspiciously.

'Oh, come on,' said Wolfbane impatiently.

They entered the little room that was decorated with blue tiles depicting dolphins. An old-fashioned tub with claw feet stood on a raised plinth. Valentine and Lucia shuddered at how clean it all was.

'Sit in the tub,' said Wolfbane.

'In there?' said Lucia, outraged. 'Ughh! If I do that I'll feel *clean* for a week.'

'Trust me,' said Wolfbane.

Reluctantly, his mother and father climbed into the tub, and Wolfbane stepped in after them. To their horror, he reached forward to turn on both taps.

'Are you mad?' screeched Valentine.

But instead of water gushing over them, the bath flipped over and began to spin at an astonishing speed. A high-pitched whine rose to a crescendo, then faded away as the spinning bathtub began to slow down.

When it finally came to a stop, Valentine and Lucia climbed out, gaping about them. There was no ceiling or walls – just an endlessly vast glowing floor. It appeared to be made of opaque glass, and was all that illuminated their surroundings. Above them, set in the dark depths of infinite space, glittered the stars of a galaxy neither of them had ever seen before.

Scattered about haphazardly, and reaching to the horizon in all directions, were extraordinary machines of all shapes and sizes. Some were as big as houses and others as small as a child's pram. The nearest looked something like a steam train without wheels. It was painted dark-green with gold edging and the surface was studded with valves and pistons. Another was a silver orb as high as a telephone box. Next to it was a monstrous contraption with wings and huge wheels with a painted dragon's head attached to the front.

Wolfbane led them through the maze of contraptions. He was searching for something.

'Where are we, my boy?' Valentine questioned as he hurried after him.

'This is Professor Newton Mars's Museum of Time Travel,' replied Wolfbane. Actually, we're in the fourth dimension, where he stores all this stuff.'

Wolfbane suddenly stopped at a contraption that looked like a small letter-box with a hood. 'Give me that piece we knocked off the Atlantis Boat,' he said, holding out his hand.

Valentine handed him a fragment of the boat's scale cladding. Wolfbane placed it in a slot at the front of the contraption. He stuck his head under a hood. There was just enough space for Valentine and Lucia to join him.

'What is this?' asked Valentine.

'It's a time-tracker,' replied Wolfbane, sighing. 'Don't you know anything?'

'I never had your advantages,' Valentine replied stiffly. 'Your mother and I made sacrifices to send you to the best boarding schools so you would be able to secure a place at Merlin College. Life was easy for you. I was educated in the university of the gutter. I'll have you know I was apprenticed to Wormwood the Sorcerer at the age of thirteen. No rugger matches, jolly teas and pillow fights in the dormitory for me. Just a nineteen-hour day and the kitchen scraps for supper. Why, I could—'

'Can't you shut him up, Mother?' Wolfbane interrupted irritably. I'm trying to concentrate. Ah! What's this?'

The swirling mass in the crystal ball concealed beneath the hood had finally settled into total blackness.

Wolfbane was puzzled. 'What on earth can we be looking at?' he said, bewildered. 'This could be the bottom of an ocean or the dark side of the moon.'

'There's something blocking its vision,' said Valentine. 'Some sort of Ice Dust interference.'

Lucia had an inspiration. 'Let's try this,' she said. Pricking her finger with a pin she had taken from Valentine's lapel, she wrote in blood on a sheet of paper from her diary: *Abby Clover's location?* She posted it through the slot and immediately the main street of Silver Springs came into focus.

'That was brilliant, my sweet,' Valentine said, impressed. 'What gave you that idea?'

'Just an educated guess,' Lucia answered modestly.

'I take it all back, said Valentine. 'I knew you weren't really a scullery maid.'

'And I know that *Cheeseman* is actually a corruption of *Chiefman,* as you've always told me,' said Lucia with a ghastly grimace of affection.

'Will you two *concentrate*,' Wolfbane hissed. 'Look! I've focused in on a newspaper office. You can read the date from the front page in the window.'

'Well, now we know where and when we want to go to, but how do we get there?' said Valentine. 'Are we going to use one of these machines?'

'Something like that. Come with me,' said Wolfbane, once again hurrying them further through the scattered contraptions.

'Look out for a large wooden horse,' Wolfbane said.

'A large wooden horse?' repeated Lucia, puzzled.

'Actually, it's the original Wooden Horse of Troy,' replied Wolfbane. Professor Mars allows the history department to store a few of their larger objects down here.'

'The wonders of a university education!' sighed Valentine, spotting the Trojan horse. 'Over there,' he exclaimed, pointing.

'Splendid,' said Wolfbane, picking up a simple object that looked like a thermos flask with a thickish flexible lead that ended in a plug attachment. 'Just what we need – a Fluid State Universal Unit,' he murmured.

'I can't see how we're all going to fit into that,' said Valentine. 'Not unless you intend to shrink us, and I never cared for that sort of thing.'

'There'll be no need for us to shrink,' Wolfbane answered and, suddenly noticing that Lucia had wandered out of sight, he called out, 'Mother, where are you?'

'Come and see what I've found,' she answered from the other side of the Trojan Horse.

Carrying the Fluid State Universal Unit, Wolfbane and his father found Lucia standing next to Ma Hemlock's spectral carriage. Complete with its skeletal driver sitting perfectly still in greatcoat and top hat, it looked like an exhibit in a natural history museum. Lucia was patting the skull of one of the horses. 'Do you remember this, Wolfbane?' she said.

'I remember nearly being killed in it,' he replied.

'You've used this carriage?' Valentine asked.

Wolfbane nodded. 'Yes – the last time we travelled in time,' he said, turning away and striding off towards the bath tub. 'Come on – we've more important things to do.'

Minutes later, they were back in Professor Newton Mars's rooms at Merlin College.

'To the Shark Boat, quickly!' cried Wolfbane, climbing out of the bath tub. 'We may have to set sail for the middle of the Atlantic Ocean.'

'Oh dear,' moaned Valentine. 'I do so hate long sea voyages.'

* * *

Back on board the Shark Boat, Wolfbane plugged the Fluid State Universal Unit into the controls, then pulled a lever. All they could hear was a low buzzing sound. 'Just as I thought,' he muttered to himself. 'The battery's flat as a Night Witch's Yorkshire pudding.'

Scowling, Wolfbane issued instructions to Lucia and Valentine. 'Mother, you make us some lunch. There are dehydrated rats and packets of dried sewer-soup in the galley. Father, I want you to make some new identities for us to use in Silver Springs, Arizona, in the year 1886. You'll find all you need in the first mate's cabin.'

'And what will *you* be doing?' asked Valentine.

'Looking for the most powerful storm I can find in the North Atlantic,' said Wolfbane. 'Now, do go and get on with it.'

Wolfbane and his parents spent the next four days at sea, roaming the Atlantic Ocean. Lucia was in a foul mood and feeling distinctly seasick, despite their being submerged for the entire voyage. Wolfbane was standing at the periscope, studying the conditions on the surface.

'Excellent!' he exclaimed finally. 'Time to assume our new identities. Show me what you've prepared for us, Father.'

Valentine led them to the first mate's cabin where he'd been working, and nodded with certain pride to the disguises he had made.

'Not bad,' Wolfbane had to admit.

'*Not bad?*' echoed Valentine. 'This is topnotch work.' He held up an entire body-suit complete with head and made of some rubbery substance. 'When you find the person you want to be, all you do is slip into this and, in a single motion, it remoulds your whole face and figure.'

'I'll take this one,' said Wolfbane.

'But that's mine,' protested Valentine.

'I thought it might be,' said Wolfbane.

'Very well,' grumbled his father, and they all slipped into their body-suits. Newly garbed, they returned to the control room and Wolfbane held up the piece of equipment he had taken from Professor Newton Mars's museum. 'This Fluid State Universal Unit,' he explained, 'was developed by Professor Mars himself. It turns just about any object you wish into a time machine.' He slid open a panel and continued. 'You see these buttons? All you have to do is set them to the place and time to which you want to travel.'

'What's stopping us, then?' asked Lucia.

'The batteries are flat,' said Wolfbane. 'I've rigged the unit to receive a recharge. Now we have to surface and attract bolts of lightning to the Shark Boat's mast on the conning tower. Electricity will pass down a conductor and into the unit.'

'Won't that be dangerous?' asked Valentine, a trifle nervously.

'Extremely dangerous,' replied Wolfbane. 'Too little power and we will be thrown into the vortex of time. Too much, and we will be cooked like barbecued-bat sausages.'

'Are you quite sure it's worth it, dear?' asked Lucia, who was still looking a ghoulish shade of green. Besides which, she had had quite enough of being lost in time.

Wolfbane's eyes blazed dark yellow. 'Any risk is worth taking if I can get to that child, Abby Clover, and her interfering friends. I would wash in scented water for the chance to have her in my power.'

Wolfbane's parents shuddered at the thought of scented water, but they were impressed by the depth of his hatred.

'I'm taking her up,' said Wolfbane, guiding the Shark Boat to the surface. They were tossed from side to side by the raging storm. Lucia and Valentine clung to a bulkhead, looking out of a porthole into blackness. Stabbing forks of lightning illuminated the massively crashing waves, which the Shark Boat was riding like some nightmare roller-coaster.

'Aghh!' Lucia groaned, looking an even worse shade of green.

As the Shark Boat was carried to the peak of a massive wave, three great bolts of lightning struck the mast and fizzed down into the Fluid State Universal Unit. Instantly, the whole interior of the Shark Boat glowed bright purple and there was an overwhelming rushing sound.

'Hang on!' yelled Wolfbane, and the Shark Boat was snatched into time.

Quincy Flowerdale's Boarding House

At Quincy's Playhouse Theatre, Sir Chadwick was inventing an explanation for how they had arrived in Silver Springs.

'We were travelling by wagon to California where we had been engaged to work in a theatre in San Francisco,' he began. 'But catastrophe overcame us.'

'An Indian attack?' asked Miss Paradine.

Starlight shook his head. 'No, bandits,' he added gruffly.

'They rode down on our wagon at night,' said Spike, joining in.

'But we fought them off,' put in Abby.

'Without weapons?' asked Mr Fitzroy, impressed.

Hilda had an inspiration. 'The Great Mandini is a fire-eater,' she said. They took one look at the streams of flames coming from his mouth and galloped off.'

Mandini looked suitably modest. 'But in my enthusiasm I set fire to our wagon and all our possessions were destroyed.'

'At least you escaped with your lives,' said Flowerdale.

'But none of our costumes,' said Hilda. 'Modesty forbids me to show you what I am reduced to wearing beneath this cloak.'

'You must come to the boarding house, Lady Street,' said Laura Paradine sympathetically. 'You are much the same size as I am, and I have dresses to spare.'

'We shall pay you back from our wages,' said Sir Chadwick.

'All in good time,' said Quincy Flowerdale. 'Now, let us repair to the boarding house where our cook will have prepared luncheon.

'Splendid,' said Sir Chadwick, beaming, and they all made their way along the main street to stop before a pretty clapboard house next to the Silver Springs Saloon.

'Bart Stoneheart owns that establishment,' said Flowerdale with a disdainful nod towards the saloon.

'No fights or gunfire this time,' Abby commented to Spike as they entered the boarding house.

Mr Fitzroy smiled. 'Even desperadoes stop for luncheon in Silver Springs. And since most people take a siesta in this fearsome heat, afternoons tend to be a little less rowdy. Trouble usually starts up again at about five o'clock, when the men on the early shift in the mine stop work.'

Flowerdale led them into a delightful living room. Satin-upholstered furniture was arranged about the polished wooden floor and there was even a small upright piano. They could smell something delicious cooking.

'Ah, Woo Ling is making Imperial Chicken, his speciality,' he said. 'I'll show you your rooms before the meal is served. I hope you can all use chopsticks.'

After the meal, Flowerdale suggested they might welcome a nap during the tremendous heat of the afternoon.

'You must take extra special heed of the sun in Arizona,' warned Laura Paradine. 'It's a wise precaution to drink a glass of water every hour or so – especially the children.'

'Why?' asked Spike.

Quincy Flowerdale blushed slightly. 'If you will forgive the indelicacy, Lady Street, have you noticed that you do not seem to perspire?'

'Why, yes,' replied Hilda. 'And I am a trifle surprised, considering the excessive heat.'

'That is because the sun is so intense, and the air so dry, the perspiration evaporates the moment it leaves your pores.'

'Remarkable,' said Mandini.

Mr Fitzroy added, 'If the source of a stream runs dry out here, a few hours later there's nothing but dust in the riverbed. It is a harsh land. Beautiful – but cruel.'

'We shall remember your warning,' said Sir Chadwick.

When all activity in the house had settled down, it was as if a hush had fallen over the whole town. All they could hear was a gentle snoring coming from Mr Fitzroy's room. Abby, Spike, Mandini and Starlight gathered in the sitting room Quincy had provided for Sir Chadwick and Hilda.

Speaking scarcely above a whisper, Starlight said, 'Wolfbane must have discovered a source of some mighty powerful Black Dust. Whatever he was using practically destroyed the Atlantis Boat.'

'But the purpose of the raid was to steal Excalibur,' said Hilda.

'That's right,' confirmed Abby. 'Spike and I were watching everything from the side of the lake during the fight. Their priority was to seize the keys to the door that led to Excalibur. They even passed up the opportunity to kill you so they could get them from Dr Gomble and Polartius.'

'Hmmm,' Sir Chadwick murmured thoughtfully. 'In that case, we may make the following deductions. Wolfbane needs Excalibur for some unknown purpose and is prepared to risk all to obtain it.'

'It certainly seems that way,' said Mandini.

'He also has a new Black Dust which is more powerful than anything we have ever before encountered. Our weapons were virtually useless against his.'

'But it also seems he has only a limited supply,' said Hilda.

'Yes,' said Abby. 'It was only Wolfbane and his parents who had the powerful wands. None of the other Night Witches were any match for you.'

'So, perhaps we may deduce that Wolfbane needs Excalibur to help him make more of the special Black Dust.'

'I thought it was impossible to do anything wicked with

Excalibur,' said Spike.

'That's quite right, my boy,' said Sir Chadwick.

'Then surely Excalibur can't be of any use to him?'

'Unless . . .' Abby said, and paused.

'Unless what, Abby?' asked Hilda.

Abby stood up. 'Remember the pageant at Merlin College,' she said. 'What was the most powerful and evil thing King Arthur fought?'

'Charlock the Bad,' answered Mandini.

'And why was he so powerful?'

'The armour he wore was forged in a river of tears,' said Sir Chadwick softly.

'I'm beginning to understand,' said Spike. 'Cutting up Charlock's armour wouldn't be considered a evil act, so Excalibur could do that.'

'Exactly,' said Abby. 'Then he could use the Black Dust he made for any evil he chooses.'

'Remember the damage to the Atlantis Boat. It looked as though it had been caused by a fist punching it,' said Starlight. 'Wolfbane was using one of Charlock's gauntlets.'

'That's it,' said Sir Chadwick. 'Charlock's armour is the very embodiment of evil. Wolfbane must have found Charlock's hidden tomb and worked out that only Excalibur can cut through the armour. He wants to use Excalibur to make more Black Dust, so he can destroy all Light Witches and spread his vile influence throughout the world.'

While he was talking, Sir Chadwick had reached into his pocket and taken out the Evil Indicator that was folded flat in its box. Almost absentmindedly, he placed it on the table and pushed the button that sprang it open. The spheres and arrows unfolded and, in an instant, everyone in the room was transfixed. The arrow indicator was trembling violently.

'Night Witches,' said Abby softly. 'Here in Silver Springs?'

'It appears so,' whispered Sir Chadwick.

'That's strange,' said Captain Starlight. 'Night Witches don't usually stray far from New England. I never heard of any out west.'

'There could be another explanation,' said Sir Chadwick. 'Wolfbane could have followed us through time.'

'How?' asked Hilda.

'Perhaps with the new Black Dust he has devised,' answered Abby.

Sir Chadwick nodded. 'If he's found another way to track us and travel in time he may even have arrived earlier than we did. That's possible with time travel. He could have been in Silver Springs for ages.'

'And he would be in disguise,' said Spike.

'We must remain calm,' said Sir Chadwick. 'If Wolfbane has followed us to get hold of Excalibur I think we can assume he has only a limited amount of the new Black Dust.'

'But we have *no* Ice Dust at all,' said Mandini. 'We are still at a great disadvantage.'

'There's only one thing to do,' said Sir Chadwick. 'I

shall appeal to the Wizards for a supply of Ice Dust.'

'Won't they be annoyed that we have time-travelled without a permit?' said Hilda.

'We didn't plan to come here. I shall state our case in my letter and let the facts speak for themselves.'

He found paper, a pen and ink in a writing table but only when the letter was finished did he realize there was no fireplace in the room.

'I don't suppose it ever gets cold enough in Arizona to need heating in these rooms,' said Captain Starlight.

'Well, we must have a fire,' said Sir Chadwick. 'This is dashed inconvenient.'

Spike was standing by the window, watching the only person working while the other inhabitants of Silver Springs were apparently resting. 'How about the blacksmith's shop?' he suggested.

'Good thinking, Spike,' said Sir Chadwick. 'Adam, perhaps you will come with me to distract the blacksmith?'

Abby and Spike watched from the window as the two men crossed the street. Captain Starlight spoke to the blacksmith while Sir Chadwick slipped his letter into the fire. Seconds later, he reached into the flames.

Within a few minutes, they had returned with the reply, which Sir Chadwick read aloud:

'Please meet our representative on the morning stage from Abilene.

Signed, *Undersecretary, Ministry of Time.'*

'Not very forthcoming, are they, Chadwick?' said Mandini.

Sir Chadwick sighed. 'Just what we've come to expect of the Wizards, I suppose. Still, at least there were no threats of dire punishment for breaking the treaty governing time travel.'

Sir Chadwick was referring to the Wizard law that was supposed to be obeyed by all Light and Night Witches. It stated that time travel was only allowed by permission of the Wizards.

'And we have informed the Wizards that Wolfbane may have deliberately broken the law. In the long run, that may be in our favour,' said Mandini.

'Well, we can't do much more,' said Sir Chadwick. 'So we might as well take our cue from the citizens of this fair town and snatch forty winks.' Smiling at Abby, he added, 'My dear, as a descendant of Sea Witches, your power over the weather is so much better developed than in the rest of us. Do you think you could arrange for a light wind to counteract the effects of this incredible heat?'

'Certainly,' replied Abby. She went to the window and concentrated on the horizon. After a few moments, and to the astonishment of the townsfolk, a delightfully cool breeze blew through Silver Springs. She was about to turn away from the window when she saw a fierce-looking bird sitting on the roof of the Silver Springs Saloon next door. It watched her with cool unblinking eyes.

'A vulture,' said Spike, who had joined her at the window.

'I wish Benbow was here,' she said uneasily. 'He'd soon chase it away.'

'He'll turn up,' Spike said with a yawn. 'He always does.'

Elsewhere in Silver Springs, behind locked doors and shuttered windows, Wolfbane, Valentine and Lucia sat in the gloom waiting for Caspar to return. They had taken off their whole-body disguises, which lay in a deflated row on the floor. Lucia was back in her black Givenchy dress. Wolfbane wore a dashing, if rather grubby, silk dressing-gown, and Valentine had a dirty towel wrapped around his middle.

'How I despise nineteenth-century fashions,' Lucia said haughtily as she prodded her disguise with an elegantly-shod foot. 'All whalebone and wire hoops. These clothes owe more to engineering than design.'

'I like them,' said Valentine lazily. 'At least the women have a bit of shape. Not just straight up and down like that thing you're wearing.'

'What would *you* know about style?' answered Lucia scornfully. 'Look at you. I've seen victims of the Black Death look more elegant.'

Wolfbane ignored his parents' bickering. He was filing his filthy fingernails into wicked-looking points with a nail-file he'd taken from his mother's make-up bag.

'What title have you chosen for yourself when you rule the world, my son?' Lucia asked him.

Wolfbane looked up, 'I haven't given the subject much thought,' he replied. 'Master, I suppose.'

'Much too plain,' Lucia said dismissively. 'How about *Emperor?*'

'Why Emperor?'

Lucia preened herself. 'Then I could be the Dowager Empress Lucia. Don't you think it has a certain ring to it?'

Just then, Caspar tapped on the window. Wolfbane leapt up to let him in.

'Well?' Wolfbane asked. 'What did you hear? Anything about the whereabouts of the Atlantis Boat?'

Caspar shook his head. 'Nothing, Great One,' he croaked.

'How long must we go on waiting?' Valentine whined. 'It's like being trapped in some ghastly paradise where nothing ever happens.'

'We shall go on waiting – and watching,' said Wolfbane savagely, 'for however long it takes. In the end, Abby Clover and her friends will pay in pain for all this tedium. I swear to it.' And with a sudden violent lunge, he drove the nailfile up to its hilt into the wall.

A Visit to the Silver Springs Saloon

In the relative cool of the evening, the new residents of Flowerdale's boarding house gathered in the sitting room for refreshments. Woo Ling had made a delicious fruit punch which they sipped appreciatively.

Quincy Flowerdale explained that the company usually enjoyed a light supper before the evening performance but tonight the Playhouse would remain shut.

'We shall need at least three days of rehearsals, I think,' said Sir Chadwick. 'Then you'll be ready to open for business again, Quincy.'

'Wonderful,' said Flowerdale. 'Well, as we all have the evening off, perhaps you would care for a buggy ride into the desert?' he asked. 'It doesn't take long to get there from the valley. I can assure you it is quite delightful in the moonlight.'

'I should like that very much, dearest,' said Hilda. 'It does sound romantic.'

'Count me in,' said Captain Starlight, grinning. 'Being a

seafaring man, I don't get many chances to see a desert.'

Mandini smiled and shook his head. 'I think we shall need some money for incidental expenses,' he said. 'If Abby would be kind enough to make me a loan of her silver dollar I shall stay in town and try my luck at the gambling tables.'

'What about you two?' Sir Chadwick asked Abby and Spike. 'Do you want to join us?'

Abby winked conspiratorially at Spike without the others seeing, and said, 'I think I'd like to stay here. I may practise the piano for a bit.'

'Me too,' said Spike, unsure of what she had in mind but sensing that Abby had a plan for something more adventurous.

'Woo Ling will be in the kitchen,' Miss Paradine said. 'He'll see the children come to no harm.'

Flowerdale and Captain Starlight went to the livery stable to hire buggies and Miss Paradine asked Woo Ling to listen out for the children.

'Are you going to see the moon in the desert, Mr Fitzroy?' asked Abby.

Mr Fitzroy shook his head. 'No, child, I think I'll go to my room and take a rest.'

Half an hour later, the adults had all set off, leaving Abby and Spike alone in the sitting room.

'What's your plan, Abby?' Spike asked.

'I thought we could have a look around the town on our own,' said Abby. 'I'd really like to see a wild west saloon.'

'I don't think they'll let us in,' said Spike. 'I can't see

them selling us glasses of whisky in the Silver Springs Saloon.'

'They won't be able to keep us out if they can't see us,' said Abby.

Spike shook his head. 'I know you can make yourself vanish,' he said, 'but you can only make me vanish by holding on to me. I don't really fancy going about hand in hand all evening.'

'Maybe I can make you vanish without holding your hand,' said Abby.

'How?' said Spike. 'You haven't even got any Ice Dust.'

'I've been practising anagram spells,' said Abby. 'I think I could make one work on you.'

'What's an anagram spell?' asked Spike, slightly alarmed.

'You mix up the letters of words to make other words,' explained Abby. 'Sir Chadwick says only very powerful Light Witches can make them work but I've managed to do it a couple of times. Shall we try?'

'All right,' said Spike. 'But make sure you get it right. I don't want just part of me vanishing.'

'I'll try a dry run first,' said Abby. She lifted the lid of the piano, tapped the keys lightly, and said:

'You row only nap.'

Immediately, the piano began to play *Greensleeves* on its own.

Spike was impressed. 'What did you say to it?' he asked.

'It was an anagram for *Play on your own*,' said Abby.

'So how about us?' Spike said, excited now.

Abby thought for a short time. 'I'll make an anagram of *Spike too*,' she said, adding, '*So to Pike.*'

She whistled the strange little tune that made her vanish. It wasn't easy, as the piano was playing quite a different tune.

Spike and Abby exchanged glances. They could still see each other quite plainly.

'It doesn't seem to have worked,' said Spike, disappointed.

'No,' said Abby. 'Sorry, Spike. I suppose I'm just not good enough yet.'

'That's all right,' he answered, glancing into a mirror on the wall. 'Hey, Abby, come here and stand beside me,' he said.

There was no sign of either of them reflected in the looking-glass.

'What do you think has happened?' said Spike.

'It must be a side effect of the anagram spell,' said Abby. 'We seem to be invisible but still able to see each other.'

'That could be useful. Let's go and test it on Woo Ling,' said Spike.

When they entered the kitchen, they found the cook dozing in a rocking chair by the stove with a large tabby cat curled up in his lap. Not wanting to disturb them they tiptoed out again.

Deciding to risk it, they left the boarding house and

stood on the sidewalk. It was evening now and a golden sunset lit the western sky. The breeze Abby had summoned earlier was still wafting along the main street, causing the flaming lanterns that lit the buildings to cast flickering shadows. Different music came from several saloons within earshot and blended with the sound of the piano still playing in the sitting room of the boarding house.

Lights were still glowing in the newspaper office and the door stood open to catch the breeze. Abby and Spike entered and watched as a man they took to be the editor sat at a large roll-top desk writing hurriedly. When he finished a page he passed it to a compositor in a long apron who took little blocks of metal characters from a series of trays and made up the words to be printed. It seemed very strange to Spike to stand so close to people who were unaware of his presence.

When they'd seen enough of the newspaper office they looked over the livery stable and the blacksmith's shop. The furnace fire was banked over now and they could see the blacksmith through the window eating an enormous supper with a lady they presumed to be his wife.

'Being invisible is a bit like being a ghost, isn't it?' said Spike. 'Everyone getting on with their lives and us not existing for them.'

'I suppose it is,' said Abby. 'Come on. Let's go and take a look in the Silver Springs Saloon.'

There was a gap wide enough below the swing doors for them to duck under without causing the doors to open, apparently unaided. Once inside, they found a place near a wall where there was little chance of anyone bumping into them.

'There's Mandini,' Spike whispered in Abby's ear, though no one could have heard him in the general hubbub. Their friend was standing by a roulette wheel, where a man was shouting, 'Gentlemen, place your bets.'

Spike and Abby looked about them. They were in a very large room with a wooden floor that was scattered with sawdust. Along one wall, running the length of the whole building, was a bar. Men in shirtsleeves served drinks with amazing speed.

The bar was crowded with customers shouting orders. Waiters carrying loaded trays were weaving among the tables scattered about the room, serving those who preferred to drink sitting down. At the far end of the barroom, where the Great Mandini stood, there was a cluster of green-baize-covered gambling tables crowded with players.

Some men were playing cards tossed to them by quick-fingered dealers. Some were betting on the fall of dice, and others on wheels that made a curious clacking noise as they turned. Brightly clad ladies with feathers in their hair took turns dancing with customers on a small dance floor.

Among them, they could see the Kentucky Kid, whose partner didn't look too happy to be dancing with the great bear of a man. Music was provided by three men playing a piano, a banjo and a cornet. A staircase curved up to a wide gallery which served as a restaurant. More waiters in long white aprons hurried between the busy tables.

Once they had got their bearings, Abby and Spike studied the customers. It was easy to tell which were the miners. Although, with a few exceptions, most of them had washed the dust from their hands and faces, they were still dressed in the same rough clothes that they wore for work. They looked quite poor but Abby was amazed by how many were gambling with reckless abandon. The card dealers and the man in charge of the roulette wheel were raking in great glittering heaps of silver dollars.

The cowboys seemed to have less money. Spike and Abby could sense their resentment at the miners' apparent riches. Abby noticed in particular a table where a brooding dark-haired man, dressed in black, sat with two others.

It was somehow clear that the dark-haired man was in charge of the saloon. People kept coming to his table to ask him questions and they were obviously very wary and respectful. His table was at the far end of the great room and the man occupied the chair with its back to the wall.

'That must be Bart Stoneheart,' Abby said softly to Spike. 'Shall we get closer?'

'Lead on,' said Spike and they made their way through the crowded room. As they reached the edge of the dance floor, the music ended and the room became slightly quieter. Most of the dancers left the floor but they saw that the Kentucky Kid and his partner, a small pretty woman, remained.

'Come on, Kid, let me go,' the woman pleaded as he continued to hug her tightly. 'You've trodden on my toes all through the last six dances. I can't hardly walk no more.'

The Kentucky Kid smiled nastily and said, 'You can only go until the dancing starts again. I'm gonna wait right here. If you don't come back to me, I'll come and and stomp on your feet so hard you won't ever want to walk again – understand?'

'I understand, Kid,' said the woman, limping away.

'Watch this,' Spike said in a low voice, going over to stand directly in front of the Kentucky Kid. Abby joined him. Spike was directly below the Kid's chin, with the man's tangled beard almost brushing Spike's head. The Kentucky Kid seemed happy to be alone in the centre of the dance floor. None of the other customers took any notice of him swaying drunkenly by himself.

Whispering in a curious, wailing voice, Spike said, 'Kid, Kid! I'm talking to you, Kid.'

The Kentucky Kid blinked. The voice was so near he swung his head down to see where it came from.

'Who in tarnation is that speaking?' he said uneasily.

'It's me, your beard, Kid,' Spike continued in the whispering voice.

'My beard?' the Kid gasped. 'Beards can't talk.'

Spike and Abby had to choke back their laughter.

'Well, I sure can,' continued Spike. 'I'm called the Beard of Vengeance.'

'The Beard of Vengeance?' repeated the Kid, his eyes

popping. 'What do you want?'

Abby was suppressing her laughter so much, tears were streaming down her cheeks.

'I'm tired of your terrible smell, Kid. I want you to wash all over, right now,' said Spike. 'Or when you're asleep, I'm going to shave myself off you and throw you away.'

With a shout of terror, the Kentucky Kid ran from the saloon, but the crowd paid little attention to his raving departure.

When Spike and Abby finally recovered from holding back their laughter, they continued to Bart Stoneheart's table. Abby and Spike were able to study the man and his companions without them having the slightest suspicion they were being watched. They were a curiously ill-matched trio.

Stoneheart was dressed completely in black. He wore a wide flat-brimmed hat, a broadcloth coat and a silk cravat fixed with a large diamond pin, but his frilly silk shirt front was grubby and his fingernails were rimmed with dirt. The two children found his face disturbing.

He had large fleshy features, a prominent nose, thick lips and jutting cheekbones. His bushy eyebrows were matched by a heavy black moustache that drooped each side of his down-turned mouth. The features could have been quite pleasant but all of the humanity seemed to have been drawn from them. His eyes might have been the eyes of a dead man.

Abby suddenly had the impression that somehow he had sensed their presence. He stared so hard in their direction, Spike and Abby held their breath, worried that he could actually see them.

The man sitting on his right noticed Stoneheart's change of mood and enquired in a drawling accent, 'Is there something causing you displeasure, Bart?'

Stoneheart glanced at him and growled, 'No.' He shifted his gaze from where Abby and Spike stood, but continued to stare about him.

The man who had spoken cut a dandified figure. His ten-gallon hat was pearl grey and matched his frock coat. The waistcoat beneath was heavy silk embroidered with flowers. He wore a flowing tie in blue silk and Abby could see two pearl-handled silver pistols at his hips.

More surprisingly, the third person at Stoneheart's table turned out to be a woman dressed like a man. Her fair hair was drawn back tightly under a cowboy hat with a snakeskin band, and she wore a green silk shirt with a fringed buckskin jacket. Looped over the arm of her chair was a cruel-looking bullwhip. When she looked up, her face was quite pretty and daintier than Abby had expected. But her looks were spoiled by the sneering expression she permanently wore.

Stoneheart's gaze had fixed on the Great Mandini, who was playing roulette and obviously a big winner. After several turns of the wheel his pile of chips had grown enormously.

'The stranger in evening clothes,' Stoneheart growled. 'It's my belief he's cheating.'

'He must be a clever cove to cheat on a crooked wheel,' answered the dandified figure with a smirk.

Stoneheart nodded and said casually, 'A man too clever by half, I would say. Have him insult you, then shoot him down without mercy.'

'Let me do it,' said the young woman, standing up. 'I'll lay a few licks of my bullwhip on him first. A quick death is too good for the rattlesnake who dares to cheat Bart

Stoneheart, Beauregard Lightfoot and Bullwhip Kate Mulroony.'

She strode towards Mandini, who was preoccupied with the spinning wheel. A sudden hush fell upon the noisy room, except for the clattering of the little white ball on the roulette wheel.

Bullwhip Kate barged into Mandini with her shoulder and he turned in surprise. She stepped back a few paces to give herself space and uncoiled the vicious-looking whip. It snaked in a long curve behind her, the tip coming to rest at Abby's feet.

'How dare you assault me in that fashion, you piece of big-city trash!' she said angrily.

Mandini raised his hat and bowed. 'Do please forgive me, ma'am,' he replied. 'If I have caused any offence, I humbly beg your forgiveness.' With another flourish he produced a bouquet of white roses which he held out as a peace offering.

Kate snapped the bullwhip. It shredded the bunch of flowers, and petals fluttered down to the sawdust. Once more, the tip came to rest at Abby's feet. Quickly, Abby stood on it before Bullwhip Kate could lash out again. While she tugged on the whip with a puzzled expression, Beauregard Lightfoot stood up and drew his pistols, but before he could cock the hammers, a great Bowie knife thudded into the table in front of him. Everyone in the saloon looked up to the gallery. A tall man wearing buckskins was standing at the rail. He had a goatee beard and yellow shoulder-length hair.

The man held up a hand and said, 'I don't usually intervene in the private disputes of others. But I couldn't help but notice that the gentleman who offered the flowers wears no weapons to defend himself.'

'Neither do you, old-timer,' snarled Beauregard. 'So stay out of this fight or I'll make *you* more work for the undertaker.'

The long-haired man smiled. 'You are correct, sir. Allow me to introduce myself. I am Colonel William F. Cody.'

A gasp went up around the saloon as people muttered, 'Buffalo Bill. It's Buffalo Bill!'

The long-haired man continued. 'What you say is true. I am unarmed.' And he stepped aside. 'But my companion has her trusty Winchester repeating rifle with her. And I can guarantee she never misses.'

Everyone in the saloon could see the pretty young woman in western costume aiming her rifle at Beauregard.

Buffalo Bill nodded to one of the card dealers. 'Will you please throw the deck of cards you hold high into the air?'

The dealer did as he was asked and as the pack of cards fluttered above him four shots rang out in rapid succession.

'Pick up the aces,' said Buffalo Bill to the dealer.

He did so, and held them high for all to see. A bullet hole was shot in the dead centre of each ace.

Beauregard Lightfoot suddenly deflated. He replaced his pistols in their holsters and slowly sat down.

Although she was seething with rage, Bullwhip Kate recoiled her whip and slumped down in her chair at Stoneheart's table.

'Will you join us for refreshments, sir?' Buffalo Bill called down to Mandini.

'Delighted, Colonel,' Mandini replied as he cashed in his winnings. They filled his hat to overflowing with gold and silver coins.

Abby and Spike lingered by Stoneheart's table just long enough to hear him say, 'Find out all you can about the fancy stranger. I will not be bested by the likes of him.'

Spike whispered to Abby that he wanted to get a closer look at Buffalo Bill and Annie Oakley. They climbed the stairs to the gallery and stood by the table. 'Do I gather from your appearance that you are also a showman?' Buffalo Bill asked Mandini as he poured him a glass of wine.

'Allow me to introduce myself. My name is Mandini. Others see fit to add the title 'Great' to the name. And that is how I appear on show bills.'

'The Great Mandini,' said Annie Oakley. 'It has a fine ring to it, don't you think, Colonel?'

'My own sentiments exactly,' said Buffalo Bill. 'Tell me, are you presently engaged? The reason I ask is that Annie and I are touring this part of the country recruiting new acts for my Wild West Show. I would deem it an honour if you would consider joining us. You have courage, Mandini. You did not flinch from the actions of those blackguards. And courage is my first requirement when I choose those with whom I work, be they rough rider or redskin.'

Mandini gave a half bow. 'I am overwhelmed by your compliments, Colonel. Were I not otherwise engaged, nothing would have given me greater joy. But, alas, the answer must be *no.*'

'So be it,' said Buffalo Bill philosophically. 'Nonetheless, it has been a pleasure to make your acquaintance.'

As the two men drank another toast to each other, Abby and Spike decided it was time to return to the boarding house.

The piano was still playing when they arrived. Abby reversed both spells and had taught Spike to play *Chopsticks* by the time the others returned from their ride into the desert.

'You should have come with us, children,' Hilda said. 'I have never seen the moon looking bigger, and the stars glittered like gigantic specks of Ice Dust.'

'What is Ice Dust, Hilda?' asked Miss Paradine.

'Oh, a new sort of glittery make-up we use in England,' Hilda said hurriedly.

'I've known some clear nights at sea,' added Captain Starlight, but never anything like this.'

'Any excitement while we were away?' asked Sir Chadwick.

'Nothing special,' replied Abby innocently, as Mandini arrived with his hat brimming with his winnings.

'This should cover our expenses for a while,' he said.

'But how did you manage to win so much?' gasped Hilda.

'Quite easy,' said Mandini. 'The croupier at the roulette wheel was obviously cheating.'

'How could you tell?' asked Quincy Flowerdale.

'It's a gift,' said Mandini with a smile. Then, waving his hands in front of Flowerdale and Miss Paradine's eyes, he said, 'You are both *very tired* and want to go to bed.' He then snapped his fingers.

Flowerdale and Miss Paradine both yawned, made their excuses and went to their rooms after saying goodnight.

'You didn't use magic for your own benefit, did you, Mandini?' asked Sir Chadwick.

'I didn't need to, Chadwick,' Mandini explained. 'The croupier wasn't very clever. I just watched his eyes. He always looked at the number he was going to select before he turned the wheel.'

Mr Fitzroy appeared at the head of the stairs in a night-cap and long dressing gown. 'Oh, it's you,' he said. 'Back from your excursion I see. I had a sort of nightmare while you were out. I dreamed that I came down here and found the piano playing on its own. Curious, eh? Well, good-night to you all,' and with that he returned to his room.

Abby and Spike avoided meeting anyone's eyes but after a brief silence Mandini said, 'Yes, a curious thing happened in the saloon too. A young lady attempted to strike me with a bullwhip but for some unaccountable reason the tip wouldn't budge. It appeared to be flattened to the floor. Almost as if someone invisible was standing on it.

Abby and Spike exchanged glances. Then, blushing, Abby said, 'That was me, Mandini. And Mr Fitzroy didn't have a dream; I made the piano play on its own.'

'And where was Spike when you were in the saloon?' asked Sir Chadwick sternly.

'I was with her,' said Spike. I'm just as much to blame.'

'You were invisible too?' said Sir Chadwick, astonished.

Spike nodded. 'Abby used an anagram spell to make me vanish.'

Sir Chadwick was so intrigued, he quite forgot to be angry. 'You're coming along in leaps and bounds, child,' he said mildly. But then he was more serious. 'However, let us have no more of you going to dangerous places without an adult. In the absence of your parents we are responsible for you both. Now, off to bed with the pair of you.' He paused for a moment, then added, 'Tomorrow, show me some more of your anagram powers.'

'There's something else about Bart Stoneheart, Sir Chadwick,' Abby said. 'I think he might be a Night Witch. He's very grubby and he smells awful.'

'I fear many people do in this town, child,' said Sir Chadwick.

'There was something else,' said Abby. I can't quite put my finger on it. But I think he sensed our presence, even though we were invisible.'

'Hmmm,' said Sir Chadwick, scratching his marmalade-coloured side whiskers. 'I suppose it could be possible *he's* Wolfbane. We shall have to keep a close watch on him.'

He studied Abby for a moment, saying, 'You seem to be doing remarkably well with your anagram spells. I wonder if you can manage one for me?'

'I'll do my best, Sir Chadwick,' she said.

'We shall need more actors if we are going to re-open Quincy's theatre. Do you think you could recall the ones who fled?'

'I'll try,' she answered. She thought for a moment before chanting, '*Suet car runt roots.*'

'What was that?' asked Spike.

'*Actors return to us,*' said Sir Chadwick. 'Now we can only wait and see if it works.'

'It will work, Sir Chadwick,' Abby said quietly.

'How do you know, Abby?' asked Hilda.

Abby shook her head. 'I'm not sure, it's just a feeling I get.'

'Thank you, my dear,' said Sir Chadwick. 'Now I think perhaps it really is time for bed.'

The children left and Mandini began to tell the story of his meeting with Buffalo Bill and Annie Oakley in greater detail. Spike and Abby each had small rooms at the head of the staircase. Just before Abby climbed into her creaking bed, she opened the window and glanced over the town. On the roof of the Silver Springs Saloon, she could see the shape of the vulture sharply silhouetted against the full moon.

The Way of the Wizards

Abby and Spike got up well before the rest of the household the following morning. It was just after sunrise but Woo Ling was already in the kitchen seeing to the stove. For breakfast he gave them thick slices of home-cured bacon with freshly baked bread. But the water in the glass jug was a cloudy light brown colour.

'I think I'd prefer milk for once, Mr Ling,' Spike said after examining the jug.

'Water's no good,' said Woo Ling. 'It tastes of mud. Would you like hot chocolate?'

'Yes, please,' they said together.

They had just finished when Sir Chadwick appeared.

'I'm going to meet the stagecoach from Abilene if you two wish to take a stroll with me,' he said. 'I shall breakfast with the rest of the boarders when I return, Mr Ling. I don't suppose you have any kippers, do you?'

'Kippers?' repeated Woo Ling, looking deeply puzzled.

'No, of course not, silly me,' said Sir Chadwick. 'Eggs

and crispy bacon it will have to be then.'

Apart from the clouds wreathing the distant mountains, the sky was as blue as cornflowers. Even this early in the morning the heat of the sun was fierce, but the breeze Abby had arranged the previous day still wafted along the main street. The only other person about was the blacksmith pumping the bellows to get his fire blazing. He nodded in a friendly fashion as they passed. A cock crowed somewhere and one of the shopkeepers came out to take down the shutters on his store front.

The stagecoach office was at the end of town where tents and shacks were dotted about randomly. A large log cabin served as the office. The door was open and they could smell freshly brewed coffee. A very old, nut-brown man in buckskins was preparing a team of horses in the adjoining corral. Despite his age he seemed very fit.

'Good morning,' said Sir Chadwick cheerfully. 'Do you expect the stage from Abilene to be on time?'

The old man shaded his eyes and looked towards the horizon. 'I surely do, stranger,' he answered.

They followed his gaze to a distant rising cloud of dust.

'My name is Chadwick Street, and this is Abby and Spike,' said Sir Chadwick.

'Washington Potts,' said the old-timer, offering a leathery hand to them. It was as sunburnt as his deeply seamed face. 'I run this station.'

'Have you lived in Silver Springs long, Mr Potts?' asked Abby.

'Since before there was a town here, child,' he grinned. 'I used to hunt in this country when I weren't much bigger than you.'

The cloud of dust was growing larger and they could see the stagecoach thundering towards them. Finally, the driver hauled on the reins and the horses came to a halt with the coach shrouded in drifting dust.

'Silver Springs,' shouted the driver. 'Ten minutes for coffee and beans before we leave for Tucson.' He and the guard swung down from the driver's seat. 'Morning, Washington. Is breakfast ready?'

'Always is,' replied the old man as he began to change over the teams of horses.

The door of the coach swung open and a chattering crowd of extravagantly dressed men and women descended. They took their baggage from the roof and set off in the direction of the playhouse. Sir Chadwick smiled at Abby. They had to be the actors she had recalled with her anagram spell.

From inside the stagecoach there was a cough, then a tall, extremely thin figure descended, carrying a leather Gladstone bag. He was holding a handkerchief over his nose and mouth and was dressed in a black jacket, striped trousers and a bowler hat. Removing the handkerchief, he revealed a long thin face with a sharply pointed nose. His disapproving eyes were bright violet and he appeared to be wearing a large false moustache.

'A Wizard,' said Abby softly, so that only Spike heard.

'Sir Chadwick Street?' he asked in an English accent.

Sir Chadwick nodded.

The figure looked at Spike and Abby and said, 'I am an Assistant Permanent Undersecretary from the Ministry of Imagination. I presume these children are Abigail Clover and Prince Altur?'

'They are,' said Sir Chadwick.

'Shall we find somewhere a little more private?' he said. 'I only have a few minutes. I'm afraid I shall be taking this dreadful mode of transport on to the next stop.'

They all walked to the far side of the corral, where the Assistant Undersecretary reached into his Gladstone bag and handed Sir Chadwick a very small package.

'What's this?' Sir Chadwick asked, puzzled.

'The Ice Dust you requested, of course.'

For a moment, Sir Chadwick could not speak. 'But this is barely a wandful,' he at last managed to splutter. 'I made it quite clear in my letter to the Ministry that we are fighting the Master of the Night Witches who is armed with some new and terribly powerful weapon. This tiny amount is woefully inadequate for the job.'

'You know Ministry policy – a wandful is all you are allowed to take back in time.'

'Don't you know that Wolfbane is trying to get his hands on the Sword of Merlin?' said Sir Chadwick.

'Well, you'd better jolly well make sure he doesn't,' said the Assistant Undersecretary sharply. 'Excalibur is entrusted to the care of the Light Witches. It's your responsibility to make sure it's returned to Merlin College.' He raised his bowler hat and said, 'Well, I must be on my way. I see the stagecoach is about to depart. Good-day to you.' And, with a brief nod to Spike and Abby, he strode back to the stagecoach and was soon lost in another rising cloud of dust.

On board the stagecoach, its lone passenger opened his Gladstone bag and placed it over his head. The Permanent Undersecretary of the Ministry of Imagination and his assistant sat in their office toasting crumpets before the fire. On a small table between them was a large crystal globe in which the head of the Wizard on the stagecoach had just appeared.

'I have delivered the Ice Dust as instructed, sir,' he reported.

'Splendid,' said the Undersecretary, buttering a crumpet. 'Was Sir Chadwick as vexed as we anticipated?'

'If anything, more so.'

'Excellent! Remember, an angry Light Witch is an efficient Light Witch. It's our job to keep them on their toes, not do everything for them.'

'As you say, sir.'

'Abby Clover and Prince Altur, are they well?'

'They appeared to be in robust health, sir.'

'Good, good. You may return.'

The head faded from the crystal and, with a sigh of contentment, the Undersecretary sat back in his leather armchair to enjoy his crumpet.

With Spike and Abby trailing behind, Sir Chadwick stalked back to the boarding house in a towering rage. Before he entered, he paced up and down for a few moments, muttering to himself until he had regained his composure.

'I'm sorry to have lost my temper, children,' he said in a better mood. 'I should have known better than to expect any more from the Wizards.'

'They're certainly a difficult lot, Sir Chadwick,' said Abby sympathetically.

Sir Chadwick struck a defiant pose. 'If that is the way they wish to handle this business, so be it,' he said firmly. 'The Light Witches shall prevail. Remember our motto.'

'I didn't know we had a motto,' said Abby.

'We didn't until this moment,' replied Sir Chadwick. 'But from this day onward it shall be, in the words of the poet Virgil, *Audentis Fortuna iuvat.*'

'What does that mean, Sir Chadwick?' asked Abby.

'Fortune assists the bold,' said Spike, and because Abby looked surprised, he added, 'Princes have to know Latin.'

Filled with new resolve, Sir Chadwick swept into the boarding house, where the others were just sitting down to breakfast. He joined them at the table and before Woo Ling could place his plate of eggs and bacon before him he was making plans for the day's rehearsal.

'I think we should alternate *Richard III* with *Romeo and Juliet*. What do you think, Quincy?'

'That sounds a capital idea, old fellow,' Quincy replied. 'But won't we be short of the necessary cast?'

'When I was at the stagecoach depot with the children we saw a group of young people who could only be actors,' said Sir Chadwick, winking at Abby. 'I think some of your original company must have undergone a change of heart, and returned.'

'Wonderful!' exclaimed Flowerdale. 'In that case, shall we go to the theatre and start work this morning?'

'The sooner the better,' said Sir Chadwick.

There was a knock on the door. Woo Ling answered it, and Hiram Prune, Mr Stout's cashier, entered, looking rather bashful. He raised his straw boater and said, 'Forgive the intrusion so early. But Mr and Mrs Homer P. Stout send their compliments and ask if all you ladies and gentlemen can come to supper this evening at seven o'clock.'

'What a splendid gesture,' replied Flowerdale. He turned to the others seated at the table. 'Does the engagement meet with everyone's approval?'

The whole company nodded their agreement.

'Then we shall be delighted,' he replied. 'Please thank Mrs Stout and say we shall arrive at the suggested hour.'

'I shall see you there,' said Hiram Prune eagerly. 'Mr Stout has been gracious enough to invite me to attend.' He backed out of the room, knocking a silver-framed photograph off a side table as he passed.

Abby and Spike accompanied the new theatre group to the playhouse. They made quite a procession through the town. Quincy Flowerdale, with his sister Laura Paradine on his arm was followed by Sir Chadwick and Hilda. Next came Captain Starlight with Spike and Abby, and Mr Fitzroy followed behind with the Great Mandini.

Although it was no great distance the procession made frequent stops so that Quincy could introduce his new companions to the less disreputable people who were part of the crowd thronging the main street.

When they eventually reached the theatre they found the players who had returned on the morning coach. Quincy Flowerdale assembled the whole company on the stage and made an announcement.

'Friends,' he began, directing his remarks to the actors who had returned, 'I am overwhelmed and delighted that you saw fit to rejoin us. Great things have happened during your brief absence. I am honoured to tell you that we have recruited some distinguished fellow Thespians from England. May I introduce Sir Chadwick and Lady Street, the Great Mandini, Captain Adam Starlight, Spike Lostboy and Abby Clover.'

There was an excited chatter of comment from the players, until Flowerdale held up his hand. 'I would like to add that, for the duration of his stay, it is my intention to place myself and the rest of the company under the direction of Sir Chadwick.'

'My dear fellow—' Sir Chadwick began but Flowerdale interrupted him.

'I'll not take *no* for an answer, Sir Chadwick. You have far greater experience than I do. I can only learn from your instruction.'

Sir Chadwick bowed deeply. 'I shall endeavour to live up to your expectations,' he said. 'So, let us begin.'

At first, Sir Chadwick asked those actors he did not know to give short recitations so he could judge their capabilities.

Spike and Abby soon became restless.

'I think we'll go and explore the town a bit more, Sir Chadwick,' Abby told him.

'Will they be safe?' Hilda asked with a meaningful glance at Sir Chadwick who was preoccupied with his new actors.

'As long as they keep out of the saloons,' Flowerdale answered.

'We promise,' said Spike.

Mandini flipped a silver dollar through the air and Abby caught it. 'That's the lucky one,' he said. Then he took two more from behind their ears. 'And these are for incidental expenses.'

'They sell very nice candy sticks and soda pop at the general store,' called Miss Paradine as they left the theatre.

On the main street, Spike dragged a toe through the thick red dust and watched enviously as a cowboy cantered past on a fine looking chestnut horse. 'I wish we had ponies,' said Spike. 'Can't you make an anagram spell and get us some?'

Abby shook her head. 'You know the rules, Spike. Light

Witches can't use magic to get things just for their own pleasure,' she sighed.

'I know,' he said despondently. 'But . . . sometimes I can understand the temptation to become a Black Witch.'

'Spike!' exclaimed Abby. 'You can't mean that.'

The shadow of a large bird passed across the dust at their feet. Abby looked up quickly, hoping to see Benbow. But it was only the vulture that had fluttered down to perch on the roof of the Silver Spring Saloon.

'I miss Benbow,' she said. 'I've never known him stay away so long.'

'How did Captain Starlight find him originally?' asked Spike.

Abby shook her head. 'It was the other way around,' she explained. 'Captain Starlight told me that, long ago, he was on board the *Ishmael* in a thick fog. He was close to a rocky shore with the wind blowing him towards dangerous reefs. He'd have been in real trouble if Benbow hadn't appeared and led him to a safe harbour.'

Spike looked up at the sky. Despite the breeze Abby had brought to the town it was still incredibly hot standing in the sunshine.

'I expect it's a bit warm for Benbow in Arizona,' Spike said. 'After all, he's a sea bird, used to cooler climates.' And seeing Abby looked concerned, he added, 'I bet he turns up any day now.'

They walked up and down the main street, looking into the newspaper office and the general store. At the mine they watched the morning shift of miners getting into the caged lift. They wandered about Flowerdale's abandoned shaft for a while but it was all boarded up. Bart Stoneheart's saloon was also shut, with the vulture perched on the roof as if it was a permanent fixture, like a weather vane. The second time they passed the blacksmith's forge, Spike said. 'It's all a bit boring, isn't it? No wonder the cowboys shoot their guns off for a bit of excitement.'

'Let's go to the stagecoach depot and stroke the horses in the corral,' suggested Abby.

'I wish we could ride them,' sighed Spike.

A few minutes later they were at the corral, holding out handfuls of hay for the horses. Sitting outside the office, Washington Potts was carving a small stick with a very large Bowie knife.

'Hello, Mr Potts,' said Abby.

'Howdy.' Mr Potts looked carefully at Spike. 'You from back east, boy? You surely are the palest face I've ever seen out west.'

'I'm from far in the south, Mr Potts,' Spike answered. 'We all look like this where I come from.'

'Is that a fact?' said Potts. 'And where would that be?'

'A place called Lantua,' said Spike. 'Where are you from?'

'Everywhere, I guess,' he replied, still whittling his stick. 'I remember coming down the Missouri river in a canoe when I was a boy. My pa was a trapper and my mother was from a tribe called the Sioux.' He looked up. 'But

I've been in these parts for more than sixty years now. When I first came here, there was nobody but me and Bart Stoneheart.'

Abby was suddenly intrigued. 'Bart Stoneheart has been here all that time?'

Potts nodded. 'He don't know I know that. Mr Stoneheart and I don't talk much.'

'But you saw him in those days?' said Abby.

'Not at first. I just used to see his signs. Footprints, ashes from camp fires, that sort of thing. But I knew he was about. For a lot of years I thought he might be a prospector. Prospectors often like to keep themselves to themselves. If they hit lucky they don't want anyone knowing where the strike is.'

He held up the stick for a moment, then whittled some more before he continued. 'Yes, sir, Bart Stoneheart sure has searched this valley. And the desert about these parts. Funny thing is, he don't look any older. The only difference is that moustache and he didn't grow that until he came into town.'

'What do you think he was looking for?' asked Spike.

'The treasure, I guess.'

'Treasure!' exclaimed both Abby and Spike.

Washington Potts nodded. 'There's a legend down in Mexico says the Spanish buried a treasure in these parts more than a couple of hundred years ago.'

Potts made some holes in the stick he had been whittling and blew three clear notes on the flute he had just carved. He handed it to Abby. 'Here, missy, you want this?'

'That's really clever, Mr Potts. Thank you,' she said. 'Will you show me how to play it.'

Abby quickly picked up how to play a tune, and since Mr Potts didn't seem to have any more to say about Bart Stoneheart, Abby whispered to Spike, 'I think we should tell Sir Chadwick what we've learned.'

Spike nodded, and told Mr Potts they ought to be getting back to the theatre.

'Goodbye, Mr Potts,' they said and began to walk away.

'Aren't you going to take them ponies with you?' Washington Potts called after them.

'What ponies?' they both answered at once.

'The ones in the other corral,' he replied. 'I thought you'd left them there.' He strolled around the stage depot.

Curious, Abby and Spike followed.

There in the smaller corral stood two pure white ponies wearing beautiful saddles decorated with silver studs.

'How wonderful!' said Spike softly, as he and Abby stood admiring the beautiful pair.

'I'm afraid they're not ours,' Mr Potts,' Abby said regretfully.

'Well, they got your names on the saddles,' Potts said.

They looked closer and, sure enough, spelled out in the decoration of silver studs on each saddle were the names *Spike* and *Abby*.

'Maybe they're a surprise present,' said Spike.

The one with Abby's name on the saddle was nuzzling her hand.

'Can you ride?' asked Mr Potts.

'I don't know, I've never tried,' said Spike, placing his foot into a stirrup and lifting himself into the saddle. Abby hesitated, still unsure, then did the same.

It was clear to Mr Potts that both children were completely at ease on horseback. They walked the ponies around the corral at first, then broke into a canter. Finally, they were galloping, until Spike headed for the fence and his pony soared over the rail to the open ground beyond. Abby followed and in a moment they were racing neck and neck, the wind in their faces, out into the valley.

Abby and Spike Put on a Show

The ponies raced tirelessly across the open country beyond Silver Springs. They leapt over dry river beds, rocks and the tumble weeds that blew across the landscape. It was almost as if the ponies were flying.

Finally, it was the children who tired. They drew back on the reins as they reached the bank of the last river in the valley and, panting from their efforts, Abby and Spike each patted their pony's neck.

'I didn't realize it took so much effort to ride,' said Spike, still slightly out of breath. 'But the ponies seem as fresh as when we started.'

They dismounted and let their mounts drink from the river. Spike watched them for a moment, then said, 'Do they look familiar to you, Abby?'

She nodded. 'I know what you're thinking. They look something like the ponies I made when I was *clouding* on the jetty at Speller.'

'They look *exactly* like the ponies you made out of the

clouds,' said Spike. 'I wonder what it means?'

'You know how it is when the Wizards get involved,' said Abby. 'You can expect anything.'

'Well, I don't care how it came about,' said Spike. I'm just happy it happened.' A thought occurred to him. 'What are we going to call them?'

'I'm going to call mine *Snow*,' Abby said, remembering their last snowball fight in Speller.

'That's not a bad name,' replied Spike, remounting. 'I shall call mine *Frost*. Let's take them back to the theatre and show them off.'

'I think we'd better walk them for a time,' said Abby. 'They may be tired after that run.'

But it was clear when Abby remounted that the ponies were still quite fresh. They snorted and pulled on their bridles until Spike and Abby once again gave them their heads.

Galloping past the stagecoach office they waved to Washington Potts before slowing to a canter, then to a walk as they approached the theatre. After tying the ponies to a hitching rail they entered to find the company taking a short break.

Inside the auditorium the heat was stifling. The men were in shirtsleeves and the ladies fanning themselves with old theatre programmes.

'I really do admire your fortitude, working in this heat, Quincy,' said Sir Chadwick, loosening his own bow tie.

'Something we have learned to live with,' replied

Flowerdale. 'And it does grow a trifle cooler in the evening.'

'It's much nicer outside,' said Spike. 'In fact, it's quite pleasant.'

Flowerdale slapped his forehead. 'This sudden breeze that's cooling our town,' he exclaimed. 'I had quite forgotten.' He turned to Captain Starlight, who had been acquainting himself with the ropes and pulleys that controlled the scenery and backdrops. 'Would you be so kind as to assist me by pulling on this rope, Captain?'

Starlight did as he was asked while Flowerdale hauled on a corresponding rope on the other side of the stage. Within seconds, they had raised the entire wall at the back of the theatre. The stage, which was on the same level as a wide flat area of ground at the back of the Playhouse, now appeared to merge with the landscape outside.

The sunlit valley, desert and distant cloud-wreathed mountains were framed like a magnificent painting. The welcome breeze flooding into the auditorium made the players sigh with relief as they gave cries of delight at the unexpected view.

Sir Chadwick nodded with approval, his showman's eye relishing the prospect of how he might use such a grand theatrical effect.

Spike murmured to Abby, 'Let's give them a surprise with the ponies while they're all taking a break.'

Abby and Spike hurried outside to the hitching rail and led Snow and Frost down the alleyway beside the theatre. They mounted their horses and galloped into view, causing the entire cast to gasp in astonishment.

Sensing the anticipation of the watching troupe of actors, Abby and Spike swept off their hats and bowed on horseback.

'What shall we do now?' hissed Spike.

'Let's find out,' answered Abby and she set Snow racing in a circle. Spike followed. Suddenly, it was as if Abby could hear a voice inside her head.

'Have no fear,' it said. *'You are protected.'*

Abby realized that while she and Spike were riding the ponies they could come to no harm. As Snow galloped at full tilt she raised herself in the stirrups then leapt up to stand on the saddle. Spike drew alongside her and did the same. Then, as if reading each other's minds, they did a forward flip, head over heels, to land feet first on the saddle once more. The audience gasped, then applauded and cheered loudly.

Spike and Abby now performed even more daring rough-riding tricks. Holding the pommels at the front of their saddles they jumped off their ponies to touch the ground before bouncing back up into the saddles. They twisted around to ride backwards with arms outstretched. Finally, throwing down their bandanas, they galloped in a full circle, then returned at full tilt to swoop down and pick the neckerchiefs up from the dust with their teeth.

There was another wild outburst of applause.

'You are veritable Cossacks!' called Sir Chadwick when they finally brought the ponies to a halt.

'Magnificent! Bravo!' shouted the other actors.

'What beautiful ponies,' said Hilda, jumping off the back of the stage to stroke them. 'Where did they come from?' she asked.

Abby made a quick and casual gesture with her hands. She held them together as fists, then shot out the index finger of her right hand with the thumb at a right angle to make an L shape. Then she made a W with the index fingers and thumbs of both hands. It was a secret sign used by Light Witches when human beings were around, and meant, *This is Light Witch business. I can't discuss it until we're alone*.

Hilda nodded as Sir Chadwick came up in great excitement. He, too, had noticed Abby's secret signal but he pretended to be concerned with other things. 'A truly superb piece of showmanship,' he enthused. 'I must devise a way of including it in our show.'

'They'll need more theatrical looking outfits,' said the Great Mandini. 'Costumes to equal the splendour of their mounts.'

Captain Starlight had been sketching on a pad he had found backstage. 'Something like this?' he asked.

Starlight had drawn an extraordinarily good likeness of Spike and Abby mounted on Snow and Frost. The children were wearing white costumes of fringed buckskin.

'What splendid draughtsmanship, Adam,' said Sir Chadwick, his voice full of admiration. 'We must have them made up just as you have drawn them.'

'We can get the Atlantis capes to look like that,' said Spike.

Sir Chadwick shook his head and murmured, 'Better to have them made. Otherwise, the actors will wonder where they came from.'

Then he spoke more loudly to Spike and Abby. 'Why don't we take the creatures for a short walk. It's always best to cool them off after vigorous exercise.'

He led them out of earshot, then asked, 'Where did the ponies come from?'

'We don't know,' said Abby. 'But I know they're magical.'

'Are you sure?' asked Sir Chadwick.

'Quite sure,' she answered. 'They anticipate what we are thinking and they don't get tired, no matter how hard they gallop. It's as if they're protecting us when we're mounted.'

Sir Chadwick looked closely at the ponies and ran his hands along their flanks. 'I think you're right,' he said. 'I can't sense any bad emanations.' He paused. 'But let's make sure with another test.'

He found a particular cactus plant which had bright fruit.

'If I'm not mistaken this is a prickly pear and horses are often very fond of them.' He put on some leather gloves and picked two of the reddish-purple fruits, wiped them of their hair-thin prickles and held one out to each pony. Snow and Frost eagerly devoured the fruit.

'Well, they're not part of a trap set by Wolfbane,' said Sir Chadwick. 'I put a speck of Ice Dust on those prickly pears. No animal sent by the dark forces would have eaten them.'

'There's something else we found out,' said Spike. 'Mr Potts told us that Bart Stoneheart has been living in the valley for at least sixty years. And Mr Potts says he hasn't changed at all, apart from growing his moustache.'

'Really?' said Sir Chadwick with a sharp intake of breath. 'How curious. He does seem to have many of the attributes of a Night Witch.' He thought again and then said, 'See if you can find out more about Bart Stoneheart from Washington Potts. Ask him if you can keep the ponies in his corral. We can pay him. Mandini has plenty of money after his win at roulette.'

As Sir Chadwick suggested, they returned to the stagecoach depot and watched Mr Potts preparing a team of horses for the afternoon coach. He said he would be happy to let them stable Snow and Frost at the stagecoach corral as long as they looked after the ponies themselves.

'Oh, but we want to, Mr Potts,' Abby answered.

'Will you show us what we must do?' said Spike.

'Sure,' he replied.

They spent the afternoon with Mr Potts who taught them how to be good grooms. They pitched fresh hay for the stalls and learned how to put on the ponies' feed bags filled with oats. Under his instruction, they gave them water, and brushed them down until he was satisfied. He spent quite a long time showing them exactly how to saddle and unsaddle the pair. They felt quite tired by the time he broke off the lessons to change teams for the afternoon stagecoach.

When he returned, he had a cup of coffee for himself and drinks for Spike and Abby. 'Soda pops,' he said. 'I keep some for any children travelling on the stagecoaches.'

'I didn't know there was so much work connected with horses,' said Spike, enjoying his drink.

'Horses have got to be tended a good deal. They always come first out west,' said Mr Potts. 'You look after your horse before yourself. And they'll look after you. I don't know why folks want newfangled means of transport – steam trains, balloons, and such.'

'Have you ever seen a balloon?' asked Abby, suddenly interested.

'I sure have,' said Mr Potts. 'Bart Stoneheart has got one. He thinks it's a secret but I've seen him in it. He keeps it in the big barn behind his saloon and he goes sailing over the desert most nights with that vulture he keeps as a pet.'

Abby and Spike exchanged glances but didn't make any comment. Instead, with a nod towards the collection of little shacks and tents clustered on the outskirts of the town, Spike asked, 'Who lives there?'

'Folks who used to farm and ranch in the valley before the rivers dried up,' said Potts. 'Most of the men work in Stoneheart's mine now. He bought their claims cheap when the land couldn't be worked any more. That man surely has made this town a worse place.'

'You really don't like him, do you, Mr Potts?' said Abby.

Washington scratched his chin. 'I get along with most critters,' he said. 'Even rattlesnakes are peaceable, providing you don't come on 'em sudden and give 'em a scare.' He shook his head. 'That Bart Stoneheart, he's different. He's the meanest critter I've ever encountered in this valley, including the scorpions. If you want my advice, stay away from him.'

'We will, Mr Potts,' said Spike.

'Well, we'd better get back to the boarding house now,' said Abby. 'We'll see you in the morning, Mr Potts.'

'Better make it bright and early,' he replied. 'Ponies are early risers.'

21

A Splendid Dinner Party

After giving Snow and Frost their evening feed and bedding them down in their stall for the night, Abby and Spike hurried home to prepare for Mr and Mrs Stout's dinner party.

When they had bathed and changed, Hilda inspected the children in the sitting room of the boarding house. Spike and Abby had been bought suitable clothes for such an occasion.

Spike looked quite at ease in his formal Eton collar, black jacket and knickerbockers. His normally tousled white hair had been slicked down with water and parted in the middle. Hilda had unplaited Abby's pigtails and curled her hair with the hot tongs Woo Ling had heated on his kitchen range. Abby wore a white dress, black stockings and dancing pumps. The dress was rather more frilly than she liked.

Hilda studied them in admiration. 'Well, you both look very presentable. But I must say, those Atlantis capes are a

boon,' she said. 'There wasn't a speck of dirt on them. I expect these new clothes will be dusty in no time.'

'Aren't Atlantis capes miraculous, dearest?' she said to Sir Chadwick who was tinkling on the piano.

'Wonderful, wonderful,' he replied without looking up from the keyboard.

Mandini and Captain Starlight entered. They had been in the yard behind the boarding house playing horseshoes with the blacksmith.

'The captain didn't miss once,' said Mandini ruefully. 'The blacksmith was most impressed – as was I!'

'It's not such a hard game,' said Captain Starlight.

'How do you play?' asked Spike.

'The idea is simple,' Mandini explained. 'You drive a short iron peg into the ground, stand twenty paces away, and hurl the horseshoes at it. With luck, and practice, they get hooked on the peg.'

'Sounds like hoopla at a fun fair,' said Spike.

'Same principle,' said Mandini. 'But infinitely more difficult with a U-shaped horseshoe.'

When Miss Paradine, Quincy Flowerdale and Oscar Wilkington Fitzroy joined them, they strolled along to the Stout family house, at the other end of the main street. It was the finest private house in town, with steps leading up to a grand pillared porch and a wide verandah on the first floor. It was even surrounded by lush gardens shaded by trees.

Mr Stout greeted them on the steps, and Mandini

remarked on the pleasantness of the surroundings.

'An accident of nature, sir,' Mr Stout informed them. 'There is a small spring beneath the property that provides us with ample water. It also fills the other wells in town.'

'A fortunate choice to build here,' said Captain Starlight.

'I was one of the town founders,' said Mr Stout. 'My wife and I came here many years ago for her health. The dry Arizona air is most beneficial for those with chest complaints.'

'So I have heard,' said Mandini.

'It's a wonder Bart Stoneheart didn't beat you to it,' said Sir Chadwick. 'He seems to have taken over much else.'

'That rascal,' sniffed their host. 'He tried. But he has yet to best Homer P. Stout.' Then he held up his hand. 'Before we go in, ladies and gentlemen, I feel I should prepare you for our faithful servants, Erasmus and Hepsibar.'

The guests exchanged puzzled glances and Mr Stout continued. 'Erasmus and Hepsibar are beloved retainers of my wife's family. They can understand your every word but they themselves do not speak. As children they were in one of the very first train wrecks in America and since then they have been unlike other people.'

He addressed Quincy Flowerdale. 'They rarely go about the town.'

'I have only seen them once or twice,' replied Flowerdale. 'But then I have not been in town long compared with your family.'

Mr Stout nodded. 'Now you are prepared, let us go through. My cashier, Hiram Prune, is helping my wife prepare the punch.'

In the large, elegantly furnished, airy room, Mr Prune was with a small, rather pretty lady in a long evening dress. She had a kindly face and silver-streaked fair hair but didn't look very robust.

After the introductions were made, an elderly couple entered the room. The man was dressed as a butler, and the woman wore a maid's white cap pinned in her hair and a white apron over her black dress.

Mrs Stout took them both by the hands as they stood at the door with heads hung. It was as if they feared the company.

'May I introduce my dear friends and servants, Hepsibar and Erasmus,' said Mrs Stout. 'They have been with my family since before I was born.'

The couple bowed slightly but did not raise their heads.

'Serve the punch, please, Erasmus,' Mrs Stout requested gently. Then to the woman, she said, 'I will come to the kitchen when we are ready for the meal, Hepsibar.'

'Excellent punch, Mr Prune,' said Mr Fitzroy appreciatively when the servants had withdrawn. 'You have made commonplace ingredients into a veritable nectar.'

'It was all Mrs Stout's doing,' simpered Hiram Prune. 'I merely followed her instructions.'

Hilda addressed Mrs Stout. 'I understand you informed Bart Stoneheart as to the proper ending of *Romeo and Juliet*, Mrs Stout,' she said.

'Please call me Emily,' she answered first, then continued. 'Yes, I know the play well. The plays of Shakespeare are often performed in Philadelphia. My parents took me frequently as a child.'

'Philadelphia!' said Mr Fitzroy with a long sigh. 'What a splendid city. I received the best notices of my career in that fair metropolis.'

'What play were you in, Mr Fitzroy?' asked Spike.

'*Hamlet*,' he replied. 'Unfortunately, news had just arrived of the 1848 gold strike in California. I think most of the expected audiences went off to the far west to seek their fortune. We had to close on the third night.'

'You have a grand piano, Mrs Stout,' said Sir Chadwick,

noticing the instrument in front of the open French windows. 'And a splendid one at that.'

'Do you play, Sir Chadwick?' asked Mrs Stout.

'A little – but I possess no exceptional talent,' he answered.

'Chadwick plays beautifully,' said Hilda.

'Perhaps you will honour us after dinner,' said Mr Stout.

'Only if the ladies will sing,' Sir Chadwick replied.

After the punch they went through to the dining room where the silver place settings laid on the snowy tablecloth glittered in the light of flickering candles.

Flowerdale sighed at the sight. 'I haven't seen a table setting as fine as this since I left home. Such refinement is a rare thing out here on the frontier, Mrs Stout.'

'The banking business must be flourishing in Silver Springs,' said Mr Fitzroy, raising a glass of excellent wine in salutation to his host.

Homer P. Stout laughed bitterly. 'This would be a far poorer table if I had to rely only on the profits from my bank.'

'Business is not good?' asked Flowerdale.

Mr Stout shrugged. 'There is some, mostly from the storekeepers. I had high hopes at one time. When the valley flourished and the ranchers and farmers appeared to be on their way to prosperity.' He held up the palms of his hands. 'But all that is gone now. Bart Stoneheart seems to have acquired all of the town's wealth – and he chooses not to keep his money in my bank.'

'I'm afraid your magnificent safe seems a trifle extravagant now, my dear,' said Mrs Stout, fanning herself, despite the breeze that wafted through the French windows.

Abby and Spike tried to appear interested but the conversation seemed very dull to them. Bored, Abby looked along the table and noticed the wax running from a candle was forming a soft thickening puddle at the base of the silver candlestick in front of Spike. She wondered if she could use the same method as she did when *clouding* and make it form a shape.

It took quite an effort but after a few tries she managed to make a funny face. She caught Spike's attention and nodded at it. He watched as Abby made it smile. Suddenly, the wax face put out its tongue. Spike snorted with suppressed laughter and earned a stern glance from Sir Chadwick.

Eventually, to the children's relief, the meal came to an end and they returned to the sitting room for coffee and brandy, and fresh lemonade for the children.

'Now, will you play for us, Sir Chadwick?' Mrs Stout urged.

'On the condition I made earlier,' he replied. 'The ladies must sing. I shall merely accompany them.'

Mrs Stout provided sheet music which had been concealed in the seat of the piano stool and soon Miss Paradine and Hilda were entertaining them with a delightfully tuneful duet.

'Wonderful harmony,' cried Flowerdale as they all applauded.

Sir Chadwick insisted Abby sing *Sunshine Millionaire*, a song he had once composed for her.

Flowerdale and Mr Fitzroy obliged with recitations and Mandini, ably assisted by Spike, rounded off the entertainment with some conjuring tricks.

As the evening drew to a close Mrs Stout offered some advice. 'I hope you will not be offended if I make a suggestion, Sir Chadwick,' she began.

'Not at all, dear lady,' he replied.

She spoke carefully. 'I'm sure Mr Flowerdale will agree with me when I say that the audience for the Playhouse, although enthusiastic, is not – shall we say – as sophisticated as those of London and the cities of our eastern seaboard.'

'Regrettably, what Mrs Stout says is true,' interjected Flowerdale.

She continued. 'The cowboys and miners who make up the majority of the audience may find a full performance of one of Shakespeare's major works rather demanding for their simple, home-spun tastes.'

Sir Chadwick nodded and, encouraged, Mrs Stout went on. 'Have you considered shortening the plays? Perhaps to their very essence. Without sacrificing any of their true splendour, of course.'

Sir Chadwick bowed. 'Mrs Stout, you are the soul of grace and common sense. I must reassure you that I will take your words to heart. I once toured with my London company to the remoter regions of the British Isles. We soon discovered that the shorter we made the play, the more attentive were our rustic audiences. By the end of the tour we could manage to stage shortened versions of *King Lear, Richard III* and *The Merry Wives of Windsor* all on the same evening.'

He turned to the others. 'In fact, this gathering has given me some other ideas, as well.'

Mr and Mrs Stout stood on the steps of their house as the guests departed. All the way home the company sang *Sunshine Millionaire* – much to the astonishment of a large group of miners and cowboys who were fighting in the main street. They paused, with Stetson hats and miners' helmets raised, to let the party pass without hindrance.

On the verandah of the boarding house, before they went to bed, Abby and Spike told Sir Chadwick what Washington Potts had told them about Bart Stoneheart's nocturnal flights in his secret balloon.

'There are unknown forces in Silver Springs, both for good and evil,' said Sir Chadwick when they had finished. 'All we can do for now is wait and watch.'

Before they went in, Abby noticed the vulture was perched in its usual place on top of Stoneheart's saloon.

From another rooftop, three baleful figures had watched Sir Chadwick, Abby and Spike as they stood on the verandah. Wolfbane, Lucia and Valentine were wrapped in their Night Witch cloaks, which allowed them to fly while giving the illusion they were bats.

'Come on,' said Wolfbane, fluttering to the ground, his parents following to stand in the dark shadows of an alleyway.

'What on earth do you think they're up to, hanging about in Silver Springs?' hissed Lucia. 'Anyone would think they were settling down to live forever in this unspeakable little slum.'

'I thought you liked slums,' said Valentine. 'You always said our happiest days together were spent in the East End of London, in those delightful days before they dug the sewers.'

Lucia reached out with a talon-like hand and stroked her husband's cheek. 'I was speaking metaphorically, my pet. Anywhere even as clean as this is a slum in my terms.'

Wolfbane noted her words and sniffed the air. 'You're right, it *is* clean here. If I wasn't wearing nose-blockers it would be unbearable. Where do you think all the rubbish goes?'

'They cart it to a place in the desert,' said Lucia in a know-it-all tone.

'How do you know?' asked Valentine.

'Caspar told me, didn't you, pet? The clever boy discovered it all on his own.'

The raven poked its head from beneath her cloak and gave a croak.

'A rubbish dump!' said Valentine with yearning. 'Just to be able to take out these nose-blockers for an hour or so.'

'What are we waiting for?' Lucia said. 'Lead on, Caspar.'

The raven soared into the air with three bat-like shapes in pursuit.

The dump was in a deep depression in the desert far from the town. The smell was appalling but it was as sweet as a rose garden to Wolfbane and his parents. They fluttered down to sit on three upturned barrels of rotting salt-pork.

'So, what do you think, my boy?' asked Valentine. 'How much longer do you think we'll have to spend in Silver Springs?'

Wolfbane remained silent, thinking.

'Until we find Excalibur, of course,' Lucia snapped.

'Has your raven searched all the rooms in Flowerdale's boarding house?'

'Thoroughly,' Lucia replied. 'There's no sign of it.'

'And no sign of their Atlantis Boat either?' asked Valentine.

'That's because it's underground,' replied Wolfbane.

'Underground! How do you know?'

Wolfbane and his mother rolled up their eyes in exasperation.

'We've searched every inch of Silver Springs, and it's nowhere to be found,' said Wolfbane, as if he were explaining to a child. 'There's only one river nearby and that's too shallow to cover it. So they must have buried it somehow – and the Sword of Merlin.'

'What can we do?' said Valentine. 'The dust around here has traces of Ice Dust in it. It would be dangerous for us to start digging holes.'

'So all we can do is stay out of sight, watch, and be ready to act. Eventually, they'll lead us to it,' said Wolfbane with mounting impatience. 'We'll snatch Excalibur and unleash the power of Charlock. Then we're really going to enjoy ourselves.'

'That'll be the day,' said Valentine dreamily. 'I know what I'm going to do when we're in power.'

'And what will that be?' asked Lucia, raising a quizzical eyebrow.

Valentine smiled. 'Nothing too complicated. I'm a simple sort of chap. I'm just going to bring back some of the good old customs that have gone out of fashion: gladiator fights, bear-baiting, human sacrifice, Elizabethan torture chambers, that sort of thing.'

Lucia carefully arranged the folds of her dress and placed a cigarette in a long holder before lighting it. 'I know what I want to do,' she said quietly. 'I'm going to start the reverse of a hospital.'

'The reverse of a hospital?' said Valentine, puzzled. 'What do you mean?'

Lucia suddenly spoke with enthusiasm. 'Hospitals take sick people in and restore them to health. I'm going to take in healthy people and make them so sick they die.'

'That's a brilliant idea,' said Valentine, impressed.

'And I'm going to form a special corps of women Night Witches,' she said with growing fervour. 'They'll wear a stunning black uniform designed by me and be known as the Dowager Empress Lucia Corps of Cursing.'

'What about you, my boy?' asked Valentine.

Wolfbane, his eyes flashing, snarled. 'All the world will tremble before me. But, first, I've some very special nightmares in store for Abby Clover and her friends.'

As he spoke a scrabbling sound came from inside the barrels they were sitting on. Tearing them open they found a pack of fat rats inside, gorging on the rotting pork.

'What a treat – fresh rats,' said Lucia, pouncing on them with glee.

Grand Opening Night

The following morning, Spike and Abby stood waiting in the newspaper office while the compositor finished printing playbills to announce the re-opening of the theatre that evening. The children were going to distribute the notices about the town.

The compositor took the last playbill off the printing press and held it up to show Abby and Spike. It read:

Quincy Flowerdale is proud to announce
The Silver Springs Playhouse will present
the following performance tonight at Eight.
RICHARD III
by William Shakespeare.
The king will be played by
Sir Chadwick Street.
Also
Feats of illusion and magic by
The Great Mandini.

Songs to move the heart
will be performed
by Miss Hilda Bluebell
and Miss Laura Paradine.
And a surprise performance from
Spike, Abby, Snow and Frost.

Mr Bradbury, editor of the *Silver Springs Recorder,* left his desk and came to look. Peering at the playbill through his spectacles, he said, 'A red letter day for Silver Springs.'

'What's a red letter day, Mr Bradbury?' asked Spike.

Mr Bradbury tugged his bow tie. 'It used to mean a Saint's day. They used to be printed in red ink on calendars,' he explained. 'But folks began to say *It's a red letter day* for any special occasion.'

'Are you coming to the performance tonight, Mr Bradbury?' asked Abby.

'I shall be there in two capacities,' he replied, sticking his thumbs in his waistcoat pockets. 'As a private citizen, enjoying an evening of culture and entertainment, and also in my role as the drama critic of the *Silver Springs Recorder*.'

'If you're coming as two people, will you buy two tickets?' asked Spike with a grin.

'I shall, young fellow,' he replied dryly. 'But Mrs Bradbury will use the other one.'

* * *

Having divided the pile of playbills in two, Abby and Spike each took one side of the main street and worked their way down, tacking the posters to verandah posts and asking shopkeepers to put them in their windows.

They ended at the stagecoach depot and took a few minutes to fuss over Snow and Frost before they went back to the theatre. There was already a crowd of people at the box office. They must have followed Abby and Spike down the main street almost as soon as they saw the posters.

On stage, things were going as normal at Sir Chadwick's rehearsals. All was in chaos. Amid the crash of carpenter's hammers and the thuds of workmen manhandling props, Miss Paradine and Hilda stood to one side of the stage singing *Our Sweethearts are Miners and Cowboys*, a song Sir Chadwick had composed for them. Captain Starlight was accompanying them on an accordion he had found in the props room.

The Great Mandini was testing a new illusion which involved making Mr Fitzroy disappear while he was suspended high above the audience. The illusion involved three huge mirrors dangling from the rafters.

Spike watched Mandini's efforts for a moment. 'We're going to have an awful lot of bad luck if that trick goes wrong,' he said.

Suddenly, Sir Chadwick roared, *'Clarence!* Will somebody be kind enough to tell me where is the Duke of Clarence?'

'I'm up here,' replied Mr Fitzroy.

'Please come down,' Sir Chadwick called in a more reasonable voice. 'I need you for the scene where you drown in the wine barrel.'

'I'm not sure how I can get down,' replied Fitzroy rather timorously.

'Pull the cord as I showed you, Mr Fitzroy,' Mandini sighed.

'Oh, yes,' he answered, and when he did so, a large pair of white wings unfolded from his costume and he glided gracefully down to the stage.

Sir Chadwick watched him with approval. 'What a magnificent entrance, Mandini. I must remember to use it in some future production.'

'I'm afraid I still don't know all my lines,' Mr Fitzroy said anxiously.

'Neither do I,' cried out several of the other actors.

'Don't worry,' Sir Chadwick answered. Then he spotted Spike and Abby. 'Ah, my bill stickers. Are you two ready? You're due to perform before the first interval.'

As he spoke, a man in a red velvet frock coat with a spiky beard and flowing hair was tugging urgently at his sleeve. Sir Chadwick turned to him. 'Yes, yes. What is it, Mr Gavin?'

'I shall have to take the photographs now if we want them to go on sale in the theatre tonight.'

'Of course,' said Sir Chadwick. He clapped his hands for attention and announced, 'Everyone in costume immediately. Mr Gavin is going to take photographs of us all.

They will be on sale in the theatre lobby after this evening's performance. As is customary in these matters, the management will receive a proportion of the sale and Mr Gavin will share the rest of the profits with the individual artist.'

Hilda told Spike and Abby, 'Your new costumes are in my dressing room.'

'That was quick,' said Abby.

'Woo Ling's family are tailors. They made them up from Captain Starlight's drawings last night.'

Spike and Abby hurried to change. A few minutes later they assembled on the stage with the rest of the performers. Mr Gavin carefully grouped everyone for a photograph of the entire cast. When they were assembled to his satisfaction, Sir Chadwick excused himself for a moment and slipped behind them. Mr Gavin impatiently flung off the black cloth covering his head and the large camera he crouched behind.

'I shall be in my place in just a moment, Mr Gavin,' said Sir Chadwick. 'The rest of you keep looking into the lens of the camera as I speak.'

Abby knew exactly what Sir Chadwick was up to. A moment later, he announced in a deep booming voice, 'This is my command. You will all know your parts perfectly.'

Abby felt a sudden tingling, as if tiny charges of electricity had passed through her body. Sir Chadwick had sprinkled the entire cast with some of his precious supply of Ice Dust. Then he took his place again in front of the cast at the centre of the stage.

'That man's voice sends a shiver down my spine,' said Laura Paradine.

'Mine, too,' said Hilda with a smile.

The entire population of Silver Springs seemed to be crowded into the theatre for the grand reopening. Abby and Spike were surprised to see the blacksmith taking the tickets in the stalls. Quincy Flowerdale explained that he employed him part-time because he was big enough to throw out any miners and cowboys who started to fight.

Sir Chadwick peered through a peephole in the curtain as the three-piece orchestra struck up. 'A full house and standing at the back of the stalls,' he announced with deep satisfaction.

'The best attendance I have ever seen,' said Flowerdale.

When Abby and Spike looked through the peephole, they saw Buffalo Bill and Annie Oakley taking their places in a box. On the opposite side of the theatre, Bart Stoneheart and his cronies were similarly seated.

'Bart Stoneheart and his gang are here,' Abby said to Sir Chadwick.

'Are they?' he replied, sternly. 'Then, I think I shall make an announcement before the curtain goes up.'

Already dressed for his role as Richard III, Sir Chadwick parted the curtains and stepped on to the stage. There was a murmur of appreciation for the splendour of his costume. Sir Chadwick raised a hand and the auditorium became quiet.

'Ladies and gentlemen, citizens of Silver Springs and distinguished visitors,' he began, with a slight bow to Buffalo Bill's box. 'Allow me to introduce myself. I am Sir Chadwick Street. Quincy Flowerdale has graciously invited me and my companions to join his splendid players, and also bestowed upon me the singular honour of producing and directing the entertainments you will see tonight.'

'I hope you know what you're taking on, fancy-pants,' jeered Bart Stoneheart. 'Remember, you're acting under my rules tonight.'

Sir Chadwick looked up at Stoneheart's box, studied him for a few moments, then spoke quite mildly. 'We shall act under the rules as they have existed since the ancient Greeks first performed plays. If you try to alter them, it will be at your own peril.' With that, he calmly withdrew behind the curtain.

Bart Stoneheart shouted after him, 'We'll show you the meaning of *peril*, fancy-pants.'

'Was that wise, Chadwick?' Quincy asked, looking concerned.

Sir Chadwick smiled as he said only, 'I have to go and make a few adjustments to my make-up. Give the sign to the orchestra to begin, if you please, Quincy.'

There was a roll on the drums and they all left the stage, except for the Great Mandini, who was on first.

His astonishing feats thrilled the audience. They gasped at his fire-eating act and applauded the skill with which he made doves and flags appear as if from nowhere. Then he read the minds of several miners and cowboys in the audience. His final illusion, in which he made Mr Fitzroy disappear from above their heads then reappear with wings to glide down on to the stage, left them open-mouthed with astonishment.

Mr Fitzroy then gave a splendidly stirring recitation of *The Charge of The Light Brigade*, and finished his act by dancing a surprisingly nimble hornpipe, with Captain Starlight accompanying him on his accordion.

Then Laura Paradine and Hilda stood in the limelight. A deep hush fell over the stalls as they sang *The Miner's Lament* and *The Cowboy's Last Round-up*.

Watching from the wings, Spike and Abby could see the miners and cowboys were enraptured, most of them sitting with tears streaming down their cheeks. When Laura and Hilda had finished the song Sir Chadwick had written for them, the storm of applause almost shook the theatre.

Before the next act, the leader of the miner's council stood up and, to rousing cheers, declared that Hilda Bluebell and Laura Paradine were officially appointed as Miners' Sweethearts.

Not to be outdone, a cowboy jumped to his feet and said that from now on Hilda and Laura would also be known as the Cowboys' Nightingales.

The curtain was lowered briefly while the stage was cleared and the back of the playhouse building raised. When the curtains parted again the audience gasped at the landscape they could now see behind the theatre. As far as the distant mountains, it was bathed in bright moonlight. This alone received a round of applause.

'Strange, isn't it?' Spike whispered to Abby. 'They can see that view any time, just by looking at it from their backyards.'

'It's what Sir Chadwick calls the magic of the theatre,' Abby answered as they mounted Snow and Frost. 'It seems more wonderful because we've framed it on stage.'

Thunderous applause broke out as Abby and Spike rode into view, and it continued as they put the ponies through their astonishing tricks, and increased even more when they performed the new one Mandini had added. At the end, Snow and Frost leaped through great hoops of fire before Spike and Abby rode them to the front of the stage. The clapping and whistling and shouting rose to a tumultuous crescendo as the ponies bowed with their front legs bent and Spike and Abby swept off their hats to bow to the audience. Eventually, the curtain fell for the interval.

The cast were all thrilled at how well the show was going. They congratulated and hugged each other extravagantly before hurrying to change for the next part of the performance. Spike and Abby quickly took the ponies to the stagecoach corral, treated them to apples, then returned to the theatre to watch *Richard III* from the wings.

The audience gasped when Sir Chadwick came on stage as the villainous king. Then they burst into roars of laughter, followed by thunderous applause.

Sir Chadwick had adjusted his make-up so that he looked exactly like Bart Stoneheart – even to the drooping moustache.

Only Stoneheart and his cronies sat in glowering silence.

Abby and Spike had seen Sir Chadwick play the role before but never with such power. He held the audience in the palm of his hand, alternately drawing hisses and cheers from the packed theatre. Bringing the play to its climax, he finally cried out in torment, '*A horse! A horse! My Kingdom for a horse!*'

The cowboys, who all loved horses, responded to this request with even louder cheers and many a pistol was fired into the copper-clad roof. It was a miracle the three mirrors from Mandini's illusion were not shattered.

Finally, the cast from the entire show came to the front of the stage to take their bows and the applause thundered on until Sir Chadwick stepped forward and held up his hand. Gradually, the shouts died down and he could speak.

'Ladies and gentlemen, we are humbled by your enthusiastic appreciation of our efforts,' he began. 'For we simple players, it makes our humdrum lives worthwhile to bring you such pleasure.'

He held up his arms and, raising his voice to reach with crystal clarity the back of the gallery, announced, 'If you have enjoyed tonight's performance, there will be new wonders tomorrow night. Other tunes performed by our songbirds, new feats of magic by the Great Mandini, even more astonishing tricks from Spike, Abby and their spirited ponies, and amazing jigs from Oscar Wilkington Fitzroy.'

Pausing dramatically, he looked directly up at the box occupied by Bart Stoneheart and his cronies. 'And I shall perform Romeo with my wife, Lady Street, as Juliet in William Shakespeare's immortal tragedy.'

There was a sharp intake of breath from the entire audience. All eyes looked up at Bart Stoneheart's box.

Stoneheart jumped to his feet and shouted, 'Now, hear me, fancy-pants. If Romeo and Juliet die at the end, so do you!' And with that, he stalked out of the theatre.

In the silence that followed, Spike spoke in a stage whisper, 'Well, that should ensure another full house tomorrow night.'

After the performance many of the miners and cowboys went to celebrate. It was hours later before the saloons finally closed and all grew quiet in Silver Springs.

In the dead of night, after the moon had set, Wolfbane, Valentine and Lucia were eating a very late supper in the purple light illuminating their time-machine Shark Boat.

'Do you like it?' asked Lucia. 'I had Caspar catch a few rattlesnakes in the desert and a horned toad or two.'

'It's not bad,' said Valentine begrudgingly. 'But a touch of deadly nightshade and perhaps a pinch of dried bat's blood might have spiced it up a bit.'

'Where in this miserable desert do you expect me to get deadly nightshade?' snarled Lucia. 'And it's not easy cooking in that tiny galley, you know.'

'I would have preferred to catch myself a few more of those fresh rats at the dump,' said Valentine morosely. 'What a rotten evening. I hate *Richard III*. It has the unhappiest ending of any play I know. Why does King Richard always have to die?'

'Perhaps Bart Stoneheart will arrange for it to have a different ending for you next time, dear,' said Lucia, goading Valentine. 'At least *he* behaves like a man.'

'Oh, do stop squabbling,' ordered Wolfbane, pushing his greasy bowl aside and scratching beneath his clothes where the lice crawled.

'I'm utterly sick of waiting for those actors to lead us to the sword,' said Lucia impatiently. 'Can't we just capture one of those wretched children and torture them until they talk?'

'It's tempting,' admitted Wolfbane. 'And it would give me the greatest pleasure to lower Abby Clover into a pit full of scorpions.'

'Or roast her in the desert sun,' said Lucia.

'With her eyes smothered in honey to attract the hornets and the red ants,' added Valentine with a horrible leer.

Wolfbane held up his hand. 'But we *can't*! No matter how enjoyable it would be, it's far too risky.'

'Why?' Valentine and Lucia both asked.

'Because, as I keep explaining to you, we only have a tiny amount of the special Black Dust. We need Excalibur so we can make more of it,' he hissed through gritted teeth.

'If we kidnap Abby Clover now, there's no telling what her friends would do. Too much is at stake to risk having them thwart our plans. You know how pathetically loyal they are to each other and how resolute they are in the face of danger.'

Wolfbane paused, drumming on the chart table with his fingers.

'No,' he said finally. 'Our victory depends on us getting our hands on Excalibur in one decisive attack.' He gestured towards the cooking pot. 'Meanwhile, let's all have some more of that rattlesnake stew, Mother.'

Dramas at the Playhouse

Late the following afternoon, when it was almost time to prepare for the evening's show, Spike and Abby were returning to the theatre after watering Frost and Snow. As they approached the Playhouse they heard voices muttering in the alleyway beside it. Peering around the corner of the building they saw the Great Mandini and Captain Starlight having a heated discussion with Sir Chadwick. There was no sign of Hilda.

'What you propose is madness,' Mandini said forcefully.

'He's right, Chadwick,' agreed Starlight. 'We have no idea how expert Bart Stoneheart is with a gun.'

'I used to be a pretty good shot myself,' said Sir Chadwick mildly.

'But you were a soldier,' said Mandini. 'This man is a professional assassin. There will be no rules of gentlemanly conduct. No seconds to see that fair play is observed. If you don't use magic he will simply murder you.'

Sir Chadwick drew himself up. 'What that creature

proposes is an affront to the whole acting profession. I will not let him intimidate me. Nor will I use magic for my own protection. I am defending my honour as an actor, not as a Light Witch. It is a personal matter. Therefore, to use magic would be breaking the code of the Light Witches. An impossible thing for me to do.'

'What does Hilda say?' asked Mandini miserably.

'She doesn't know – and I don't want either of you telling her. I shall take every precaution.'

Spike and Abby slipped away and walked further along the main street.

'Sir Chadwick is jolly brave,' said Spike. 'I heard Mr Potts say Bart Stoneheart was as quick as a rattlesnake with a six-shooter.'

'Sir Chadwick is a hero,' said Abby. 'And Bart Stoneheart is not going to shoot him tonight.'

'But you heard Sir Chadwick say he can't use magic to defend himself,' said Spike.

'No, but I can,' said Abby. 'Stand still. I'm going to make us disappear.'

Moments later, unseen by any of the occupants, Spike and Abby entered the saloon. Stoneheart was playing cards with Beauregard Lightfoot. There was no sign of Bullwhip Kate Mulroony.

The children crept closer, and Abby held her hands above Stoneheart and Lightfoot's heads, saying, *'May shun tilt dig tin.'*

The children quickly stepped back several paces.

'What did you say?' asked Stoneheart suspiciously.

'Nothing,' said Lightfoot, dealing another card.

'I could have sworn you said, "My son is tilting."'

'What does that mean?' said Lightfoot.

'How should I know?' replied Stoneheart, growing angry. 'It wasn't me who said it.'

Just then Bullwhip Kate strode up to the table.

'Time to go to the theatre,' she said.

Stoneheart threw down his cards and, drawing one of his pistols, he spun the chamber to check it was loaded. Satisfied, he replaced it in his holster and attempted to rise. But he was unable to leave the chair, no matter how much effort he put into the struggle. Amazed, Bullwhip Kate watched as Beauregard Lightfoot struggled in the same manner.

'It's that conjurer. Doing his magic tricks,' gasped Lightfoot. 'He's put some kind of hex on us.'

The crowd in the saloon, most of whom were preparing to leave for the Playhouse, watched Stoneheart. Seeing their interest, he put a restraining hand on Lightfoot's arm.

'Sit still,' hissed Stoneheart. 'I don't want word of this getting around the town, or I shall be a figure of mockery.' He beckoned to Bullwhip Kate and whispered, 'You go to the theatre. Take care of Chadwick Street. Say I was too proud to take part in a gunfight with a fancy-pants actor, so I sent a woman.'

'I'm as tough as any man,' snarled Bullwhip Kate, offended.

'I know you are,' said Stoneheart. 'So get out there and prove it.'

As they slipped out of the saloon, Spike asked Abby what her anagram spell had said.

'*Stay until midnight*,' Abby answered. 'But now we've got Bullwhip Kate to deal with, I think I may have made things worse.'

'How?' said Spike.

'You know what a gentleman Sir Chadwick is,' said Abby. 'He would have fought Bart Stoneheart. But there's no chance he would shoot a woman – unless she were an evil Night Witch.'

'We'd better get to the theatre,' said Spike, as the sidewalk filled with people heading for the Playhouse.

The show went just as well as the previous evening's performance, despite the threat of ultimate violence. Buffalo Bill and Annie Oakley, who were still in town, occupied the same box as they had on opening night. Before the curtain rose, they had called backstage and offered to buy a drink in the bar for any of the cast who were free during the interval.

There were murmurs of surprise from the audience as they noticed Bullwhip Kate Mulroony was alone in Bart Stoneheart's box. But word quickly spread that Stoneheart was only coming to see the last act of *Romeo and Juliet* and, eventually, the audience settled down.

When the show started, the audience gasped at Mandini's latest display of magic and illusion. Much appreciation was shown for Mr Fitzroy's Irish jigs. Even the accompaniment, provided by Captain Starlight on the accordion, earned a special round of applause.

A storm of hoots and whistles and clapping greeted Laura and Hilda. Throughout their songs the miners and cowboys held up and waved the photographs they had bought from Mr Gavin the night before.

To balance the tragic content of *Romeo and Juliet*, Sir Chadwick had included a few cheerful songs in Laura and Hilda's repertoire. They'd even had a large poster printed with the words of *Sunshine Millionaire* so the audience could join in.

Abby and Spike's performance earned even wilder whoops and cheers than it had the night before. Frost and Snow obviously enjoyed the applause and even added a few touches of their own to the act.

Any time the ponies were still for a moment between tricks, Snow would take Frost's tail in his teeth and give it a tug, then pretend innocence when Frost looked around. One of the cowboys laughed so much he fell off his seat into the aisle, and lay there writhing with mirth until he was kicked by one of the miners.

During the interval, Spike and Abby went for refreshments with Captain Starlight and Mandini. They were met in the theatre bar by Buffalo Bill and Annie Oakley. Buffalo Bill gave them glasses of lemonade, and was full of praise for their rough-riding tricks.

'I wish you youngsters would join my Wild West Show,' said Buffalo Bill. 'There's people all over this great country who would appreciate the antics of those ponies of yours. Just name your price and I'll put your names up in lights.'

'We're very flattered, Colonel,' said Abby, speaking both for herself and Spike, 'but we must stay here with the show in Silver Springs.'

'Well, I shall just have to get over my disappointment,' he said with a smile. 'But why don't you come up to our box and watch the rest of the show with me and Annie?'

'I've got a box of mighty fine candy that comes all the way from Chicago,' said Annie.

'Do you know, I've never seen a play from a box,' said Abby.

'And I've never had candy from Chicago,' said Spike, so they accepted the invitation.

Although Sir Chadwick was presenting a considerably shortened version of *Romeo and Juliet*, he and Hilda were so brilliant in the leading roles the citizens of Silver Springs were moved to tears – with one exception. Bullwhip Kate. All through the performance she sat with her feet resting on the balustrade of Stoneheart's box, tossing peanuts into the air and catching them in her mouth.

There had been a certain amount of tension in the audience as they anticipated the arrival of Bart Stoneheart but when he didn't show up no one bothered to glance up at the box any more.

But as Sir Chadwick and Hilda came forward to take their curtain calls, there was a sudden loud crack of Kate's bullwhip and all eyes turned to see her standing in the box with her lash snaking down into the orchestra pit.

'Bart Stoneheart told you to give the play a happy ending and you ignored him,' she stormed. 'He told me to tell the folks you're just a prancing, primping showboy and he wouldn't dirty his hands by punishing you himself. So I'm here to do the job.'

She cracked her whip again. 'First, I'm going to give you a whipping. Then I'm going to shoot you down like a yellow prairie dog.'

Hilda attempted to stand in front of Sir Chadwick but he swept her around behind him.

From Buffalo Bill's box on the opposite side of the stage, Abby and Spike watched as Kate Mulroony raised her whip again. Buffalo Bill started to reach for one of the pearl-handled Colt revolvers he now wore at his sides but Abby was quicker. Without thinking, she snatched his other revolver from the holster and shouted, *'This she toot rag melt,'* as she cocked the gun and fired.

The Colt pistol was huge in her hand but it felt as light as if it were made of feathers. She didn't even feel the recoil from the massive gun, which should have knocked her off her feet. Abby's shot cut Kate's whip clean in two. For a moment, she gazed at the half left in her hand and then with an unladylike oath, threw the remains of the whip aside and snatched for her own pistol.

Abby's second shot knocked the revolver from Kate's hand before she had a chance to level it at Sir Chadwick. It had all happened so fast, people in the theatre were still looking about them to see where the shots had come from. Quickly, before anyone noticed, Abby slipped the gun back into Buffalo Bill's holster.

Kate stood frozen in disbelief, looking open-mouthed at the hand from which Abby had shot her pistol. She had not seen Abby fire, and imagined some conjurer's trick had been played on her. Slowly, her expression turned to one of rage. She shook a fist at Sir Chadwick, shouting, 'You lily-livered side-winder. Next time, I'll make *sure* you fight like a man.' And, with that, she stomped out of the box.

Sir Chadwick bowed and, to great applause, escorted Hilda from the stage.

'That was mighty pretty shooting, little missy,' said Annie Oakley.

Buffalo Bill nodded. 'And we won't tell anybody about this,' he said.

'Why not, Colonel?' asked Spike.

Buffalo Bill looked serious. 'Because there are many bad men in the west, son. If they heard that a girl called Abby Clover could shoot that well with a pistol, they'd come here to try and outshoot her in a gunfight.'

'Really?' said Abby and Spike.

'He's right,' said Annie Oakley.

'But what about you, Annie?' asked Abby. 'No one in the world shoots better than you.'

Annie smiled. 'I use a rifle. Bad men don't seem to find that a challenge. It's only folks who are fast on the draw with a pistol they want to kill.'

'I think we'd better go backstage,' Spike said. 'Thank you for letting us sit in your box, Colonel Cody. It was a jolly good job you did.'

'Goodnight, and thanks for the candy,' said Abby.

When they rejoined the actors they found Hilda and Sir Chadwick in their dressing room with Captain Starlight and Mandini.

'I was *sure* that dreadful woman was going to shoot you, Chadwick,' Hilda was saying, still upset.

He gave a laugh but there was a degree of relief in the sound he uttered. 'I knew all was well when I heard a voice shout out *This she toot rag melt*.'

Hilda looked puzzled. 'I heard that, too. What on earth does it mean?'

'It's an anagram,' said Spike. 'I worked it out. It means, *Let me shoot straight*.'

'So it was you who saved Chadwick, Abby,' said Hilda. 'I'll never be able to repay you.'

'I hope you didn't mind me interfering, Sir Chadwick,' said Abby.

He laughed. 'Feel free to do so any time,' he replied lightly. Then he became serious. 'But did anyone see you shoot so well?'

'Only Buffalo Bill and Annie Oakley,' said Abby, and she told them of their warning.

'There's a great deal of common sense in that man,' said Captain Starlight. 'He deserves his reputation as a hero.'

'Well, all's well that ends well,' said Sir Chadwick.

When the midnight hour struck in Bart Stoneheart's saloon Bullwhip Kate was pacing angrily in front of Stoneheart and Lightfoot who were still unable to rise from their chairs. She was relating the events at the theatre.

'That slick city-actor-man used some damned conjuring trick on me,' she stormed. 'I'm going to get me a Bowie knife and skin the varmint like a buffalo.'

Just then, a clean-shaven Kentucky Kid passed her on

his way to the bar. She snatched the large knife from his belt and held it up to his face, demanding, 'Is this sharp?'

'Sharp enough to shave with, Kate,' the Kid replied, uneasily stroking his smooth cheeks as he eyed the gleaming blade almost touching his nose.

Suddenly, Stoneheart and Lightfoot rose slightly from their seats and thumped back down again. They both practised standing up and sitting down a couple of times, then Stoneheart sat back. His expression was so terrible, Kate's own anger faded away.

'Give the Kid back his knife,' he hissed.

The Kentucky Kid took it from Kate and scurried away.

Stoneheart continued, 'Tell a couple of the boys I want them to follow Chadwick Street tomorrow and shoot him down. *And* any of the other actors they can get at the same time.'

'I'll do it with Kate,' said Lightfoot.

Stoneheart shook his head. 'They know you two, and will be on their guard. I don't want any slip-ups this time. I want that fancy-pants in a pine box by noon.'

It was after midnight when Abby went to the kitchen to get a glass of lemonade. The mixture was warm when she poured it from the stone bottle and for a moment she longed for a few lumps of ice. She took the drink to the darkness of the verandah and stood at the top of the steps enjoying the cool breeze. Music was still coming from the Silver Springs Saloon, where some of the last customers were singing *My Darling Clementine*, but it was a softer version than usual.

Abby was enjoying the song when she heard a gentle sob come from the shadows. It was Laura, clutching a handkerchief as she gazed at the saloon.

'What's the matter, Laura?' Abby asked, concerned.

Laura tried to smile but another sob was all she could manage. 'Oh, dear,' she replied. 'I'm so unhappy.'

'Why, what's happened?' asked Abby.

'It was watching *Romeo and Juliet* tonight. It put me in mind of my own predicament,' Laura answered. She sighed and gazed at the saloon again.

'So, if you're Juliet, who is your Romeo?' asked Abby, gently.

'Beauregard Lightfoot,' Laura replied after a pause.

'Lightfoot!' exclaimed Abby. 'Bart Stoneheart's friend?'

Laura nodded hopelessly.

'Does Quincy know about this?' Abby asked.

'No, and you must never tell him. Swear to me you won't. Quincy would challenge him to a duel if he thought Beauregard had been dallying with my affections.'

'When do you meet?' asked Abby.

'We don't any more,' said Laura. 'Before Quincy fell out with Bart Stoneheart we would see each other on the main street. He always used to raise his hat.'

'You used to talk?'

'No, never. But I dropped a handkerchief once and Beauregard picked it up. He still wears it in the top pocket of his waistcoat, next to his heart. So I know how he feels about me.'

Abby could see Laura was deeply unhappy. On an impulse she muttered '*Wet vole nit*' into her glass of lemonade. 'Here, drink this,' she said, offering the glass to Laura.

'Thank you,' said Laura, sipping the drink. 'I feel better now, knowing someone shares my secret.'

Abby went back to her bed. She was in the next room to Spike and the wall between them was so thin they could speak to each other quite easily.

'I heard Laura's secret,' said Spike sleepily. 'My window is open.'

'Did you hear what I said?' asked Abby.

'The anagram spell?' replied Spike. 'You said, *Let love win*.'

'I hope it works,' said Abby. 'Goodnight.'

Danger at the Bank

The following morning, after breakfast in the boarding house, Abby and Spike watched Sir Chadwick and Quincy Flowerdale counting out a large pile of money on the dining-room table.

'More than three thousand dollars,' said Flowerdale. 'Our fortunes are certainly looking up.'

'It's a lot of cash to keep about the house,' said Captain Starlight. 'Shouldn't we put it in the bank?'

Sir Chadwick raised an enquiring eyebrow at Flowerdale, who nodded his agreement. 'A capital idea,' he said. 'Such a sum would tempt many a desperado in this town if they knew it was lying around here.'

'Would you care to come with me, Quincy?' Sir Chadwick asked.

Quincy shook his head. 'If you don't mind, I won't. I have a coat fitting with Woo Ling's brother. It is such a pleasure to be able to afford some new clothes.'

'I'll go with you, Chadwick,' said Starlight who had been burnishing the horseshoes with which he and Mandini played in the yard. He tucked them into his belt and took one of the two large sacks of silver dollars on the table. Sir Chadwick carried the other.

'We might as well come too,' said Abby. She and Spike had fed and groomed Frost and Snow before breakfast and had not yet planned the rest of their day.

Sir Chadwick and Captain Starlight led the way down the main street towards Mr Stout's bank. Sir Chadwick jingled one of the sacks of money and said, 'I have a plan, Adam.'

'Go on,' said Starlight.

'Now Quincy is in the money again, I'm going to suggest he re-open his silver mine.'

'So we can tunnel from it to the Atlantis Boat?' said Abby quickly.

'Correct,' replied Sir Chadwick. 'It will give us the ideal opportunity.'

'A fine idea, Chadwick,' agreed Starlight. 'The sooner we get to the Atlantis Boat the better.'

'It's been worrying me for some time,' Sir Chadwick continued. 'I'm sure Wolfbane and his crew are about, but they're keeping well concealed. I shall be less concerned when we have the Sword of Merlin back in our possession.'

Captain Starlight looked up into the clear sky with a slight frown, and Abby knew what he was thinking.

'Benbow's been away a long time, hasn't he, Captain?' she said.

Starlight smiled reassuringly. 'He's an independent bird. When he wants to come back no power in the world will be able to stop him.'

As they approached the bank three cowboys were dismounting. They had bandanas tied across their faces as protection against the dust, and took their time tying their horses to the hitching rail as Sir Chadwick, Starlight, Abby and Spike entered the bank. They had almost reached the counter when the cowboys crept up behind them with their revolvers drawn, and pushed Spike and Abby aside.

Quickly regaining her balance, Abby pointed at Sir Chadwick and Captain Starlight, and shouted, '*For mere bits echo tears*.'

Suddenly, the bank was filled with the howling sound of a ravenous wolf pack and a strange greenish-yellow light. Startled, the three cowboys looked uncertainly about them. Then they screamed in horror as a terrible transformation overcame Starlight and Sir Chadwick.

Starlight's head grew scales. His clothes fell away and his body changed into that of a gigantic rattlesnake. It was about to strike.

Sir Chadwick's clothes also fell to the ground as his body convulsed into that of an enormous scorpion. The creature scuttled towards the cowboys, its great sting poised, its claws snapping.

Screaming with fear, the cowboys' trigger fingers tensed and gunshots wrenched the air. They tossed the guns aside and fled from the bank. Immediately, Sir Chadwick and Starlight were returned to normal, and they dashed out after the bank robbers.

The sound of gunshots had drawn the attention of the people on the main street. They watched the three terrified cowboys run from the bank, leap on their horses and gallop away as Sir Chadwick and Starlight burst out through the door after them. Starlight studied the fleeing bank robbers for a moment, then casually drew the burnished horseshoes from his belt.

The escaping cowboys were already halfway down the main street by the time Starlight hurled the iron missiles. They whistled through the air with deadly accuracy to strike each cowboy on the back of the head. They tumbled off their horses like coconuts falling from a shy in a funfair.

The watching townsfolk let out a great cheer and

several men rushed forward to drag the unconscious cowboys back to the bank.

'What a magnificent piece of work,' said Homer P. Stout, who had hurried to Starlight's side. Holding up one hand to silence the crowd, he pointed with the other at the cowboys lying limply in the dust.

'My cashier, Hiram Prune, tells me these dastardly cowards attempted to rob the bank. Thanks to Captain Starlight they are apprehended.'

Even more cheering followed.

Starlight held up a hand. 'These men should be in jail,' he said.

'We've got the jail,' shouted the blacksmith, 'but no sheriff. I vote we appoint Captain Starlight.'

More cheering broke out and shouts of 'Starlight for sheriff!' echoed down the main street.

Banker Stout stepped forward. 'I propose we have a citizens' meeting in the general store in half an hour, to appoint Captain Adam Starlight sheriff of Silver Springs.'

His suggestion was followed by more cheering from the crowd.

'You seem to have been elected by popular acclaim, Adam,' said Sir Chadwick, smiling.

'In that case,' replied Starlight, 'you can give me a hand to get them into jail.'

'And you can have my silver dollar for luck,' said Abby, handing him the coin.

The cowboys had now struggled to their feet but were

still too stunned to put up a fight. Subdued, they walked in silence to the abandoned sheriff's office where a rusty key was produced and the robbers locked in a cell.

While they were still looking about the dusty office, Buffalo Bill and Annie Oakley stuck their heads around the door.

'Your companions at the boarding house said we'd find you here. We're about to depart,' said Buffalo Bill. 'We've just come to say goodbye.'

'Are you catching the stagecoach?' asked Sir Chadwick.

Buffalo Bill nodded. 'Next stop, Tucson.'

There were handshakes all around and Annie Oakley said, 'I'm mighty sorry you young 'uns won't be joining us in the Colonel's Wild West Show. It would have been real fun to have you along.'

'I know it would, Annie,' said Abby. Then she asked Buffalo Bill, 'Have you ever thought of taking your show to England, Colonel? I'm sure the people there would love it.'

'England, eh?' said Cody, stroking his beard thoughtfully. 'Now that's an idea.'

'Why stop at England?' said Spike. 'The whole of Europe would like to see the Wild West Show.'

'A world tour!' said Cody, his eyes gleaming. 'That's a capital suggestion,' he said as he and Annie waved goodbye and made for the stagecoach depot.

In the dusty sheriff's office, Sir Chadwick said to Abby, 'Your anagram spells are getting more and more powerful, child.'

'So it was Abby, was it?' said Starlight. 'I wondered what had happened. At first I thought Wolfbane had got to us.'

'No,' said Sir Chadwick. 'Abby mixed up the letters of the words *Become their worst fears*. So you and I changed into what the cowboys most feared, Adam. But it was extraordinary that she could alter *me* in such a fashion. I don't mean to belittle you, my dear fellow,' he said, smiling at Starlight, 'but I am something of an exception. The Master of Light Witches is a pretty tough subject on which to cast spells. Even for a friendly Light Witch.'

'I couldn't think what else to do, Sir Chadwick,' said Abby. 'I hope you're not angry.'

'On the contrary, child,' he replied. 'I am delighted you are making such strides.' He stopped for a moment and thought. 'I wonder if . . .' he began, then his voice trailed away.

'You wonder what?' asked Starlight.

Sir Chadwick spoke slowly. 'The Wizards leave us here with only one wandful of Ice Dust between us. But all the time, Abby's anagram spells grow more and more powerful, almost in compensation.' He shook his head. 'No, even the Wizards couldn't be that devious. Surely they wouldn't put us in so much danger just to hasten Abby's development as a Light Witch.'

'It seems to me they do anything they feel like,' said Spike. 'They've never worried too much about us being in danger.'

* * *

The general store was crowded for the town meeting. Sir Chadwick and Starlight sat each side of Quincy Flowerdale in the front row. In a low voice, Sir Chadwick was suggesting something to Flowerdale, who vigorously nodded his head in agreement.

Banker Stout stood up and proposed Captain Starlight as sheriff. The Captain accepted the post, and stood before everyone to have the star pinned to his jacket. Quincy Flowerdale rose to his feet.

'I'd like to make an announcement while you are all gathered here,' he began. 'From the day after tomorrow I intend to re-open my silver mine. This will stop Bart Stoneheart's monopoly as the major employee in Silver Springs and provide more jobs for the poor folks in the shanty town.'

'Excellent news,' cried Banker Stout, clapping his hands with pleasure. 'Things are looking better and better in Silver Springs.'

But the news was not greeted with the same degree of enthusiasm at the back table in Bart Stoneheart's saloon.

'What kind of cowards did we send to kill those actors?' asked Stoneheart bitterly. 'They ran away like little children from a spider.'

'Everything seems to be going their way for those actors,' Lightfoot said as he dealt cards to Stoneheart and Bullwhip Kate. 'If they reopen Flowerdale's mine, it will drive up wages. We'll need more cheap workers.'

Stoneheart considered his comment. 'There's still plenty of ranchers and farmers in the valley,' he said. 'Perhaps it's time they were forced back into town.'

'It might not be so easy with this new sheriff,' said Bull-whip Kate. 'And that actor, Sir Street or whatever he's called, I don't think he's as stupid as we thought. In fact, there's something mighty funny about all those English actors – including the kids. They ride those ponies too well. It ain't natural.'

'Maybe, maybe,' said Stoneheart, studying his cards. 'But I've still got a few tricks to play – tricks they couldn't dream of in their worst nightmares.'

A Voice in the Night

A day and a half later, the townsfolk of Silver Springs were gathered before a flag-decked platform erected in front of Flowerdale's mine. Notable citizens sat either side of Quincy Flowerdale, giving the ceremony a dignity befitting the occasion.

As sheriff, Captain Starlight had a place on the platform next to the Great Mandini, who was there in his new role as general manager of the Flowerdale Mine. Several storekeepers also shared the honours.

A team of miners had laboured in shifts for twenty-four hours to make sure all the mining equipment was in good working order. Now the mine was to be opened officially by Banker Stout.

Wearing blue uniforms decked with gold braid, the three-piece band from the theatre played stirring marches, and Mr Gavin took photographs. From the steps of his saloon, Bart Stoneheart and his cronies watched with grim faces.

Eventually Banker Stout stepped forward and one of the bandsmen blew a fanfare on his cornet.

Mr Stout began. 'This is certainly a happy occasion for Silver Springs,' he declaimed in his squeaky voice. 'Once more, our fair town has another mine which will provide sorely needed work for our less fortunate citizens.'

A cheer went up from the crowd and Mr Stout held up a hand to quieten them. 'You know me as a man of action, not words. So, without further ado, I declare the Flowerdale Mine open for business.'

There was an uproar of cheering, and the band struck up a rousing tune as Mrs Stout cut the blue ribbon strung across the mine entrance. Eventually the crowd dispersed and Abby, Spike, Hilda and Sir Chadwick strolled back towards the theatre.

'How long do you think it will take Mandini to tunnel to the Atlantis Boat, Sir Chadwick?' asked Abby.

'It's hard to say,' he replied. 'It might take weeks. If only we had a decent supply of Ice Dust it would be much easier.'

'Can't Abby use an anagram spell?' asked Spike.

Abby shook her head. 'Anagrams only seem to come to me in an emergency, when someone is in danger or really upset,' she said as they arrived at the Playhouse.

Because they put on six performances a week, the company was kept very busy rehearsing. After the opening night, Sir Chadwick had not used any of his emergency supply of Ice Dust to ensure the actors knew their parts. Consequently, most of them had to work very hard, learning new plays and inventing different ways of keeping the audience entertained.

But Hilda and Laura's songs were so popular, the cowboys and miners insisted they sing the same tunes night after night. They yielded to popular demand, and also added an occasional surprise. The crowd always wanted Abby and Spike to put Frost and Snow through the same routines, but the rest of the cast were always frantically learning new lines.

Spike and Abby helped a lot by listening to their readings and providing them with their cues but it was all very tiring. When they got home from the theatre they had a hot drink, went straight to bed, and slept soundly until a cock crowed at dawn, telling them it was time to get up to water and feed Snow and Frost at the stagecoach corral.

After the performance that night, Abby and Spike went to bed and were, as usual, soon sound asleep. But Abby had a strange dream. She could hear a voice calling her and she knew it came from the cloud-wreathed mountains on the far horizon. The dream seemed so real, she got out of bed and leaned out of her window. Spike was doing exactly the same in his room.

'I had an odd, dream, Abby,' he said. 'I could hear a voice calling my name from the mountains.'

'So did I,' answered Abby, whispering so as not to wake anyone else in the house.

'Do you think we should tell the others?' asked Spike.

Somehow, Abby knew the voices were meant just for

them. She shook her head. 'You know, I think it might be whoever sent us Snow and Frost,' she replied. 'If they had wanted anyone else to come they would have called their names as well.'

Just then, bathed in moonlight, a vast balloon rose silently into the air above Bart Stoneheart's saloon. The vulture that was usually perched on the roof was circling the great orb with slowly flapping wings.

Spike and Abby could see three figures in the basket suspended under the balloon.

'Stoneheart, Bullwhip Kate and Beauregard Lightfoot,' Spike whispered.

But Abby was more interested in the decoration on the fabric – a great eye pierced by a dagger.

As they watched, Stoneheart continued to float towards the desert and the distant mountains, the balloon kept aloft by the hot air rising from a fire in a great iron kettle beneath it.

'I think we should follow them,' said Abby.

They dressed hurriedly and ran to the corral where Snow and Frost were stabled. By the time they were mounted, the balloon was far across the valley – a mere dot in the moonlit sky.

When they were clear of the town, Spike and Abby urged the ponies into a gallop and, once again, they seemed to fly across the ground. They raced so fast, Abby was puzzled that there was no sound of pounding from the ponies' hooves. She looked across at Frost and noticed that no dust was rising as he galloped. Swinging wide in her saddle to look beneath Snow, she saw that no dust rose from his hooves either. Spike shouted, 'Won't they be able to see us from the balloon?'

'Gosh, yes. Pull up,' Abby answered, realizing he was right.

They stopped by a prickly pear cactus that grew on the bank of the last river in the valley. While Frost and Snow munched at the fruit, Abby made a great effort with her disappearing spell. She wanted to include Snow and Frost as well as Spike.

'I think that's worked,' said Abby without much conviction. She and Spike could still see each other and the ponies, but there was no way of knowing if they were invisible to the rest of the world.

'If only we had a mirror,' said Spike.

Snow and Frost snorted, shook their heads, and started moving towards the river.

'Of course,' said Abby. 'We can see if we're reflected in the water.'

They peered from the bank and saw nothing but the moon and stars in the flowing surface of the stream. Remounting, they continued their pursuit of the balloon.

Snow and Frost galloped tirelessly across the great landscape of the valley, soaring over obstacles and uneven ground and gaining on the balloon that was now quite close to the mountains.

Glancing back over her shoulder, Abby could hardly

make out the town. There was only a gleam of moonlight where the moon reflected on the copper roof of the theatre but there was no other sign to show where Silver Springs stood at the other end of the valley.

Stoneheart's balloon was following the course of the river and as they got closer, Spike and Abby could see there were no foothills to the mountains. They just rose abruptly from the flat floor of the valley like vast jagged black teeth.

The balloon climbed even higher to hang suspended about halfway up the tallest peak. From the mountain base flowed the last river to cross the valley. Spike and Abby had now arrived at its source. Dismounting, they watered the ponies where several small springs ran from cracks in the mountain to form a wide pool that flowed into the river.

High above them, the balloon was tethered to shrubs growing on the mountainside. Leaving Frost and Snow to drink, Abby and Spike waded to the far side of the pool to see if they could get a better view of what Stoneheart and his two accomplices were up to.

There was a deep silence except for the sound of tapping from above. Everything looked eerie in the silvery light of the moon. The tapping sound stopped and from somewhere far away there came the howl of a coyote.

Abby and Spike saw the balloon cast off and silently float away. Then, from high above them, came the sudden cracks of three shattering explosions. Like mighty claps of thunder they echoed along the mountain range.

Directly above Abby and Spike, the face of the mountainside trembled and bulged. To their horror, they realized that thousands of tons of rock were about to engulf them.

Snow and Frost were still on the far side of the pool.

'Run, Frost! Run, Snow!' Abby and Spike shouted.

The ponies immediately turned and galloped away.

The Secret of Cloudy Mountain

Helpless, Spike and Abby watched the avalanche come crashing down towards them. Abby knew she could save herself by using her magic trick of *tobbing* to get herself out of the way, but she couldn't leave Spike to face the danger alone. She tried desperately to think of an anagram spell but couldn't. The rocks torn from the mountainside were about to engulf them, when a familiar sight suddenly brought hope.

Benbow!

The huge albatross swooped down, legs thrust out. Spike and Abby each seized one and, just in time, he flew them out of the path of the thundering avalanche.

'Benbow!' shouted Abby. 'Where have you been?'

The great bird gave a squawk of triumph and flew them higher and higher up the mountainside. They could see Stoneheart's balloon in the distance now. It had been cast free of its mooring and was hovering a safe distance away from the mountainside and the mischief Stoneheart had caused.

They looked below and saw the river already drying up as the springs now lay buried beneath a massive pile of fallen rocks.

Benbow continued to fly higher. They had almost reached the peak when he suddenly turned and flew towards the mountainside as if he were about to dash them against the rocks.

Spike and Abby braced themselves for a collision, but it never came. Instead, with a twisting motion, Benbow entered a great crack that had been concealed from their view. They let go of Benbow's legs and found themselves on the floor of a vast cave. From far within its depths, light came from a flickering fire which cast dancing shadows on the ragged walls and ceiling of the mighty cavern around them.

Benbow flew deeper into the cave. As they followed him they began to hear chanting – a song like nothing they had ever heard before. It rose and fell over and over again. Curious, they walked towards the glow of a fire. There was smoke in the air but it smelt sweet.

Abby stopped abruptly, and grabbed Spike's arm. 'Look at that!' she gasped.

The floor of the cave was covered in a great treasure. Piled as high as men, fantastic stacks of silver bars gleamed in the firelight. Among the heaps of silver were the skeletons of soldiers dressed in armour – the kind worn by Spanish conquistadors hundreds of years before. Abby picked up one of the heavy silver bars. The date stamped into it was 1650.

Only then did they see who the singer was. An ancient man sat cross-legged by the fire, arms folded and eyes closed. He was dressed in a buckskin shirt covered with intricate decorations made with hundreds of coloured beads, and he wore a single eagle feather in his long white braided hair. His face looked as old as the mountain rocks that surrounded them.

Beside him sat Benbow, wings folded, gazing into the fire. Although she knew the great albatross had powerful magical abilities, Abby had been worried by his long absence. Now a flood of relief and affection swept through her. Abby did not have to speak – Benbow could read her thoughts. He nodded gently at her. The ancient man stopped singing and opened his eyes. He smiled and it was as if he were a friend Spike and Abby had known all their lives.

'I am Talking Eagle,' he said. 'I have waited for you a long, long time.'

The Tale of Talking Eagle

Talking Eagle gestured with a sweep of his hand for Spike and Abby to join him. They sat cross-legged on a blanket and looked about them. In the firelight they could see the piles of silver reflecting flickering light on to the rocky surface of the cavern. The heaps of silver ought to have blackened over time, but Abby could feel magical forces in the cavern. Even the ancient armour shone as if it had just been polished.

'How did you know we would come, Talking Eagle?' asked Abby.

'I saw it in a dream,' said the old man. 'I saw many things in dreams. That is why I sent the sacred ponies to you.'

'*You* sent Frost and Snow?' said Spike.

Talking Eagle nodded. 'I knew they would eventually bring you here.'

'Why do you want us?' asked Abby.

'It was meant to be,' he answered as he scattered dried

leaves on to the fire to produce more of the sweet-smelling smoke. 'Listen, and I will tell you my story. I was born long ago, far to the north, where the great snows come in winter,' he began. 'When I was a boy, I had the first dream.' His eyes flickered towards Benbow. 'This great bird from the sea came and showed me that I must make a long journey south to where the snow never falls.' He paused to scatter more dried leaves on the fire.

'So I left my tribe. I passed through forests wider than a hundred skies, crossed mighty rivers, great plains of grass and over mountains. The moon was round many times before I came to the burning desert. I walked on, following the bird's desire until I could go no further. I lay down to give myself up to the Great Spirit.'

Talking Eagle was silent for a time, then he began again. 'But I woke up and I was no longer thirsty. Instead, I was in this cave. The place of the dead men and their treasure.'

'And are you the only person who knows of its existence?' said Abby.

Talking Eagle shook his head grimly. 'Another man – he who flies over the desert – seeks it. But he can never find this cave.'

'Why?' asked Spike.

Talking Eagle stood up. 'I will show you,' he said, leading them back to the cave entrance. There, he reached out with his hands and heaved against something. To their amazement, Abby and Spike saw he had swung a vast mirror, shaped like a dish, towards them.

Just for a moment, the mirror caught the reflection of Stoneheart's vulture hovering close to the mountainside. Unfortunately, none of them noticed it.

Unaware that the hideous bird had seen the cave mouth, Spike turned to Abby. 'It's like Mandini's illusion when he makes Mr Fitzroy disappear,' he said. 'Instead of seeing the entrance to the cave you see only a reflection of solid rock.' He stepped forward and rapped the mirror with his knuckles. It rang like a bell. 'It's solid silver,' said Spike, surprised.

'Did you make this?' Abby asked.

Talking Eagle shook his head.

'Who did, then?' said Spike.

'The Little People of Big Spirit,' Talking Eagle told them. 'It was they who found me in the desert and brought me here.'

Spike and Abby exchanged glances.

'And who are the Little People of Big Spirit?' Abby asked.

'They live by the lake,' said Talking Eagle. 'I live here in the cave.'

'Lake?' repeated Spike. 'Where is the lake?'

'Come, I will show you,' said Talking Eagle.

He led them through chamber after chamber in the depths of the mountain until they stood in a cavern lit by a pale blue light that shone up from a great pit in the floor.

On the far side, standing on a plinth of rock as tall as Abby, was a strange gruesome-looking object. As they moved closer they heard a faint throbbing sound. Embedded in a block of crystal was a black human heart. And it was beating.

'What does this mean?' whispered Spike.

'I do not know,' said Talking Eagle. 'It has always been here.'

Passing the sinister heart, they came to the mouth of the cave on the other side of the mountain.

Blinking as they emerged into the daylight, they saw thick white clouds above them, and down below were the placid blue waters of a lake.

Talking Eagle pointed to its surface and said, 'The lake used to be lower but the man who flies has blocked up all the rivers and streams that once ran freely from the foot of the mountain.'

'It was Stoneheart who made the valley dry,' said Spike.

'So he could ruin all the farmers and ranchers and buy their land cheap,' concluded Abby.

'Where are the Little People of Big Spirit now, Talking Eagle?' Abby asked.

Talking Eagle pointed at the misty surface of the lake. 'They live down there. If you wish to explore the waters, use these.' He held out two small oblongs of crystal. 'If you put them in your mouth you will be able to breathe underwater.'

'Where do they come from?' asked Abby, taking one of the crystals.

'The Little People of Big Spirit make them so they can

swim in the depths of the lake,' replied Talking Eagle.

As Abby and Spike were examining the crystals there was a sudden series of cries. Abby recognized Benbow's warning call.

The three hurried back into the cave, where they could hear the sound of beating wings. At first, the children thought it was Benbow approaching, but before they had time to protect themselves a dark creature was upon them.

Stoneheart's vulture! The vile bird swooped towards Abby and Spike with a screaming cry, its talons outstretched and its razor-sharp bill ready to tear at their flesh. Abby gazed into the vulture's staring yellow eyes only for a moment before Benbow swooped down and with one blow of his powerful wing knocked it against the wall of the cave.

But Abby had already lost her balance. As she flung out her hand towards Spike, she knocked the black heart, which toppled off its pedestal and down into the pit.

Clutching Spike's hand, they teetered momentarily on the edge before they too tumbled in. Down and down they fell towards the source of the eerie blue light.

The Mystery of the Lake

Spike and Abby plunged into the icy water that glowed with a sapphire blue light. Desperately, they tried to swim back up to the surface but a powerful force was pulling them further and further down.

Abby remembered the oblong of crystal and thrust it into her mouth. Immediately, she could breathe again. Spike was next to her, twisting and turning as they plunged deeper towards the source of the sapphire light. Abby pointed to the crystal in her mouth. Spike nodded and bared his teeth to show he was already using his.

The water gradually became warmer as the force continued to pull them down. Finally, the long shaft ended. They had descended to the lake-bed, which was thickly coated with a sparkling white substance. And still the force was pulling them towards the source of the sapphire light.

Shoals of rainbow-coloured fish swam close to them. There was something very familiar about this place. Abby

felt as if she must have visited it before. Then it dawned on her – their surroundings were almost identical to the bed of the great lake in Spike's homeland in the Kingdom of Lantua, the greatest known source of Ice Dust in the world!

Excitedly Abby scooped up a handful of the white sparkling powder and let it run through her fingers, while Spike put up both thumbs in triumph and mouthed the words 'Ice Dust!'

Ahead, they saw a rock shaped like a small volcano in the bright sapphire glow. From it poured the light and the white sparkling Ice Dust that lay thickly about them. And, caught in the flow that gushed up from the little volcano, was the black heart Abby had knocked off its pedestal.

As they watched, the heart danced in the pure light like a ball caught on a spout of water. To Abby and Spike's utter amazement, the heart slowly turned from pitch black to a glowing pinkish-red.

Without knowing why, Abby swam forward, took the heart from the gushing jet and placed it in her pocket. She indicated 'Up' to Spike and they struck out for the daylight above.

Dawn had broken and a pale sun shone through the clouds concealing the surrounding mountain tops as they broke the surface of the lake. They swam to the side, where a wood grew down to the water's edge, and pulled themselves up on to the bank.

'Do you think Stoneheart knows about this place?' asked Spike.

Abby shook her head. 'I don't think so, there are such strong Light Witch forces here, Spike.' She pointed up. 'Those clouds were made by magic, not nature. It's my guess they were created as a sort of barrier so Stoneheart couldn't see the lake from his balloon, but now that vulture—'

'Look!' said Spike, pointing.

Beyond the trees there were what appeared to be small fields with rows of crops growing. Closer to Spike and Abby, little boats were tied up at a tiny jetty at the water's edge.

As they had tumbled into the lake, their Atlantis capes had taken on their original shape. Now Spike and Abby shook themselves like wet dogs and the capes immediately threw off the water and reformed as their western clothes. They could smell wood smoke. Then they saw the first little figure.

A man no taller than Spike's shoulder stood beneath a pine tree gazing at them with a grave expression. He wore a tall black hat with a flat brim and a large white lace collar lay over his long black belted coat. His trousers were gathered at the knees over black stockings. His shoes had large silver buckles.

'Didst thou come from Talking Eagle?' he asked.

'Yes,' replied Abby. 'My name is Abigail Clover and this is Prince Altur of Lantua. I call him Spike.'

'Art thou the chosen ones Talking Eagle saw in his dreams?' said the little man.

'I suppose we are,' said Spike. 'Who are you?'

'My name is Hornbeam,' he answered. 'I am the leader of my people.'

'Are you an elf, Hornbeam?' Abby asked.

'You know of elves?' he said.

'We have many friends who are elves,' said Abby.

'I would like to believe thee,' said Hornbeam. 'But it is not always wise to trust the word of human beings. Canst thou prove thou knowest the ways of elfish folk?'

Abby looked about her. 'Can you prove you are an elf?' she answered. 'If you are, where are your elfberry trees?'

At these words, a smile came to Hornbeam's solemn features and he waved behind him. Suddenly he was surrounded by more little people and their children. The men were dressed like Hornbeam, and the women all wore a white cap and long black dress with a wide white collar. The children were dressed in miniature versions of the clothes their parents wore.

'This is my wife, Myrtle,' said Hornbeam.

A pretty elf curtsied to them, and Spike and Abby bowed in return.

Then Hornbeam pointed behind him. 'There is the path to our village. Perhaps thou wilt join my family for breakfast.'

They followed the elves up some small stone steps set into the hillside, and through the wood to emerge in a village of little clapboard houses that were surrounded by orchards of elfberry trees. There were also farmyards filled with miniature pigs, cows, horses, chickens and ducks.'

'I've never seen such small animals before,' said Abby.

'We have been here a long time,' said Hornbeam, ushering them into one of the houses. 'Human beings breed their stock to be large; we just did the reverse.'

A few minutes later, Spike and Abby found themselves in a tiny kitchen. They felt very large when Hornbeam indicated for them to take a seat at a small pine table. The furniture was beautifully made. The floor was bare scrubbed board, and there were delicate wooden chairs set around the table. A long dresser held fine blue and white china and there was an iron cooking range against the opposite wall. Myrtle went to the stove and took out a tray of tiny flat cakes that smelt delicious.

Two elf children stood watching them with their hands crossed over their chests. When Hornbeam nodded they also sat down at the table.

'Forgive my children if they stare at thee,' said Hornbeam. You are the first human beings they have ever seen.'

'Oh, I'm not a human being any more,' said Abby. 'Well, I am . . . but I'm also a Light Witch.'

'I'm a human being,' said Spike, smiling at the children, who smiled back shyly.

'You say you know other elves,' said Myrtle.

'Yes,' answered Abby. 'We know town elves who live in London and wood elves who live in Darkwood Forest, near my home.'

'Where dost thou call home?' said Hornbeam.

'A place called Speller, in England.'

'Speller!' Hornbeam and Myrtle chorused. 'Why, that surely is the famous English Sea Witch port.'

'You've heard of it?' asked Spike.

'Oh, yes,' replied Hornbeam. 'It is known among our people. But how didst thou come to the Cloudy Mountains?'

While Myrtle served them breakfast, Abby and Spike told their story. When they came to the end, Hornbeam shook his head. 'Night Witches,' he said. 'So, they are still up to their evil ways.'

'But how about you?' said Spike. 'How did you come here to this secret place?'

'I shall tell you a fire story,' said Hornbeam. First, he addressed Myrtle. 'Wife, be kind enough to make the coals brighter.'

The Curse of Samuel Cherry

Myrtle placed more wood on the hearth next to the cooking range and pumped a set of bellows to make a roaring little fire.

'Look into the flames,' said Hornbeam, 'and you shall see the story happening as I tell it.'

'We've done this before,' said Spike. 'A town elf called Wooty once showed us an ancient saga.'

Hornbeam smiled. 'It is good to know they still practise the old crafts in England.' Then he began. As he spoke, Spike and Abby watched the story unfold in the flames, just as it happened long ago.

'We came from Massachusetts more than two hundred years ago. We were helping two Light Witch explorers called Samuel Cherry and Caleb Crabgrass. They were seeking a source of Ice Dust in North America.'

As Abby and Spike looked into the flames they could see the two Light Witches and the elves marching into a great wilderness of forests and mountains, then journeying by

canoe along mighty rivers.

'We crossed vast prairies of grass where buffaloes in their millions roamed and deserts were as wide as oceans,' Hornbeam continued. 'Finally, after years passed, we came to the valley that lies at the foot of the Cloudy Mountains.

'Here, we made two discoveries. The land beneath the valley is filled with silver, more than we could imagine. But we were not the first to find it. Before us, the Spanish had come and mined the valley and the Cloudy Mountains.'

Spike and Abby saw Spanish conquistadors in the fire, transporting great loads of silver on the backs of mules.

Hornbeam continued. 'The silver treasure turned the minds of the Spaniards and they fell out among themselves. Half of them hid in Talking Eagle's cave with the silver they had mined, and the others attacked them to make it all their own. The two sides fought until all were dead – only the silver remained.'

'How do you know they were all killed?' Spike asked.

Hornbeam produced a parchment. 'This was an account of all that happened. It was written by the last Spaniard while he lay dying of his wounds.'

Spike and Abby saw the battle and the last of the Spaniards dying in the cave.

Spike interrupted. 'What did the Spaniards make of the pit of light and the lake?' he asked.

Hornbeam held up a finger. 'The pit and the lake were not yet revealed when we found the cave,' he said. 'But there was Spanish gunpowder in abundance. Huge barrels of it among the treasure. Then Caleb Crabgrass began to argue with Samuel Cherry about keeping the silver for themselves. So we knew Caleb Crabgrass had taken the Dark Path.'

'What's the Dark Path?' asked Spike.

Abby answered him. 'It's when Light Witches lose their way and start to want wealth and power,' she answered.

'You are right, child,' said Hornbeam. 'The treasure had turned poor Caleb's head. He wanted more and more. He took gunpowder and set off a great explosion at the back of Talking Eagle's cave. When the smoke had cleared, the pit of light was revealed together with the opening in the cave that now looks down on the lake.'

'And then you found the Ice Dust?' Abby asked.

'More than we ever dreamed of,' said Hornbeam. 'And it was finding it that caused Caleb Crabgrass to finally abandon the Path of Light. He said with the silver *and* the Ice Dust, he and Samuel Cherry could rule the world.'

Samuel pleaded with him to put evil thoughts aside but Crabgrass had secretly taken one of the Spanish swords and performed Night Witch magic upon it. He had found some Ice Dust that had been crushed by the rock fall after the explosion. Caleb mixed it with dried scorpions and the blood of snakes to make Black Dust.'

Abby and Spike watched spellbound as all this unfolded in the flames.

'What happened next?' asked Spike.

'Caleb sent the sword he'd bewitched to kill Samuel

Cherry. But Samuel had taken precautions. His pockets were filled with pure Ice Dust. Although the sword impaled Samuel, he had enough Ice Dust on him to work his own spell before he died.

'He filled his hands with Ice Dust and seized the blade of the sword impaling his body. He cursed Caleb Crabgrass, then he called on the sword to cut out Caleb's heart and encase it in crystal so it would go on living. He also took away Caleb's memory so that he would never know where the treasure cave was located, or that they had found a lake of Ice Dust beyond the Cloudy Mountains.

'Caleb wandered off into the desert. With his dying breath, Samuel Cherry told we elves to make the silver mirror so we could hide the entrance to the cave.' Hornbeam leaned forward to stir the fire with a tiny poker. Then he looked up. 'From that day on, Caleb has roamed the valley and the desert, forever in search of the lost treasure and his missing heart, which he had replaced with a stone.'

'And Caleb Crabgrass became *Bart Stoneheart*,' said Spike.

'So, that is the name he chose for himself,' said Hornbeam. 'It is very suitable.'

'Why did you stay here?' asked Abby.

Hornbeam looked around him. 'We are happy here. The elfberry saplings we brought with us thrived near the waters of the lake. What more could we want? But we knew someone would find us one day, and had to make sure it was someone we could trust. We called for Talking

Eagle because we could feel his dreams from so far away. And in the end he knew it was thee, Abby Clover, who would come to the valley.'

'Other Light Witches will follow,' said Abby. 'The Night Witches destroyed Bright Town. The Light Witches of America need the Ice Dust more than they ever did.'

Hornbeam smiled. 'The Light Witches of America will keep us safe.'

He nodded to Myrtle, who brought two large leather bags and handed them to Abby. 'You have need of this Ice Dust,' Hornbeam said. 'Come back if you need more.'

'Thank you,' said Abby. 'We shall find a way to repay you.'

Hornbeam had gone to a cupboard beside the dresser. From it he produced two beautiful little muskets and two leather satchels. The muskets were intricately decorated with silver chasing. They were more like works of art than weapons.

'Take these,' said Hornbeam. 'They are special. We elves have some powers. Our gunsmith worked on them for many years. Talking Eagle told us they would be needed one day.'

As Spike and Abby examined them, Hornbeam told them, 'Muskets can usually only be shot once before you have to reload. But look at this.' He flipped open a compartment in the butt of one of the muskets, and into it he slotted an oblong box which he had taken out of the leather satchel. 'It is now loaded and will continue to fire until the box is empty.'

Spike examined one of the rifles. It was simple to reload.

'One more thing,' said Hornbeam. 'The bullets are made from silver and Ice Dust. Thou wilt know how to use them well.'

Spike and Abby bid farewell to the elves, who kept waving from their elfberry orchards until they were out of sight. Hornbeam led them around the lake and then to a narrow tunnel.

'This will bring thee to the foot of the mountain overlooking the valley,' he said. 'Good luck.'

Passing through the tunnel they eventually reached a narrow crack through which daylight flooded. They squeezed through to find themselves standing close to the gigantic heap of rocks brought down by the avalanche.

Talking Eagle was there, waiting for them.

'You found the Little People?' he asked.

'We did,' said Abby.

'Did you find the black heart?'

Abby handed it to him. 'It's changed a bit now,' she said.

Talking Eagle nodded with an understanding smile and carefully placed it in a pouch at his waist, then pointed over his shoulder. Waiting in the shade of the rocks were Frost and Snow, grazing on prickly pears.

'Where's Benbow?' asked Spike.

'You will see him again soon,' replied Talking Eagle.

Mounting the ponies, Spike and Abby waved farewell and galloped back across the hot valley towards Silver Springs. The sunlight was so fierce, the bed of the last river had already dried to dust.

Wolfbane Reveals Himself

As Spike and Abby neared Silver Springs they saw an astonishing sight. A vast mass of people were slowly making their way towards the town in wagons, on horseback, and many on foot. Farmers and their families were herding their livestock. Ranchers and cowboys were driving herds of cattle. The last settlers in the valley were leaving their parched lands to head for Silver Springs, where there was still water.

It was a sorry sight. The people looked defeated, like an army that had lost its last battle. As they approached the edge of town, they found Bart Stoneheart had set up a reception for them. He sat, flanked by Bullwhip Kate and Beauregard Lightfoot, at a long table at the beginning of the main street. Set above them were signs reading:

CATTLE BOUGHT HERE

BEST MONEY PAID
FOR LAND CLAIMS

TOP PRICES FOR LIVESTOCK

JOBS FOR GOOD WORKERS
IN STONEHEART MINE

People were already queuing to sell him their possessions and take up the offer of jobs in his mine.

Abby stood up in her stirrups and pleaded with them in a loud clear voice. 'Please listen to me, folks. There's still plenty of water in the valley. Bart Stoneheart set off an explosion that caused an avalanche and blocked off the river.'

'That's a dirty lie,' snarled Stoneheart, leaping to his feet. 'Keep your mouth shut if you don't want me to teach you a stern lesson, missy.'

Ignoring him, Abby shouted, 'The water is trapped inside the mountains.'

'What she says is true, right enough,' said a cowboy who was covered in dust and sat on a weary looking horse. 'I was there at the foot of the mountains just after sunrise. I near wore my horse out getting back here.'

'You see,' shouted Abby. 'There *is* still water.'

The people now looked to the rider for confirmation. He shook his head. 'It's there, sure enough. But half the mountain came down at the source of the river. You could blast for a year without shifting it.'

'There you are,' shouted Stoneheart. 'Cowboys never lie. There's no way you can live out in the valley any more. So, who will accept my generous offers and sign up with me?'

By this time, many of the townsfolk of Silver Springs had joined the crowd. Abby and Spike dismounted and some of the ranchers and farmers crowded around them, asking questions. It was obvious that most people were reluctant to take up any of Bart Stoneheart's offers.

Quincy Flowerdale shouldered his way through the crush and shouted, 'Any man who wants a job is welcome at my silver mine.'

Banker Stout emerged from the crowd, offering to help. 'And if anyone wants a loan to tide them over, come to the bank. Meanwhile, you can water your stock on my land. But you'll have to take it in turns.'

Bart Stoneheart was shaking with anger at these developments. Overturning the table before him, he drew both his pistols and levelled them at Spike and Abby.

'You can't gun down children in front of the whole town, Bart,' hissed Bullwhip Kate. 'It would not go well with you.'

But Stoneheart had lost his reason. His face quivered in rage and his face turned purple. With bloodshot eyes popping, he screamed, 'I am Bart Stoneheart! I can kill anyone I want to.'

He cocked the hammers of his pistols but, before he could shoot, Captain Starlight and Sir Chadwick arrived and quickly stepped into his line of fire.

Bullwhip Kate and Beauregard Lightfoot drew their guns.

Boiling with rage, Stoneheart swung his arms sideways and aimed his pistols at Snow and Frost who were tied to a hitching rail. The people behind the two ponies scattered. But before Stoneheart could squeeze the triggers, Abby and Spike had levelled their muskets.

They both fired at once, their Ice Dust bullets shattering the barrels of Stoneheart's pistols. He was left holding their now useless handles. Hurling them aside, he almost convulsed with rage. Finally, he recovered sufficiently to stalk off back towards his saloon, with Bullwhip Kate and Beauregard Lightfoot hurrying after him.

As the cheering died down the crowd turned their attention to Banker Stout and Quincy Flowerdale who began making notes of the requests for help.

There were great comings and goings in Silver Springs throughout the day. Crowds of men were signed on as miners by Flowerdale, who was helped by Mandini. The streets were filled with livestock waiting to take their turn to water at the spring on Banker Stout's property. Also, a stream of customers queued at the bank to arrange loans.

The Playhouse was filled to capacity again that evening and the audience gave a special cheer to Flowerdale and Banker Stout for such practical demonstrations of their good citizenship.

Later, when the town was quiet and all decent people were in their beds, Bart Stoneheart stood alone in the doorway of his saloon, moodily smoking a particularly vile-smelling cigar by the light of the last lantern burning in Silver Springs. He was gazing with undisguised loathing at the theatre when a voice suddenly croaked at him from the shadows.

'Would you like to see Abby Clover destroyed, Mr Stoneheart?'

'Who's there?' asked Stoneheart, startled. He drew the new revolvers he had bought that afternoon and pointed them in the direction of the voice. 'Show yourself or I'll blast you where you stand.'

A strange little man came out of the shadows with a curious hopping motion. He wore a long cloak which reached to the ground and a black silk top hat. The face now revealed was narrow with a vast beaky nose. Tiny round yellow eyes gazed, unblinking, at Stoneheart.

'Who are you?' asked Stoneheart, still pointing his revolvers.

'My name is Caspar,' said the

little man. 'Caspar Raven. I have been sent here to invite you to a meeting that will be to your great advantage.'

'Meeting? Where?' said Stoneheart.

The little man gave an evil chuckle. 'Not far. Put on this blindfold and come with me. You will realize your heart's desire.'

At the expression 'heart's desire', Bart involuntarily clutched the place where his own stone heart nestled.

'Why should I trust you?' he asked.

The little man chuckled again, and said, *'Live ma I.'*

Stoneheart stepped back. In the long distant past, as a Light Witch, he had been taught the most secret words Night Witches used to identify themselves.

'Live ma I,' he whispered, knowing what it spelt backwards. Then, without further hesitation, he accepted Caspar's blindfold.

Stoneheart was surprised by the short distance the little man had led him before there was the thud of a great door closing behind him. A dreadful smell, which caused him to flare his nostrils with pleasure, filled the air: rotting food, old socks, stale cabbage water, and much worse. Bart Stoneheart felt more at home than he had in centuries.

'You may remove the blindfold,' said an unfamiliar voice.

Stoneheart did so and in a dim purplish light he saw Homer P. Stout, his wife and Hiram Prune smiling at him.

'You!' Stoneheart gasped incredulously.

'Not quite,' said Wolfbane, who looked exactly like

Banker Stout. 'You'll find the people you think we are in here.' He opened a large locker and standing inside, moulded into waxworks, were the real Mr and Mrs Stout together with Hepsibar, Erasmus and Hiram Prune.

'We came to Silver Springs some time ago and took their places,' said Wolfbane, shutting the locker on the waxen figures. 'But we had to make clockwork versions of Erasmus and Hepsibar.'

'Where are we?' demanded Stoneheart. What is this?' He reached out and struck the black steel wall near him.

Wolfbane smiled. 'You know it as Banker Stout's safe. In fact, it is a Shark Boat fitted with a Fluid State Universal Unit to allow it to travel through time.'

'This is a great deal to take in,' said Stoneheart.

'Take a seat, my dear fellow,' said Wolfbane. 'We both desire the same thing – the death of Abby Clover and her friends. We can be of great use to one another. But first, you must tell us what a Night Witch is doing in this dreary little town. Then we shall explain why we are here.'

Lucia opened a bottle of deadly nightshade brandy and they all sat around the chart table in the Shark Boat as Stoneheart told his story; then Wolfbane explained how they had pursued Abby and her friends across the world and back through time.

'So, what are your plans for this valley, Stoneheart?' Wolfbane asked.

'When I own all the land,' said Stoneheart, 'I'm going to blast that mountain open. All that pent-up water will tear across the valley in a great tidal wave. It will rip up the earth and wash it away – most of the town too – leaving all the silver exposed. And, as an added bonus, there should be a satisfactory loss of life.'

'Won't it just flood the valley?' asked Valentine.

Stoneheart shook his head and produced another of his dreadful cigars. 'I had the ground surveyed. There's a gentle slope. The water will just run off towards Tucson. With any luck, it might even drown a few people there.'

Lucia leaned forward and struck a match for him. He inhaled the choking aroma appreciatively.

'I do so like a man who smokes,' she purred. 'It makes the air around one so . . . *breathable*.'

Ignoring his mother, Wolfbane considered Stoneheart's idea and nodded approvingly. 'A sound plan. But first, I want you to do me a favour.'

'What is it?' Stoneheart asked suspiciously.

'Don't put your plan into action until I give you the word. We've got to find the Atlantis Boat first.'

'Why?'

Wolfbane sat forward. 'Once we have Excalibur we can shave off enough black powder from Charlock's armour to send Abby Clover and her friends into *The Chaos* for ever.'

'That doesn't sound so bad,' said Stoneheart, puzzled. 'I often enjoy a bit of chaos when life in the west becomes too tame.'

Wolfbane became a trifle impatient. 'I keep forgetting that, as a Night Witch, you've been on your own for a long time. I'm not talking about ordinary common or garden *chaos.* I'm talking about *The Chaos.*' He stood up and said, 'Come and look in here for a moment.'

Stoneheart followed him along the hull of the Shark Boat to where a navigator's table stood against a bulkhead. Set into the table was a large black crystal ball.

'Look into this,' instructed Wolfbane.

Stoneheart stared down into the black depths. Gradually, the swirling mass inside the ball settled into a clear image. He could see a series of disturbing scenes – a world made from the nightmares of the insane.

Stoneheart could see the inhabitants of a small town that at first seemed quite normal. But as he watched, trees sprouted through the roofs of houses, roads became raging rivers, the ground cracked open and gushed lava. He saw people hunted by dogs, and cats that flew in the sky, orchards that grew giant insects instead of fruit under a grey dismal sky filled with falling stars.

Stoneheart looked up from the crystal and smiled at Wolfbane. 'And you say we can send Abby Clover and her friends to this place?' he asked.

'Once I find Excalibur,' Wolfbane replied.

'You don't know where it is?' said Stoneheart.

'No. But, I think I shall quite soon.'

Soon after Stoneheart's glimpse into *The Chaos*, Wolfbane thanked him for his visit and asked Caspar to see him to the door.

'A promising relationship,' Valentine commented as soon as they were out of earshot.

Wolfbane nodded. 'He's a little primitive for my taste but there's the makings of a proper Night Witch in him.' Changing the subject, Wolfbane then said, 'Tomorrow I want you to go to Flowerdale's mine as Hiram Prune and apply for a job.'

Valentine was aghast. 'A job!' he spluttered. 'Me, work in some dreadful little tinpot mining office?'

'I'm not talking about a job in the office,' said Wolfbane contemptuously. 'I want you to sign on as a miner. Tell them you're tired of sitting in a little cage counting money. That you want to earn a man's wage by honest toil.'

'That'll be the day,' Lucia sneered.

'What is the purpose of this folly?' said Valentine.

Wolfbane slapped his hand against the hull to emphasize his point. 'I'm sure the Atlantis Boat is buried somewhere, and Excalibur with it. The reason Chadwick Street and his friends were so eager to open Flowerdale's mine again wasn't to dig for silver but to dig for the Atlantis Boat. That's why we can't see it in the crystal. Because it's buried underground.'

'Brilliant deduction, darling,' said Lucia. 'So, if your father works down the mine we shall know which way they are tunnelling and get there first from Stoneheart's mine.'

'I knew *you* would understand, Mother,' said Wolfbane.

Good News from the Great Mandini

As Stoneheart crossed the main street the lantern outside his saloon seemed to be the only one burning in Silver Springs. But in Flowerdale's boarding house, Abby, Spike, Mandini and Captain Starlight had gathered in Sir Chadwick and Hilda's room with the curtains carefully drawn so that no chink of light could show through. Captain Starlight sat at the writing desk working on the Evil Indicator with Abby's special penknife. The others watched his skilful hands making adjustments to the delicate mechanism.

Finally, he sat back and said, 'That should do the trick. I've located the energy field detectors and reversed the settings.'

'You are clever, Captain,' said Abby.

'It wasn't so hard,' he replied. 'Night Witches give out negative fields of energy and Light Witches give out positive fields. I simply switched the settings over.'

Mandini picked up the Indicator and watched as the

arrow swung around in an arc. 'This will prove very useful, Adam. I've studied maps of both Flowerdale and Stoneheart's mines. It's like a gigantic maze down there. There are so many twists and turns in the tunnels, after walking for ten minutes or so you could be facing in any direction.'

'It's picking up your presence at the moment,' Starlight said. 'But when it comes closer to Excalibur the energy field will be so strong it will only point in the direction of the sword on the Atlantis Boat.'

'Excellent,' said Sir Chadwick. 'So you will take it down the mine with you tomorrow, Mandini, along with the Ice Dust Abby and Spike brought us. You should be able to break through to the Atlantis Boat pretty quickly.'

'And we can go home at last,' said Abby.

'As long as Wolfbane doesn't spring any nasty surprises,' said Hilda.

The following evening, when the Great Mandini had returned from his duties at the mine, he came to Sir Chadwick's room to report. But first they called for Starlight and the children to join them before they prepared for the night's performance.

'We've made excellent progress,' Mandini said enthusiastically.

'How did the Indicator work?' asked Starlight.

Mandini smiled. 'As you predicted. It gave a clear direction to the north-west. But it took some coaxing to get the men to work on a new tunnel. Some of them seemed to think I was a little crazy.'

'Why?' asked Abby.

'Because we hit a very rich seam of silver in the main shaft yesterday. They were pleased with the bonus they were going to earn. I had to promise the miners digging in the new direction they would earn the same money as those who had already found silver.'

'How are you using the Ice Dust?' asked Sir Chadwick.

'First, I hypnotized the men so they believed I was planting dynamite charges. Then I made the area they were to excavate as soft as sand and as light as duck down. You have never seen a tunnel dug faster. And you would never guess who was the most enthusiastic worker – Hiram Prune! Says he signed on for the high wages. Well, he certainly earned them today. I think we'll reach the Atlantis Boat tomorrow.'

Across town, in Banker Stout's house, an exhausted Valentine was reporting to Wolfbane and Lucia. He slumped down in one of Mrs Stout's pink velvet chairs and wiped his grimy hands on the armrests. 'I can't say I like this kind of dirt,' he said, looking down at his dusty clothing. 'It has no smell, and I feel so weak there must be traces of Ice Dust in the ground. Be a dear, Lucia, and run me a nice bath of bog water. A foul soak is just what I need.'

'Tell us what happened at the mine before you even think about taking a bath,' warned Wolfbane.

'Do we have a map of Stoneheart's mine?' Valentine

asked. 'You have no idea how confusing it is down there.'

Wolfbane produced one but Valentine shook his head. 'I can't make head nor tail of all this.'

Lucia sighed and snapped her fingers. The map rose in the air and became three-dimensional images of all the tunnelling works taking place beneath of Silver Springs.

'Ahh, that's more like it. Look, this is Stoneheart's mine,' said Valentine. After a moment's study he pointed to another shaft from which various branches sprouted. 'This is Flowerdale's mine, and this is the new tunnel Mandini insisted we begin digging today.' He sat back with another sigh. 'You can have no conception of how hateful the work is. I dug frantically, just to get it over with as soon as possible.'

'It's heading in the direction of that old shaft,' said Lucia, pointing.

'That's where the Atlantis Boat must be,' said Wolfbane.

'Why don't we get Stoneheart to open the old tunnel? It shouldn't take any time at all from his side,' said Lucia.

Wolfbane shook his head. 'No, it isn't that easy. Stoneheart explained every inch of his mine to me. They sealed off that shaft with an explosion. It brought half the roof down. It could take weeks to excavate it by manpower alone.'

'So what shall we do?' asked Lucia.

Wolfbane strode across to the window and looked out far beyond the town towards the desert. 'I shall prepare a spell. It is time to put our trust in the worst of Night Witch power.'

32

The Army of the Damned

Before the performance the following evening, Mandini returned from his duties at the Flowerdale mine and arranged for a meeting in Sir Chadwick and Hilda's dressing room. As soon as Abby, Spike and Captain Starlight arrived, Mandini produced his map of the tunnelling beneath Silver Springs.

'We have reached a crucial stage in the operations,' he announced. 'My calculations show we are no more than an arm's length from where the Atlantis Boat is resting in an abandoned shaft in Stoneheart's mine.

'How did you calculate that?' asked Sir Chadwick.

Mandini pointed to his map. 'Quite simple.' He put his finger on the new tunnel they had been excavating with the aid of Ice Dust. 'The Indicator, which, thanks to Adam, now only points to the Atlantis Boat and Excalibur, has given us the exact direction in which to work.'

He then pointed to the old main shaft in the Flowerdale mine. 'But if you stand in this tunnel, the Indicator points

this way. So, if you draw lines from each point in the directions shown by the Indicator they cross just here. And that, as you can see, is very close to where we have now reached.' He looked about him at the excited faces.

'I let the men go half an hour earlier this evening because I was worried we might break through too soon.'

'Could we tunnel through tonight, after the show?' asked Sir Chadwick.

'Easily,' answered Mandini.

'Then tonight it is,' said Sir Chadwick. 'We go to work when the town sleeps.'

Later that night, the friends had again gathered in Sir Chadwick and Hilda's room. They wanted the household to have settled down before they set off for the mine. Abby and Spike sat at the table with Mandini performing card tricks for them. Sir Chadwick and Hilda were reading and Captain Starlight was drawing in a sketch book. They all looked up when they heard the grandfather clock chime midnight in the sitting room below.

'We'd best give it another hour,' said Sir Chadwick and they continued with their various occupations.

But elsewhere in town, as the clock chimed midnight, evil was afoot. Wolfbane, Lucia and Valentine, accompanied by Bart Stoneheart, made their way stealthily to the barn where Stoneheart kept his hot-air balloon.

'I don't see why Beauregard and Bullwhip Kate have to

be left,' grumbled Stoneheart.

'This is Night Witch business,' hissed Wolfbane. 'Get used to knowing that your loyalties must now be to your own kind.'

'They've served me well in the past,' said Stoneheart, who was slightly surprised to feel a sudden pang of affection towards his usual companions.

Wolfbane, Valentine and Lucia climbed into the basket with Stoneheart so he could show them how to fire up the pot to inflate the giant silk balloon.

'How do you control its direction?' asked Wolfbane.

Stoneheart showed him a small steam engine that drove a propeller.

'I want you to take us to about the centre of the valley,' Wolfbane instructed. 'I'll tell you when to stop.'

They soared aloft and across the valley, which was already withering into desert. The grass and trees were wilting brown and the bed of the last river now looked as dry and dusty as all the others.

Eventually, they reached a place that satisfied Wolfbane. He instructed Stoneheart to drop a grappling hook on a rope to moor the balloon to the ground.

All was silent around them, except for a faint wind that moaned across the dead valley. High above, the stars glittered like fragments of shattered glass and the moon was a vast glowing orb in the indigo blue sky.

Wolfbane nodded his satisfaction and reached down into a bag he had brought with him. From it he took what looked like a large black finger and a long black robe which he draped around his shoulders.

'From the gauntlet of Charlock,' he said reverently, holding the black finger of armour aloft.

The smell that wafted from Wolfbane's black robe reminded Stoneheart of a decaying bison he had once found in the desert. He sniffed appreciatively. Looking closer, he saw that the robe was embroidered with strange writhing snakes and demons. The garment slithered and swirled about Wolfbane's body as he chanted:

'You evil spirits now grow near,
And take a form that all shall fear,
Now shape yourselves to look like men,
But each shall have the strength of ten,
You all are made for demon work
Come forth from Hades where you lurk!'

The last line was delivered as a shout and as it died away, there came another sound – a sudden thumping, like the muffled beating of a heart, but multiplied a thousand times over.

Stoneheart turned his head from side to side, trying to detect the origin of the sound, but it seemed to be coming from all directions.

'Be patient,' said Wolfbane. 'My children are coming.'

Stoneheart looked towards the far edge of the valley, where it rose to level out once again into the desert. In the crystal clear night air he could just make out puffs of dust clouds.

It was as if hundreds of head of cattle were heading towards the valley. Stoneheart turned around and saw the same sort of dust clouds coming from the opposite direction. And the strange thumping sound continued.

The dust clouds reached the edge of the desert and began to descend the walls of the valley. They were approaching the balloon from all directions, but still Stoneheart could not see exactly what was coming.

At last, he began to make out shapes. At first, he thought they were men but they were so misshapen they might have been some other species of animal that had learned to walk upright on hind legs.

The creatures shambled towards the balloon, and Stoneheart felt as if a sudden chill wind was blowing. The shapes he saw were taller than men but there was something inhuman about the relentless way they moved, and all the while the thumping grew ever louder.

As they began to gather beneath the hovering balloon, Stoneheart could finally see these dreadful creations had been fashioned from the cacti that grew in the desert. Wolfbane's spell had made them a monstrous host for the army of Night Witches in his command.

The Battle in the Mine Shaft

At one o'clock, by the light of the moon, Abby and Spike led the group out of the boarding house to make its way to Flowerdale's mine. As a precaution, Sir Chadwick had insisted that Hilda, Mandini and Abby fully charge their wands. Spike carried his musket, and Captain Starlight had a belt full of horseshoes coated in Ice Dust.

When they reached the mine shaft, Mandini did not start the steam engine that operated the elevator. Instead, he used a single speck of Ice Dust from his wand to operate the machinery so they could descend in silence.

After disembarking from the cage, Captain Starlight, Mandini and Sir Chadwick took pickaxes and spades from racks near the lift shaft.

'This way,' Mandini instructed, setting off along the wide tunnel leading to the new shaft that branched off towards the Atlantis Boat.

As they reached the head of the new tunnel Abby was

feeling deeply unhappy. An odd throbbing sensation seemed to be pulsing through her head as regularly as the rhythmic beating of a drum.

'I feel a bit strange, Abby,' said Spike, rubbing his forehead.

'So do I,' she said, turning to Sir Chadwick.

He was holding up his hand. 'I feel it too, Abby,' he said. 'I think we all can.'

'The sooner we get to the Atlantis Boat the better,' said Captain Starlight, swinging his pickaxe.

Sir Chadwick and Mandini joined in. Abby, Spike and Hilda used the spades to clear away the rubble, and load the rocks and earth into a nearby wagon. But all the time they worked, the throbbing grew more insistent inside Abby's head. She felt more weary than she could ever remember.

Sir Chadwick, Captain Starlight and Mandini hacked on until their pickaxes suddenly felt no further resistance, and the old tunnel that held the Atlantis Boat was revealed. The men sank to their knees, exhausted. The throbbing had become almost unbearable.

Suddenly realizing it must be the work of Night Witches, Abby held up her arms and shouted, '*Leave red nag.*'

Spike, who in spare moments had been practising re-arranging the letters of words, instantly knew the phrase Abby had uttered was *'Reveal danger'*.

He stared about him. Areas of faint shimmering light seemed to be clinging on to all of the friends. The light became stronger and the shapes more distinct. To their horror, they realized what they were.

Demons! Demons with horned heads and tails. Their bodies shaped like men with the loins and legs of goats. They clung with teeth and talons dug into the bodies of their victims.

'*Occubusi!*' shouted Sir Chadwick. He drew his wand and stabbed at the vile creature clinging to Hilda. The demons squealed and spat as the friends twirled and stabbed with their wands to free themselves of the loathsome creatures.

When all the demons lay weakened and squirming on the ground, Sir Chadwick pointed his wand and shouted, 'I command you to return to Hades.'

The squealing creatures were engulfed in a sudden bloom of fire, then there was nothing.

'What were they?' asked Spike, shivering suddenly, as if one of the monsters still clung to him.

'Occubusi,' replied Sir Chadwick. 'Summoned from the underworld by a very powerful Night Witch spell.'

'Wolfbane must be close,' said Hilda.

Sir Chadwick nodded. 'And he knows where we are. He must have sent those things to delay us.'

'I feel better now,' said Abby. 'But I can still feel that thumping sensation.'

'There's something else coming,' said Sir Chadwick. 'And it is dreadfully powerful. We *must* reach the Sword of Merlin on the Atlantis Boat.'

As he spoke, the whole side of the tunnel suddenly fell

away, revealing a massive cavern lit by flaming torches . . . and filled with Wolfbane's nightmare army of cactus men!

The throbbing noise continued along with a hideous scraping sound as their spiked bodies grated against one another. The cactus men raised their misshapen arms, and great spikes sprouted from the ends as if they carried swords in each hand. From the tip of each spike dripped a yellow venom.

Wolfbane, Lucia and Valentine had discarded their disguises. With Stoneheart at their side, their own vile selves stood on a pile of rocks, urging on their demon force.

'Form a battle line,' shouted Sir Chadwick. 'Abby, Spike! Be swift! Fetch Excalibur from the Atlantis Boat.'

'And my harpoon,' yelled Captain Starlight.

Clashing their spike swords together rhythmically, the cactus men pressed forward to attack.

Sir Chadwick, Hilda, Mandini and Starlight retreated a few steps back into the mouth of the tunnel leading to the Atlantis Boat. The cactus men could now only come at them a few at a time through the narrow gap. Wands ready, the Light Witches and Starlight prepared themselves for the first assault.

The battle began. Light Witch wands flashed as they sliced through the arms and trunks of the shambling cactus figures. But as one was felled another quickly took its place. The battle raged with relentless ferocity. To his dismay, Sir Chadwick saw that some of the cactus men were hacking at the walls to widen the tunnel. If they succeeded the four of them defending it would soon be overwhelmed by sheer numbers. Some of the stabbing cactus spikes penetrated the guards of the defenders and they were soon covered in bloody wounds. The Light Witches chanted a protective spell:

'Poison, poison cannot slaughter,
Deadly venom turn to water.'

It was a special war call used to neutralize any killing potions an enemy might use in battle. But it could not stop the cuts of the cactus swords. Only courage made the Light Witches fight on. Slowly, their strength was ebbing away as they fought the vast forces arrayed against them.

Hilda was deeply wounded in the leg and sank to her knees. Mandini went down but was still thrusting with his wand. Starlight suddenly felt his harpoon being thrust into his hands by Spike, who then began to fire Ice Dust bullets from his musket.

Roaring his battle cry 'Remember Bright Town!' Starlight sliced through two cactus men with one sweep of his weapon. But still more pressed on. All at once, the cactus men halted.

Abby had rushed into the fray and stood before the friends, wielding Excalibur.

'Kill her! Kill the child,' Wolfbane howled.

Once again, the Sword of Merlin seemed to be weightless in Abby's hand. It was as if it were part of her body and the weariness she had felt earlier was completely gone. Moving forward, she cut through the cactus men as if she were walking in the countryside slashing at weeds with a stick.

The creatures kept advancing but now the Light Witches were standing their ground. Then, led by Abby, they began to press forward and the drumming throb began to fade.

Stoneheart could see that Wolfbane's attack had failed. 'Their magic is greater than yours,' he shouted. 'Your plan is worthless. I'm going to destroy the valley as I intended.' Leaping from the pile of rocks he ran back along the tunnel into his own mine shaft.

Wolfbane, Lucia and Valentine stayed briefly, but seeing that Abby, armed with Excalibur, was too strong for the cactus men, they fled as well.

When the last of Wolfbane's army were destroyed, the Light Witches and their friends looked about. The remains of the creatures had already begun to dissolve into dirty pools of water. At last they could examine the Atlantis Boat. Its hull was as good as new. While it had rested at the bottom of the mine, the magical craft had repaired itself.

'I'm tempted to go aboard and return to our own time right now,' said Sir Chadwick with a sigh. 'But we still have duties and obligations we must fulfil here in Silver Springs.'

'What exactly do you think Stoneheart meant when he shouted he was going to destroy the valley?' Hilda asked as Sir Chadwick applied a poultice of Ice Dust to her wounds.

'We'd better get up to the surface and find out,' said Mandini.

The Might of Excalibur

Dawn was breaking when Abby and her friends reached the surface. Standing in the main street, they could see Bart Stoneheart's balloon in the far distance above the valley, heading towards Cloudy Mountains. With a sudden whoosh of flapping wings Stoneheart's vulture rose into the air from the roof of the saloon.

Sir Chadwick put his hand on Spike's shoulder. 'Do you think you could bring down that bird with your musket?' he asked.

'Easily,' said Spike.

'Give me your bullet,' said Sir Chadwick. 'I don't want you to kill it.'

Spike took the round of Ice Dust ammunition from the magazine and handed it to Sir Chadwick. He passed his wand over the bullet and handed it back to Spike.

He brought the rifle up to his shoulder in one swift motion and hardly seemed to aim. There was a sharp report and the vulture tumbled from the sky near the

stagecoach corral.

They all hurried to where it lay in the dust. It was blinking malevolently at them as they approached.

'I think we need your skills of hypnotism, Mandini,' said Sir Chadwick.

'Certainly,' he replied.

'Will it be able to talk?' asked Spike.

'Possibly, if it is a Black Witch familiar, as I suspect it is,' said Sir Chadwick.

Mandini crouched over the bird and moved his hands swiftly before the creature's eyes.

'Fancy being able to hypnotize a vulture,' said Spike, impressed.

'What is Bart Stoneheart's plan for the valley?' asked Mandini.

The vulture did not speak.

Abby leaned forward. 'Benbow doesn't speak,' she said, 'but Captain Starlight reads his mind.'

'That's right,' said Starlight.

Mandini pressed his fingers to his forehead to concentrate and then said, 'I'm beginning to get something.'

'That's even more impressive,' said Spike.

Mandini began to speak the vulture's thought aloud. He told them how Stoneheart was going to blow off the side of the mountain and flood the valley to get at the silver beneath the earth.

'That would be a catastrophe,' said Hilda. 'What can we do, Chadwick?'

Abby still held Excalibur. She could feel its power strengthening her arm. Spike looked at her, knowing what she had in mind. In an instant, they were running towards the stalls where Snow and Frost were stabled.

'We'll try to stop them,' Abby called back.

'Good luck,' cried the others, as Stoneheart's vulture flapped its wings and soared into the sky.

The ponies galloped across the valley at magical speed. Spike was carrying his musket and Abby Excalibur. The sun rose as they hurtled on, the ponies devouring the distance. Ahead, they could see Stoneheart's balloon.

'I think we might catch him in time,' shouted Spike.

Abby was about to agree, when she noticed something on the edge of the valley, coming from the desert. It was the head of a wagon train which stretched back to the horizon. The leading wagon was just turning down a defile to enter the valley.

If Stoneheart dynamited the mountain, all the people would be killed. Abby knew she had to warn them.

Changing direction, she and Spike raced the ponies towards the covered wagons.

'Stoneheart's balloon was even closer to the mountain range. 'It's going to be a close run thing,' called Spike.

The ponies ran like the wind, soaring over all obstacles. As they approached the wagon train, the wagon master and the scout rode out to meet them.

'You must turn the wagons,' shouted Abby. 'They're

going to blow open the mountain and flood the valley. All of you will be drowned.'

The wagon master and the scout did not stop to question Spike and Abby. Instead, they turned their horses and raced back to the wagon train. As they got closer they shouted a warning to the wagons to get to higher ground.

'I think we're too late to warn Talking Eagle and the elves,' said Spike. 'The elves will be in the greatest danger. Hornbeam told me they all fish in the lake each morning.'

Stoneheart's balloon was almost at the foot of the Cloudy Mountains.

'I can send them a message,' said Abby and she concentrated on the clouds above the peaks.

Spike watched the clouds reform to spell out the words:

BEWARE! STONEHEART IS GOING TO
BLOW UP THE MOUNTAIN AND
FLOOD THE VALLEY WITH THE
WATER FROM THE LAKE.

'I hope they read it,' said Abby anxiously as they waited with Snow and Frost pawing the dusty ground.

In the distance, the wagon train had been turned about and almost everyone was back on the higher ground of the desert.

Then came a thunderous explosion. Even though they were a very long distance away, Spike and Abby felt the shock waves hit them.

In the clear air, they saw the whole side of the mountain billow up to hang suspended for a moment, before splitting asunder with a thunderous roar. A gigantic waterfall gushed forth as the lake water burst out in a roaring cataract. It smashed into the ground and surged towards them in an enormous turbulent tidal wave.

'We're too late,' said Spike.

But something strange was happening to Abby. She was suddenly filled with a willpower far greater than her own. She knew exactly what to do. A great shock ran through her body as she held Excalibur aloft.

From the clouds that remained above the mountains, three jagged streaks of lightning forked out to strike the sword in her hand. Spike saw Abby suddenly glow with faint blue light. She pointed Excalibur towards the tidal wave hurtling towards them and shouted:

'Mountains, rivers made to last,
Exist again as in the past.'

The message Abby had written in the clouds dissolved, and the sky turned yellow, then strange shades of lilac and purple. There was a sudden hush as if the whole universe was holding its breath. In that moment of total stillness, the tidal wave halted and to Spike's astonishment, went into reverse.

He watched, amazed, as huge boulders and tiny fragments of the shattered mountain slowly reformed its previous shape as if there had never been an explosion.

The sky returned to its usual colour, and Abby and Spike could even hear bird songs.

'Look,' shouted Spike, pointing with his musket. Rivers and streams once more sprang from the base of the mountain and flowed out over the valley.

Above their heads, Abby and Spike could see Stoneheart's balloon heading for Silver Springs.

On board the Shark Boat concealed in the Silver Springs bank vault, Wolfbane, Lucia and Valentine were working furiously. Valentine sat at a workbench covered with tools and the two gauntlets from the armour of Charlock. Wolfbane and Lucia were making alterations to a large gun that was designed to fire through the ports of the boat.

'How are you managing with the ammunition?' Wolfbane asked Valentine, without looking up from his own task.

'I think I've almost solved the problem,' replied Valentine. 'It's impossible to cut them, you know.'

'Of course it is,' snarled Wolfbane. 'If we could have cut up the armour we wouldn't have had to go to all this trouble in the first place.'

'Got it!' said Valentine triumphantly. 'I see now how this chainmail hooks together. Most ingenious. I've got the knack now.'

'Well, get a move on,' said Wolfbane. 'There isn't much time.'

'My badness!' exclaimed Valentine. 'I've never noticed before – Charlock had six fingers. Or five fingers and a thumb to be precise.'

'Stop burbling!' shouted Wolfbane. 'Can you make the ammunition or not?'

'All done,' Valentine answered smugly. 'We now have two Colt revolvers loaded with bullets made from Charlock's armour.'

'You could kill any Light Witch with those,' said Lucia admiringly.

'Who is going to do the job?' asked Valentine.

'I think we'll leave that pleasure to Stoneheart. Even he should be able to shoot Light Witches in the back from point blank range.'

'So, what's the plan?' asked Lucia.

'Just give me a moment,' said Wolfbane as he struggled to fit the bits of Charlock's chainmail armour into a magazine he had constructed on the side of the gun. He then attached leads to the various pieces of armour. Finally, he was satisfied.

'Got it!' he said, pleased. 'The armour gives enough power to the gun to generate a beam of evil distilled to a breathtaking intensity.' He slapped the side of the gun and chuckled. It sounded more like rats scrabbling in a sewer pipe than laughter. 'It will be more than enough to hurl Abby Clover and what's left of her friends into *The Chaos*.'

'Come to the crystal,' he commanded Valentine and Lucia.

They all gathered about the navigation table and Wolfbane waved his hands to reveal the image of Spike and Abby galloping towards the town.

'Abby Clover has the Sword of Merlin,' hissed Lucia. 'How can we defeat that?'

'Watch and learn, Mother,' said Wolfbane, with a sweep of his hand towards the crystal.

Lucia looked again. She saw two small children in the path of Abby and Spike's galloping ponies. A boy lay on the ground as if he were ill and a little girl was waving at Spike and Abby, obviously pleading for them to stop.

They reined the ponies to a halt and the girl cried out, 'We're from the wagon train. We were left behind. My brother is very ill.'

Spike and Abby dismounted and knelt beside the little boy. Abby placed Excalibur by her side and reached out to lay a hand on his brow. As the boy looked up at Abby his face suddenly changed. His nose grew into a great black beak. It was Caspar, Lucia's raven, but he was a monstrous size. Two claws, big as a man's hands, seized Abby's arms before she could snatch up Excalibur. Fighting to free herself from the creature's clutches, she twisted and turned desperately.

Spike aimed his musket but he could not get a clear shot. Casting the musket aside, he threw himself on to Caspar, who was trying to peck out Abby's eyes. All three rolled on the ground. Abby struck her head on a rock and lay, stunned. Caspar wriggled free from Spike and gave a croaking chuckle of triumph. Spike saw why.

The girl had transformed herself too – into Stoneheart's Vulture. The vile birds each seized one end of Excalibur and soared up into the sky and headed towards Silver Springs. By the time Spike had retrieved his musket the birds were out of range.

'You see,' shouted Wolfbane, hovering over the crystal. 'All is not lost. Victory *will* be ours.'

He gazed into the crystal again, shouting, 'Fly on, my beauties. Fly on. Bring Excalibur to me!'

An Assassination is Planned

At the cave mouth on top of Cloudy Mountain, Hornbeam and Talking Eagle looked out over the valley towards Silver Springs. Abby's warning in the clouds had given them time to reach safety. Beneath them, the rivers were once again coursing across the landscape.

'It is time for us to go to town,' said Talking Eagle.

'It will take us many days to walk the distance,' said Hornbeam.

'I think not,' said Talking Eagle, taking down the great silver mirror dish and balancing it on the edge of the precipice.

'Sit beside me,' he instructed Hornbeam as they climbed aboard. Silver Eagle pushed off from the cave's mouth and the mirror began to slide down the mountainside.

They were soon hurtling towards the bottom so fast the feather almost blew out of Talking Eagle's headband.

'Hurrah!' shouted Hornbeam, exhilarated by the speed of the ride.

'Hold tight,' called Talking Eagle as they hit a bumpy patch before sailing over the edge of an overhanging rock. They soared out into space and down, until the silver dish landed with a mighty splash in the largest river at the base of the mountain. The fierce current now raced them towards Silver Springs.

Because of the extraordinary clarity of the air, Sir Chadwick, Hilda, Captain Starlight and Mandini had seen Abby's message in the clouds from the steps of the Playhouse. And so had the people gathered on the main street. The townsfolk had also seen the results of the spell Abby had

performed when she reformed the mountain after the explosion. They had gaped in astonishment when the river gushed past, and they were all now chattering in jubilation.

The Light Witches and Starlight could see Stoneheart's balloon drifting back towards the town.

Sir Chadwick gave a great sigh of relief. 'When Abby returns with Excalibur, we can take care of Stoneheart and hunt down Wolfbane. Then we can leave,' he said. 'But first, I think some mass hypnotism on your part may be a good thing, Mandini. Can you make these people forget they saw Abby's spell?'

'With pleasure,' he replied, and he shouted down to attract the crowd's attention.

Sir Chadwick, Hilda, Starlight and Mandini returned to the boarding house, unaware that Abby had lost possession of Excalibur.

'We must remain vigilant,' said Sir Chadwick. 'The tide has turned in our favour, but Wolfbane is still on the loose. Keep your wands handy and be ready for anything. As soon as Abby and Spike get back we shall hunt down Wolfbane's crew.'

After landing his balloon, Stoneheart made his way to the bar where Bullwhip Kate and Beauregard Lightfoot were playing cards with the Kentucky Kid.

'I've got four aces,' said the Kid, reaching out to scoop up the huge pile of chips in the pot. Before he could touch them, Stoneheart seized his collar and dragged him away from the table.

'Get out,' said Stoneheart.

'But Bart,' whined the Kentucky Kid, 'that's the first hand I've ever won in your saloon.'

'And the last,' snarled Stoneheart. 'Get out and never come back.'

'Where have you been, Bart?' Kate asked as the Kid slunk away.

Stoneheart didn't answer immediately but reached for the whisky bottle in front of Beauregard. When he'd taken an enormous gulp straight from the bottle, he looked down at the tabletop and replied, 'Watching the death of my dreams.'

'Maybe you'd like to take revenge?'

Stoneheart swung round to see Wolfbane holding out two pistols.

'I have seen your plans dashed like my own, Wolfbane,' Bart said bitterly. 'We have no chance for revenge while that accursed child Abby Clover has the sword.'

'Oh, but she doesn't,' replied Wolfbane.

Hope flashed across Stoneheart's face

'This is what I want you to do,' said Wolfbane. 'Your two companions,' he said, nodding at Lightfoot and Bull-whip Kate, 'will go now and challenge Sir Chadwick Street, the Great Mandini and Captain Starlight to a gun duel on the main street.'

Beauregard and Kate looked a little uneasy.

'That Starlight is pretty fast with those horseshoes,' said Beauregard. 'I've got my reputation to consider.'

'Three of them and two of us?' said Bullwhip Kate. 'I'm not sure I like those odds either.'

'Tell your cowardly underlings there's absolutely nothing to fear,' said Wolfbane contemptuously.

'And how can you guarantee that?' asked Stoneheart.

'Because when they face the actors, you will be on the balcony behind Sir Chadwick Street, Mandini and Starlight. Before they have a chance to act, you will shoot them in the back with these guns.'

He handed the pistols to Stoneheart.

'I prefer my own,' Bart replied.

'I have prepared special bullets for these,' said Wolfbane.

Stoneheart took the guns and weighed them in his hands. Sensing their phenomenal power, he said to Beauregard and Bullwhip Kate, 'Go and call those rats out on to the street.'

In the boarding house, the residents, with the exception of Spike and Abby, were seated around the breakfast table. Mandini was suggesting to Flowerdale that it would be better for the mine to remain shut for the day. He said there were some safety repairs he intended to carry out personally. It was the story he and Sir Chadwick had agreed to tell Quincy Flowerdale, to give themselves time to tidy things below ground and move the Atlantis Boat to the su0rface.

'As you see fit, Mr Mandini,' said Flowerdale. 'You are in charge of all matters at the mine.'

'Abby and Spike are taking longer than I thought they would,' said Hilda, looking anxious. 'They should have been back by now.'

Captain Starlight looked up from buttering a slice of toast and said, 'Yes, you're right.'

There was a sudden splintering crash of glass, and a stone hurtled through the window. Bullwhip Kate was shouting in the street, 'There's three yellow dogs hiding in Flowerdale's Boarding House – Mandini, Starlight and Chadwick Street. Put on your guns and meet us outside Stoneheart's saloon or we'll burn down the theatre.'

'Barbarians,' said Sir Chadwick, calmly turning towards Flowerdale. 'I shall be obliged for the loan of a revolver, Quincy.'

'And I require the same favour,' said Mandini.

'I will be honoured if you will allow me to accompany you, gentlemen,' replied Flowerdale.

Sir Chadwick shook his head. 'It would serve no purpose. I would prefer you to stay here and guard the ladies.'

'As you wish,' Quincy replied with a bow.

Captain Starlight declined the offer of a gun. Instead, he checked the burnished horseshoes in his belt. Within a minute they were walking on to the main street.

The townsfolk were already taking cover. It was clear from their stance that Beauregard Lightfoot and Bullwhip Kate were expecting gun play.

The crowd parted at the approach of Sir Chadwick, Mandini and Starlight who walked three abreast. When they drew level with their backs to the saloon, Captain Starlight stepped forward and spoke. 'Lay down your guns. I am arresting you both for a breach of the peace.'

At that moment, Abby and Spike galloped on to the main street. Caspar and the vulture were overhead, still clutching Excalibur.

Immediately, Abby and Spike realized a gun fight was about to take place, and they could see Stoneheart standing on the balcony with guns drawn, ready to shoot Sir Chadwick, Mandini and Starlight in the back.

High above Abby's head, Caspar and the vulture circled with Excalibur.

It seemed inevitable that Stoneheart would kill her friends. But suddenly a white flash, swift as a shooting star, smashed into Caspar and the vulture.

'Benbow!' Abby cried out in relief.

Released from their grasp by the blow, the Sword of Merlin tumbled through the air. Abby galloped forward and caught the sword just as Stoneheart fired both guns. Moving at such an incredible speed no one could actually follow her actions, Abby swung Excalibur and struck the bullets aside.

Stoneheart was about to fire again when Abby hurled the sword. It flashed in the sunlight and pierced Bart Stoneheart where his heart should have been. He gazed down at the hilt protruding from his chest, then plummeted forward over the balcony to lie motionless in the red dust of the main street.

Everyone was so shocked by the fate of Bart Stoneheart, no one noticed Lightfoot draw his gun, but all heads turned at its sharp report. Captain Starlight was thrown back by the impact of the bullet hitting his chest, but he did not fall. He staggered back a few paces, clutching his breast pocket. From it he withdrew Abby's silver dollar, now badly dented. He looked at it for a moment, then dropped it into the dust.

Lightfoot was about to fire again when Laura called from the sidewalk, 'Beauregard, for my sake, please don't shoot!'

Lightfoot paused, uncertain, looked at Laura, then slowly put the gun back in its holster.

Bullwhip Kate had also reached for her gun, but Starlight was too fast. He pulled a horseshoe from his belt and, with deadly accuracy, knocked the six-shooter out of her hand.

The crowd parted once more as an extraordinary couple arrived on the scene.

It was Hornbeam and Talking Owl. Having been carried into Silver Springs on the newly restored river, they were now rolling the great silver mirror before them.

They were just in time to see Bullwhip Kate looking down on Bart Stoneheart's still body. As Abby withdrew Excalibur, a tear trickled down Kate's cheek and splashed on to the wound in Bart's chest.

'He could have been a fine man if he hadn't been so full of hate,' she said. 'I'm sorry I never had the chance to take a straighter path with him.'

'Me too,' said Beauregard Lightfoot. 'I came from a fine old Virginian family. And I've brought nothing but shame on them.'

Talking Eagle stepped forward. 'Do you both feel true sorrow for the waste of your lives?' he asked.

Kate and Lightfoot nodded hopelessly.

'Then maybe you deserve another chance,' said Talking Eagle.

'What's the point?' said Kate. 'Bart's dead. I just wish I was there in the dust with him.'

Talking Eagle rested the mirror against Hornbeam and, stepping forward, he knelt down beside Stoneheart and tore open his shirt. He took something from his pouch and thrust it into Stoneheart's chest.

Abby and Spike were the only ones to see it was the purified heart they had taken from the Ice Dust fountain in the lake.

Stoneheart began to stir and, after a moment, he slowly sat up. His face had lost its bitter cast. He even looked kind and quite friendly. Caleb Crabgrass, the Light Witch, had returned from the past.

Laura came from the sidewalk to stand beside Lightfoot. Without speaking, he raised his hat and took her hand in his own.

'Another one of your anagram spells hits the mark,

Abby,' Spike grinned. 'Love wins, after all!'

While Captain Starlight stood with Sir Chadwick and Mandini, Hilda came to join them. She was accompanied by Quincy Flowerdale.

'Do you think Wolfbane is still about, dearest?' Hilda asked calmly.

'I really can't say,' said Sir Chadwick. 'If we had the Evil Indicator set to evil, we could sweep the town for a dark presence.'

Starlight stepped forward. 'I'll take Excalibur down to the Atlantis Boat for safekeeping. While I'm there I'll reset the Evil Indicator. Then we can hunt for Wolfbane.'

'Capital idea,' said Sir Chadwick.

'No time to lose. I'll get on with it,' said Starlight, taking the sword from Abby and heading for Flowerdale's mine.

While they had been talking Mr Bradbury, the newspaper editor, approached them with his notebook open. 'Perhaps you can tell me exactly what happened here today, Sir Chadwick,' he said. 'There seem to be a lot of conflicting reports.'

'Always delighted to help the press,' said Sir Chadwick. 'But I have another exclusive for you.' He led Mr Bradbury over to Bart Stoneheart.

'This gentleman has declared he is forsaking a life of villainy.'

'Is that a fact, sir?' asked Mr Bradbury with sudden interest as he made rapid notes on his pad.

'It is,' said Bart. 'And to prove it, I intend to give my saloon away.' He beckoned into the crowd. The Kentucky Kid, unsure the signal was for him, pointed a questioning finger at himself.

Bart nodded. 'Yes, you, Kid,' he said. 'I hereby make you a present of the Silver Spring Saloon.'

The Kentucky Kid's chest seemed to swell to twice its usual size, but he was too overcome to speak.

'And what profession will you pursue from now on?' Mr Bradbury asked Bart.

Stoneheart actually blushed and looked sideways at Kate. 'Well, I've always hankered to tread the boards as an actor. But life has had a way of taking me in other directions.'

'Same here,' echoed the amazed voices of Bullwhip Kate and Beauregard Lightfoot.

Laura beamed and squeezed Lightfoot's arm.

Bart Stoneheart swept off his hat and bowed to Quincy Flowerdale. 'Sir,' he began, 'I have done you many a disservice and I beg your forgiveness. I only hope you will grant me the opportunity to make amends.'

Quincy was nonplussed. He looked at the way Laura was clinging to Lightfoot's arm and said, 'Laura, what does this mean?'

Laura spoke so all the townsfolk could hear. 'Quincy, I love Beauregard Lightfoot. We were star-crossed lovers but a miracle has taken place and now I can take my place at his side.'

Quincy shook his head. It looked as if he were about to protest but instead he gave a shrug. 'The Code of the West says everyone deserves a second chance. So be it. Let bygones be bygones,' said Flowerdale magnanimously. 'You shall all have places in my company, if you so desire it.'

Mr Fitzroy was about to say how well the day was turning out, when there was a splintering crash.

Along the main street the front of the bank had burst open as if pushed by a massive hand.

'Another exclusive!' shouted Mr Bradbury, flipping his notebook over to a fresh page.

The whole town gaped as an ugly black snout, shaped like the head of a shark, thrust through the great hole in the

bank. Slowly the rest of the body emerged, driven on squeaking caterpillar tracks. The object swung around and the crowd scattered, leaving Sir Chadwick, Hilda, Mandini, Abby and Spike standing together.

From a porthole near the snout, a sinister looking gun poked out. As the Shark Boat trundled towards them the hatch opened.

'You are done for, Light Witches,' Wolfbane screamed. 'Take one last look at the world before I hurl you all into *The Chaos*.' There was a rumbling sound from inside the Shark Boat and the whole machine began to tremble at the dreadful force it was about to unleash.

'Fire!' screamed Wolfbane from the turret.

But before the beam of evil could be unleashed, Talking Eagle and Hornbeam rolled the great silver mirror in front of Abby and her friends.

The mirror came to rest as a purple beam flared from the barrel of the gun. Striking the centre of the silver dish, the beam gathered into a great ball and was repelled back towards the Shark Boat, instantly engulfing it in purple light.

With a mighty explosion, the Shark Boat vanished completely. At first it seemed nothing was left but a foul smell wafting across the main street, but Abby and Spike saw the crystal ball from the Shark Boat's navigating table. It lay spinning in the dust. Gazing down at the ball they could see Wolfbane, Lucia and Valentine inside the Shark Boat, screaming to get out as they hurtled into *The Chaos*.

Spike gave the ball a kick and it dissolved into a dark smudge of dust.

The townsfolk stood with open mouths at this extraordinary turn of events.

'I think this calls for another touch of mass amnesia,' Sir Chadwick murmured to Mandini.

'Immediately,' he replied. And, taking the pistol from Sir Chadwick's belt, he fired into the air to gain the attention of the townsfolk.

'Ladies and gentlemen,' he boomed. 'May I show you something?'

Sometime later, the friends gathered at the boarding house to say their farewells. After some more of Mandini's surreptitious hypnosis, Quincy Flowerdale and the other actors all now believed that Abby, Spike, Captain Starlight, Mandini, Sir Chadwick and Hilda were catching the stagecoach to Tombstone. However, the Atlantis Boat was awaiting them in the newly restored river where Sir Chadwick and Abby, with the help of Excalibur, had moved it earlier. The valley was already showing signs of looking lush and green again.

The real Banker Stout and his wife were once more in their house, reunited with their real servants. Rehearsals for a new production of *Romeo and Juliet* had begun, with Bart Stoneheart and Bullwhip Kate playing the leading roles.

Although Abby and her friends did not know it, back in

Torgate, Mandy and Nigel had been released from their imprisonment in space and time when Wolfbane and his parents had been hurled into *The Chaos*. The twins were wandering along the pier, better behaved than they had ever been.

When Sir Chadwick, Hilda, Mandini, Starlight, Spike and Abby finally left the boarding house they met Talking Eagle and Hornbeam on the bank of the river.

Abby and Spike were a little concerned. 'We haven't been able to find Snow and Frost,' said Abby. 'We thought they might have gone back to the corral, but Washington Potts hasn't seen them.'

'They are magic creatures, child,' said Talking Eagle. 'They come and go as they please.'

'Like Benbow,' said Abby sadly. 'We haven't seen enough of him recently.'

'You will in good time,' the great Indian said with a smile. He looked much younger somehow.

Just for a moment, Abby's memory stirred. Talking Eagle's long thin face and pointed nose suddenly reminded her of somebody else she had known. She hadn't noticed before that he had violet-coloured eyes, the same colour as a Wizard's!

'Have you ever been anywhere else, Talking Eagle?' she asked. 'Outside America, I mean.'

'I have been many places at many times, child,' he said enigmatically.

Hornbeam shook hands with everyone, and Sir Chadwick said, 'Look out for the American Light Witches in the future, Hornbeam. They'll be along some day for that Ice Dust you've been guarding so well.'

'We shall be ready,' said the little man. 'A safe journey to thee all.'

Talking Eagle and Hornbeam stood on the river bank and watched as they all climbed aboard and closed the hatch. There was a sudden humming sound, and the Atlantis Boat vanished.

Benbow and the Circle of Time

'We're here,' said Spike, gazing into the navigation crystal on board the Atlantis Boat, which showed the location and the date. 'And there's still three days before Christmas.'

'My parents won't even have missed us,' said Abby.

They opened the hatch and looked out on the lake at Merlin College. Snow was falling. It lay everywhere, heavy on the trees and the college buildings. The bodies of all the people Wolfbane had bewitched still lay as Abby had left them, buried on the lawn.

As Abby stepped ashore Sir Chadwick handed her Excalibur, saying, 'Would you like to do the honours and wake them up? Hilda is making hot drinks. They might be a trifle chilled after their sleep.'

Holding the great Sword of Merlin aloft, Abby intoned :

'Now is time warm winds to blow,
Bring us back the friends we know.'

The heaps of snow on the lawn began to stir and, gradually Dr Gomble and the college dons sat up, rubbing their eyes. Charity and Elijah were the last to wake. Hilda handed them each a mug of hot chocolate, which they drank gratefully.

'So, thou didst escape the Night Witches, Chadwick,' Charity said, blinking.

'Even better news for you and Elijah,' he replied. 'Since you were bewitched, we have found a vast source of Ice Dust in America.'

'America!' gasped Charity. 'That cannot be.'

'When you see it you will believe it,' said Sir Chadwick.

Dr Gomble looked about him and said, 'I think we shall postpone the pageant this year. We have had enough excitement at Merlin College.'

He took a sip of cocoa and said, 'Why do I feel great things have happened while we slept? Can you enlighten me, Chadwick?'

'We travelled back in time, defeated Wolfbane, and discovered a great source of Ice Dust in Arizona,' Sir Chadwick told him.

'I look forward to hearing a full account,' said Dr Gomble, glancing towards the trees. 'Good gracious me!' he exclaimed. 'Strange animals are loose in the college grounds.'

Abby and Spike followed his gaze. Immediately, they rushed across the lawn to the edge of the wood where Snow and Frost stood waiting for them.

'I feel the hand of Wizards in this business,' said Dr Gomble. He sighed. 'Will we ever understand them?'

He turned to Sir Chadwick. 'Shall we all retire to the common room? I'm most anxious to hear all that has happened.'

Forming a loose procession, the dons led the adults into the college, leaving Abby and Spike trotting happily about the grounds on Snow and Frost.

After the Atlantis Boat had departed from Silver Springs, Talking Eagle and Hornbeam walked back to the main street. Talking Eagle paused, stooped down and picked up the dented silver dollar that Captain Starlight had dropped there in the dust. He held it up momentarily before throwing it into the air. There was a flash of white and Benbow swooped down to catch it.

'Let it all begin, great bird,' Talking Eagle called out.

And Benbow flew off on his long journey through space and time, to drop the dented dollar in Speller Harbour for Spike and Abby to find.

UNITED
OF AMERICA
ONE DOLLAR

The Witches of the Wild West